MOVING DAY

Also by Jonathan Stone

The Cold Truth

The Heat of Lies

Breakthrough

Parting Shot

JONATHAN STONE

MOVING DAY

A THRILLER

THOMAS & MERCER

Published by Thomas & Mercer, Seattle

www.apub.com

Amazon, the Amazon logo, and Thomas & Mercer are trademarks of Amazon. com, Inc., or its affiliates.

ISBN-13: 9781477818244
ISBN-10: 1477818243

Cover design by Stewart A. Williams

Library of Congress Control Number: 2013919401

Printed in the United States of America

*For Roger and Abbie—with boundless pride
at who you've become*

For Sue—with boundless thanks for who you are

T he doorbell rings. Stanley Peke moves to the big, gracious front door slowly. He finds himself moving everywhere a step slower these days. He opens the big door, and there stand four huge men in crisp green uniforms, an immense white truck behind them.

The day has come. The day he has vaguely known would come since he and his wife moved in forty years before.

The man in front with the clipboard smiles. A short, broad man. A short, broad grin. "Good morning, Mr. Peke, sir. Nice day for it, isn't it? Just give us your John Hancock right here, sir, and we'll get started."

Peke frowns a little. "Thought it was tomorrow."

The man with the clipboard frowns now, too, looks down at the clipboard, shakes his head gently, pleasantly, and, looking back up at Peke, says cheerily, "No, sir, it's today. The twenty-fourth." Even checking the clipboard one more time, just to be sure.

Peke can tell, though, just beneath the crisp cheerfulness, what the man is thinking: that Peke, despite his hale, healthy appearance, must be a little forgetful. A little senile.

"Who is it?" his wife, Rose, calls out from the kitchen.

"The movers. They're here."

"I thought it was tomorrow," Rose says unsurely, coming around the corner, a frown of mild consternation that probably very much mirrors his own of a few moments ago.

Because I told you it was tomorrow, Peke thinks guiltily. But he doesn't say it. Doesn't want to further embarrass himself in front of the foreman. At seventy-two, he is physically robust, the envy of his friends, but he finds that he occasionally forgets things. Little things. He's noticed that he sometimes misplaces his keys, his wallet, but he'd just as soon not worry his wife. It shows that what they're doing—heading for the easy, breezy perfections of Santa Barbara—is the right thing. That keeping track of the details of running a big home is—at their age—starting to get a little beyond them. "Nope. It's today," Peke informs his wife authoritatively, and turns and winks at the man with the clipboard.

A day he's known would come someday. A day that's been coming for forty years.

Forty years, three children.

Forty years of birthday parties in the den and on the back deck; graduation dinners and holiday feasts in the bright dining room with the facing bay windows; even a daughter's wedding on the back lawn.

Forty years of life's triumphs, setbacks, and celebrations. Family crises, and resolutions.

Today is moving day.

》》》

Peke watches. Long retired now, a happy, half-attentive homebody, like Voltaire's Candide, cultivating his garden after his adventures in the world, he has nothing else to do now, really, but watch. So he watches them move every piece. Moving the pieces more carefully than they would if unobserved, he's sure.

Almost everything is already packed, of course. The company sent a crew to do most of the packing a week before. Obviously, that's how it's done nowadays. First a packing crew, then a moving crew. The packing crew must go job to job, just packing. Specialists. More efficient. The world has changed mightily in the forty years they've been in this house. And for the last week, he and Rose have been wandering among the cartons as if through a cardboard graveyard.

The last few things, though, the big things, this crew packs. He can see they know what they're doing. They take care of the big Empire mirror, swaddle it in protective layers, then build a protective wooden box around it. Such care is amusing, considering how haphazardly the mirror came in here. He and Rose got it at an estate sale. They were kids, really. (Or so it seems now, from this perspective.) They'd just bought the house. Nobody wanted it, a big, gaudy, old thing like that. Didn't even have a price tag on it. The people just wanted it taken away. Rose mentioned to him recently that it's worth a fortune today. He's sure she's exaggerating, but he's continually surprised at what old things fetch. You watch that show on PBS, and it's astonishing.

He watches them pack the big oils. When they had lived in the Village before buying the house out here, she'd purchased a few of these crude-looking canvases, saying it was good to support the local artists. He'd argued that he didn't see any evidence that these exuberant flings and smudges of color qualified as art. Abstract Impressionism, she'd exuberantly explained. They had to put the big canvases in storage, because they were too big for the Village apartment, and he told her how foolish it seemed to buy things you put right into storage. Now they own some canvases that by all rights should be in museums. Museum people have come by over the years. The damn things are still too big even for these walls, but they do draw their share of oohs and aahs at dinner parties, and you

3

can't have them in storage anymore—you'd have to have your head examined.

He watches them struggle, the four movers all together, with the Spanish armoire. He remembers the island vacation where she picked it up. He remembers arranging for a trailer to fetch it at Idlewild (before it was called Kennedy). Just a single, undistinguished terminal building at the end of a runway amid dank, swampy fields. Arranging it from overseas—the phone connection in those days was impossible. Shouting into the phone. Getting cut off a dozen times. He remembers all that.

They're a good crew, he sees, working together, the foreman calling out the directions calmly and accurately, everybody's eyes on doorways, on doorjambs. He can see he'll have nothing to complain about.

He watches them struggling with the highboy. Some famous maker in Philadelphia, he remembers. There was debate and some research done, some years ago, about whether it belonged at one point to John Adams. He forgot all about that until this moment, because he forgot all about the highboy. It's not the kind of thing you think about.

The two younger movers, as they pass him, look over and smile pleasantly. He can't tell if that's company training, or if they're just decent men who see an old couple moving out after a lifetime. Seems like the latter. Seems sincere. But he isn't so naive about the world to think they might not merely be pasted-on smiles.

Cartons of dishes. Passed down from Rose's mother, and her mother's mother. And removed much like this, no doubt, when they'd left their homes in Cambridge and on the Cape. Into the smaller, squarish, paneled trucks of a couple of generations ago.

He watches the books. Cartons and cartons of them. The green-uniformed men in a steady bibliographic parade, hefting and transporting the cartons like heavy, cubic drums in front of them, or balanced on shoulders, one or two cartons at a time. His favorites in there somewhere. His leather-bound Montaigne. His Dante folio.

And then the truly valuable: the family pictures, still on the walls. Christmas in the rain forest. April in Paris. The five of them and their hosts atop the Great Wall. In Moscow on business. His life passing before his eyes, he smiles to himself. His life passing orderly before his eyes, carried by green-uniformed men.

"Must feel weird," says the black one, smiling, pleasant, stopping for a moment, as if reading Peke's thoughts. Thoughts easy to read, after all, in an emptying house. A house soon to have in it nothing but thoughts.

"I'd rather watch the furniture carried out than have the furniture watch me carried out," Peke quips. He means it only to amuse, to somewhat forgive his idle standing around. But he sees the momentary alarm cross the face of the black mover. He shrugs. "It's a day that comes for all of us." Sounding like too much grim wisdom, unfortunately. Particularly with his mild foreign accent.

"How long you lived here?" asks the black man, perhaps only politely, perhaps genuinely curious.

"The whole time," says Peke, smiling, pleased at his own friendly wit, and the black man smiles back appreciatively.

>>>>

At the truck, the foreman with the clipboard is supervising the loading. Surveying the space and the items, fitting things together ingeniously. He looks up, smiles at Peke, looks back to his work. You can see the man has a talent for it. And has been lucky enough to discover that talent. Peke has been lucky like that, too. It was at a desk, it was manufacturing, but the business grew, always steadily grew, and he was fortunate enough to be doing the right thing at the right time, and it gave him this house and this life.

Peke watches the man fitting, refitting, thinking ahead. A three-dimensional puzzle to solve. It probably isn't a bad living, thinks Peke. He begins to compute in his head what the move is costing, times the number of people a crew might move in a week, minus the capital costs of the truck, minus the percentage you shared with the moving company, but still . . . you could raise a family decently. You could do fine.

>>>>

He watches as they continue loading. Every item has its moment in the sunlight—in many cases for the first time in forty years—and then, in another moment, is wrapped snugly in blankets, like a precious child, and tucked into the truck. He watches until he can't watch anymore, and he wanders out back to the patio, sits, and scans the *Times*, until at last they come and take the patio furniture, too.

>>>>

Late in the afternoon, looking out the kitchen window, he sees the four of them pull from the truck and position two steel rails and then, with exquisite care, coax the old Mercedes SL convertible up into the truck. It feels almost ceremonial, because it is one of the final items.

And then they're done. The foreman with the clipboard rings the doorbell. The other green-uniformed men are arrayed behind him, just as when they arrived.

"That's it. You just initial it here, saying no damage was done to the floors or doorways."

"And you've got the exact address?" Peke looking over his bifocals at them.

"Yessir, we do," crisply. "And we stay in touch with our office as we go, so you can always check in with them." The broadly built foreman drums his index finger on the clipboard as he reads through the shipping manifest once more, double-checking the sheaf of papers himself.

"Here's your receipt," he says, pulling the top, yellow copy off and handing it to Peke.

Following it with his hand for a handshake, and his quick, efficient grin. "See you at the other end," he says with a smile. His eyebrows lift. "And, uh, you're all set for tonight? With a place to stay?" Peke detects the note of concern. A sudden sliver of uncertainty. That since Peke confused which day, maybe he has also confused or even neglected his own sleeping arrangements.

Peke smiles. "Staying right here," he says. The foreman looks puzzled, his concern deepening. "On an old mattress. With a candle. Same way we spent the first night in this house. With nothing but our name." And now the movers presumably know what is packed in the big carton at the back of the garage that Peke instructed them to leave there.

The foreman with the clipboard nods, smiles with understanding. "Wow," he says. He seems to be pausing, really thinking about it. "Huh. Well . . . enjoy it."

Peke lights the candle. He positions the mattress. He builds a fire in the fireplace. The mattress, the candle, the fire. It was all they had when they moved in forty years before. (The house much smaller, simpler then, before they added and renovated and transformed it into the stately gray-shingled palace it is today.) They will re-create that night. Though not in all its details. He smiles. Not with all that youthful energy. But in effect, in feel, it is the same.

As he lies down next to her on the mattress, lowering himself carefully to the floor (the floor where he hasn't been, it occurs to him, since he played with his infants years ago and since a back spasm one midnight a decade earlier), he can still remember so vividly how he lay down next to her on the mattress in this room in front of this fire forty years ago. What a strange moment—time disappearing, time upended. Forty years like a single day. A finger snap. A blink. He is seventy-two, she seventy, and though they tease each other about the new pills available, their affection now takes the place of their sex, but their sex was vivid enough that the memory satisfies.

They say little. They hold each other. Her flesh against him— after a half century of his male rumination and regard—is truly more familiar to him than his own. They fall asleep to the candle and the fire.

He gets up in the middle of the night to urinate, to empty his old man's bladder. He walks through the silent house. The house is empty, couldn't be more empty. The house is full, couldn't be more full.

Each room echoes in its emptiness.

Echoes with memory.

>>>

In the morning, a short time after they awaken and dress, the doorbell rings.

Peke moves to the big, gracious door slowly, as slowly as he finds himself moving everywhere these days. Peke notices now, sees through the skylights, that outside it is an identically cloudless day to the day before, to moving day.

He opens the door, and standing there is a different foreman with a clipboard, another team of green-uniformed men, and another white truck.

They seem slightly, indefinably, less crisp than yesterday's crew. He's confused. "You . . . you were here yesterday."

The clipboard man looks at him, with a mirroring expression of confusion. "Well, no, we weren't, sir. You're scheduled for today." The man looks at his clipboard, then at Peke. It is precisely the same look that the short, broad foreman gave him yesterday, Peke sees. Like Peke is a little senile. Peke is put off by that. "Look, your guys were here yesterday," he says more insistently. With irritation.

"Sir, these are our guys," the man says with a matching insistence. "And they weren't here yesterday." The clipboard man looks past Peke into the gracious entrance hall and the living room behind it, and sees that they are both empty.

"Tell me I'm not seein' what I'm seein'," he says.

Police trace the receipt Peke was handed to a printing shop in Wheeling, West Virginia. The printing bill was paid with cash, and it leads no further. The flimsy yellow receipt is checked for fingerprints—fingerprints other than Peke's. Peke can't remember whether the man ever touched the receipt fully or not. The results come back. Apparently, the man did not.

"Usually, of course, the residents don't stay in the house. They're not so romantic," says the detective. "So usually it's only discovered a week later. When you're waiting for your belongings. And they never come. And who knows where these people are a week later."

Stanley and Rose Peke have a lifetime of memories from the big house in Westchester.

And nothing else.

The white truck moves sleekly along I-80.

They'll reach Montana in less than forty-eight hours.

America, thinks Nick. *What a place.* No wonder the Russian mobsters, the Cuban sea scum, the crazy Dominicans, the bug-eyed Syrians, the slopes and sand niggers . . . no wonder they all want in. Well, this is something they can't pull off, at least. This is a little tricky for them. Higher up the crime chain. The truck. The smiling, uniformed crew. This is a niche.

He's been at it a couple of years. It's pretty good. Some of the moving companies now send stern warnings in red lettering along with their shiny sales packets, but these are old people—they don't understand. If they read the warnings at all, they obviously forget them by the time Nick rolls up. Or else they're overwhelmed by the crisp green uniforms, blinded by the sparkling white truck.

The big white truck. Like an earthbound cloud. A little bit of white rolling heaven. Crisscrossing the black ribbon highways of the greatest land on Earth like it's Nick's backyard. America!

Of course, he knows that stealing the worldly goods, the memories, the lifetime of an elderly couple in a single deceitful morning and afternoon isn't exactly the American dream. But the sunny salesmanship of it, the bright-eyed, cheery hucksterism—well, that's American, isn't it? Pulling up in a shiny eighteen-wheeler now, instead of that rickety wooden cart with snake oils on the back. It's the American grifter tradition. A long-established, if not quite honorable, piece of Americana.

The American grifter tradition—he smiles at the notion. The criminal's need to glorify his craft, to make it more than it is—he recognizes and suppresses that impulse in himself. He doesn't deceive himself. He's smarter than that.

Oh, he's no highbrow, and no evil genius, but he's no idiot either. He's a species that he's quickly come to see is exceedingly rare—an intelligent criminal. Intelligent enough, anyway, to stay out of jail long enough to get good at it. Intelligence is the exception in his world. But there are a few who possess it, and he's one.

Growing up in deprivation (a deprivation that, in truth, was not so much a daily trial of living as a suffocating flatness of life), he was always fascinated by finer things. A sculpture—inexplicably unscarred by graffiti—in the park where he'd meet his dropout friends. An ornate stained-glass window in the sorry church he was dragged to, before he refused to go anymore. The elaborate pewter chalices on the altar. Who possessed the time, and patience, and talent—who knew the safety and serenity in life—to create such intricacy? To craft these subtle pleasures?

Such objects were like missives from some other, greater, twinkling civilization he was drawn toward across a noisy, seething universe. And this—this cargo, this dark highway, this ingenious little system of his—was the way he'd found in adult life to deal in that civilization's glittering currency.

Growing up in deprivation, he saw that he frightened people with his intelligence. It was unwelcome, out of place, belonged in that paint-peeling foster home and that faded neighborhood even less than he did. It made his sour, dull foster parents nervous (hell, as a kid it made him nervous—this *difference*), and they said no good would come of it. And were they right? Hard to say.

It's his intelligence and his yearning, he knows, that have landed him in this truck and in this life, though he can't sort out whether it's his intelligence or his yearning that has the upper hand. Though there is a third trait that is a by-product of both and may override them both: his essential aloneness.

Which probably accounts for his success at this as much as anything, he thinks. As one who is adjusted to his own aloneness, he feels no impulse to boast, or confide, or share—all fatal flaws in the life of crime.

By now he's accepted his aloneness, his predilection for self-distance and isolation. And this is just right for a loner. The long, silent hours. The wide-open spaces. The continual movement. Rather than, for instance, standing on the same street corner day after day, peddling drugs, in broad view on an urban stage, expected to entertain and impress the locals. Or sealed up in some apartment, waiting for untrustworthy buyers where they can always find you, like a sitting duck.

It's low-tech, too. In these freewheeling days of cybercrime, of stealing information off the Internet, of complicated telecom scams, of digital identity theft, it's about the last low-tech scam he knows of. That's admirable, he thinks. It's simple. It relies on the American highways. The glittering black ribbons of interstate. Like black ribbons wrapping the gifts America is offering.

And it's safe. Old people, for Christ's sake. It's self-selecting: these people are selling and moving in general because they can't manage their current lives anymore. Nobody gets hurt. Not physically. Not even financially. Except the insurance companies, of course. People like this are all insured, but the insurance companies are so big, one operator like Nick hitting randomly, irregularly, isn't enough to get them to mobilize. As far as the police go, well, nobody's gotten killed, after all. Not so far, anyway. The only injuries are psychological. The stolen memories—that's the part the old people want back most—and cops don't have the manpower to go after memories.

And there are so many rich old people in America. Every single town in America has its little establishment of them. Go into any stinky little American town anywhere, and it's got its fancy section, its local wealth. Pockets of money, whatever pocket of America you're in. The amazing thing isn't that there are wealthy people—it's how many. The sheer number! Literally thousands upon thousands.

America! What a stupendously successful experiment it's turned out to be. So many rich. Scattered so vastly. That's why Nick is never caught.

Like sheep spread across an immense meadow—and a wolf emerges periodically from the woods to pluck them at will, Nick thinks.

Driving west, into the setting sun.

It's highway robbery, redefined.

In mid-Pennsylvania, just before Harrisburg, they pull off the interstate. Now, near midnight, they make their way along service roads, past a line of industrial buildings whose exact function is unclear in daylight and utterly oblique at night. But it is a path on which an eighteen-wheeler at midnight is not the least bit suspicious. It is a corner of industrial America where an eighteen-wheeler is merely part of the landscape, even at this late hour. Particularly at this late hour.

The night. It's one of the things Nick likes best about the scam. One of its simplicities. You load up all day, then take off and drive all night with the advantages of darkness. The advantages of speed, and relative invisibility, and law enforcement at low ebb. It's a time when truckers dominate the interstates anyway.

They make a right turn and head toward a row of warehouses. Nick takes his cell phone out of his uniform pocket, dials, waits patiently until it is answered.

"It's Nick," he says. Which is sufficient, he knows.

Nick pulls the white truck in behind the row of warehouses, turns in toward one warehouse among them. He stops at the shut chain-link gate. Atop the gate and along the entire chain-link fence, razor wire perches thickly coiled, glistening like a snake of menace in the moonlit night.

A small metal shack stands inside the gate. A stocky Hispanic man pokes his black-capped head out from inside it.

The chain-link gate opens electronically, with an initial jolt. Nick cajoles the truck carefully into the huge lot. There is a handful of other sixteen-wheeled-trailer bodies, cabless, in the lot already. Slumbering allosaurs of the American road.

Nick pulls in slowly, brings the big truck to a halt behind one of the trailers.

His crew piles out. LaFarge. Chiv. Al. All three take out cigarettes. No smoking in the cab with Nick.

The black-capped Hispanic—Jesus *(Hay-sus)* is his name— hustles out from the guard shack, carrying a large, deep carton awkwardly in front of him and struggling with a stepladder hooked over one shoulder. He is pockmarked, sorry-eyed, indigent-looking. And with his graying hair, he is older than one might expect for this kind of rendezvous.

For greeting, Nick merely nods.

Jesus bends down to the carton. Lifts out an industrial paint-sprayer, wriggles the apparatus onto his back.

Whereupon LaFarge stubs out his cigarette, comes over and bends down to the carton, and hitches on a second paint-sprayer. Besides Jesus—an auto-body-shop spray-painter by day—LaFarge is the only one allowed to do this work. Any of the others, including Nick, would make a mess of it.

First, three strips of guide tape are placed, quickly and expertly, down one entire flank of the truck, demarcating two white strips between them.

And then the paint sprayers—smoothly, wordlessly, hissing mildly—are walked by Jesus and LaFarge down the flank to make two thin red stripes.

Now, above the double stripe on one side, using the stepladder, Jesus tapes up the stencil he's already cut, to carefully spray the big, simple red letters in a glossy metallic quick-dry lacquer that will do its final drying on the road.

It's a nice, dry, beautiful night.

In rain, they would have pulled the truck into the warehouse. Would have had to wait a couple of hours for the lacquer to dry. A little riskier. A little longer. Lights on. But tonight is dry.

Chiv scurries up into the cab of the truck. Emerges with a flattened paper bag, from which he pulls two STATE OF OHIO truck license plates. He hunches down at the rear of the truck to switch the license plates.

They've never had any trouble. Not an ounce. But better safe than sorry, to keep it that way, is Nick's philosophy.

Now Jesus and LaFarge stretch the guide tape along the other side.

They spray smoothly. LaFarge—a former tagger in the Bronx—is the only guy Nick can think of for whom that offbeat skill has translated into actual, if not legal, employment.

Now Jesus tapes up the stencil on this side. In tiny, graceful arcs begins to spray.

"You fuck!"

The word from Nick is like a rifle shot in the previously still night.

"How the fuck do you spell 'Ohio'!?"

The spray-painter jumps back from the truck, turns to Nick, stricken. His eyes wide, as if swollen, a broad cartoon of utter fear.

Nick smiles wide. Shakes his head. "Naw, it's right. Just messin' with your wetback brain. You got it right."

LaFarge, Chiv, Al, laughing, choke and wheeze out cigarette smoke.

Nick looks up at the side of the truck and finds himself actually feeling a note of pride. Ohio Produce. A fine concern. Tonight, they are Ohio Produce.

Previously, Western Auto Supply. Before that, Iowa Growers Transport. Metro Distributors. Bailey Industries.

Sometimes the red stripe, sometimes two green ones, other times blue. That and the logo did the job. You didn't have to paint the whole goddamn truck.

Though they did that, too, once a year. One time, yellow. Another time, sky blue. For promise. For clear sailing.

Ohio Produce. Western Auto Supply. The made-up corporate entity, the manufactured manufacturers, existing only for hours. Then, on safe arrival, scraped off.

Iowa Growers Transport. Metro Distributors. The corporate names like a bland song of the American road. Nick and his crew had been employed at each of them for only a day or two. *Can't keep a job. Unreliable fuck-ups, aren't we?* Nick smiles.

In twenty minutes, Jesus stands back, unshoulders the spray-painter.

The paint is tacky to the touch. It will air-dry, final-seal, over the next hour, air-assisted on the road. That's the new technology.

Nick stands up. He likes this quick stop in industrial America. An industrial America his privileged victims generally never see, or understand, or even think about. That's part of why he likes it, he knows. Because this is his, and not theirs.

Now, for payment. Nick opens the right-side back gate of the truck. It swings out and clangs against the truck side, echoing against the night as he rolls the interior horizontal gate open. Jesus, suddenly less sullen, suddenly shedding years, climbs up. He and Nick disappear inside the dark truck as if into a narrow shop at a Middle Eastern bazaar. Merchant and buyer.

With the low assistance of Nick's flashlight, Jesus browses the truck. When he looks toward items that are covered, Nick describes them to him.

The auto-body spray-painter settles quickly on the Nakamichi stereo sitting between two Louis XIV chairs. Nick can see it: the glum spray-painter arriving back at his ghetto walk-up with the brushed-aluminum Nakamichi, listening to salsa on it, the bland, unquestioning look of his worn-out wife. A stereo like this is argu-ably a lot for painting a name and some stripes on a truck. It's worth a lot and easy to move. But in this case, Nick knows, it's easy to be generous. The Louis chairs are probably worth ten times as much. But of course the paint-sprayer doesn't even consider a chair. Chairs are just to sit in.

No cash changes hands. A deal that's cleaner than cash. Nick likes that, too.

In another couple of minutes, after savoring last tokes of tobacco, they are all back in the truck cab, out the gate, hunched shoulder to hunched shoulder, a military night operation. The truck painting is probably unnecessary, but Nick doesn't discount its symbolic value—demonstrating to the crew the importance of being careful. To protect their franchise. In that alone, the effort might be worth it. If trouble ever comes, Nick knows, it will more than likely arise from some unforeseen incompetence of LaFarge, Chiv, or Al.

While the painting may be unnecessary, it's almost traditional by now, a ritual part of the trip. Like a favorite roadside stop on a family outing. At a certain point you just do it because everybody expects it. It's simply part of the journey.

He looks at them—Chiv, LaFarge, Al—in the rearview mirror. Some outing. Some family.

Pulling back out onto I-80. Heading west.

Peke still has the Mercedes sedan. He still has money in the market and in the bank. He still has his wife. He still has his kids, and their futures, and their quick, easy smiles and comfort in the world, and his grandchildren with their bright eyes and adorable faces. He still has what he was wearing the day before.

"Oh, Daddy," his daughter Anne says on hearing.

The others, Daniel and Sarah—she from some far-flung terminus of modern life, he in an office Peke can picture precisely, each of them reduced to a slight, tinny voice over the wire—simply listen, stunned, offering suggestions hollowly, knowing their ever-competent father already has it as well in hand as anyone could. He is wordlessly proud that none of his three children indicates any thought of selfishness—of heirlooms gone, of their rightful inheritance of expensive artwork looted. They seem to be concerned primarily and genuinely with the effect on their parents, and with nothing beyond that.

All three have been living their own lives for years now, as Peke and his wife have always hoped and wished for them. Their parents' life is remote to them. They all accept that at this moment, oddly, there is nothing more for them to do.

Rose's reaction, though wordless, is the most pronounced. This was her home, her roost, as it is so often a wife's more than a husband's. She has gone silent. Has drawn in. She says nothing because there is nothing to say. She seems to feel nothing, because, he knows, there is too much for her to feel. She seems to be in a kind of limbo—fully recognizing the fact but not yet accepting it, functioning without feeling. It seems that she wants no discussion of the event—no grieving, no wistful philosophy, no recrimination or assignment of blame. He has always thought of her as highly resilient, but in truth her resilience has never been tested. For Rose, it seems the event is simply still too close. In truth, he can't tell how she will handle it, because she is not handling it yet.

A further conversation with the police brings little else. Peke learns (one of those little facts that he's sure he will now know forever) that there are 246,000 semi tractor-trailers on the American road at any given time, and to most Americans, of course, apart from their signage, the vehicles are indistinguishable from one another. This sleek white one is likely not so sleekly white anymore, says the detective.

"I mean, can you describe the truck to us at all? Any markings? Any distinguishing features?" the detective asks, his weariness undisguised, as if knowing already that Peke cannot. As if knowing already that Peke barely even looked at or considered the truck. "That's the beauty of the scam," says the officer, with a thin smile that hovers between admiration and resignation, which Peke resents.

Stanley Peke has been shrewdly alert all his life. His shrewdness, his alertness, have indeed brought him his life. And for a moment, he was stupid. And one stupid moment, it seems, one lax moment, wipes out all the shrewdness of a lifetime.

For days, he's furious. He inhabits the fury, sleeps with it, wakes with it, lies in bed with it, waiting for it to burn itself out enough for him to sleep. He's ready to get into the Mercedes and spend the rest of his years, if it takes that, driving around the continental United States, looking for them. Looking for the truck. Looking for wherever they took it. He'll find it, too. That is the intensity of his rage. Irrational. Fanciful. Consuming.

The slick deception returns to him in individual elements. The foreman's concerned look. Peke had thought it was concern about his senility. Yes—checking, assuring, that Peke was senile and gullible enough. *And, uh, you're all set for tonight? With a place to stay?*—the seemingly concerned questions had been only the thief noting Peke's schedule and plans. *Staying right here? Wow. Huh. Well, enjoy it.* The foreman-thief calculating that it gave him just one night's head start until the scam was discovered, but that was plenty, more than enough. *No, sir, it's today. The twenty-fourth.* Earnestly checking the clipboard. Employing the authority of the written word. Peke relives every moment of precisely how it was done. He witnesses again every one of those smiles. Inauthentic smiles, he'd correctly sensed. But he'd thought it was only company policy, company edict, that was behind their inauthenticity. And that general cheerfulness? Perhaps the one thing that was real. The cheerful realization that their slick trick was going to work. Work again, no doubt—as practiced, as polished, as it seemed to be. The rage wells up in him again.

Though another line of thought is always alongside that rage, on a parallel, logical track: *It's only our things. We have plenty of money. We can live simply. What have we really lost? We don't possess our memories physically, after all, and those are certainly worth more than the rest of it, and we still have those. We have reached the stage of life where we want—need—to simplify our lives. Doesn't this do just that? Force it, accelerate it, but simplify nonetheless?*

Of course, he knows that this criminal—this thief—probably counts on exactly that attitude. (Rage needs focus, and the focus of his rage has narrowed to the quick-grinning, too-earnest foreman, presumably the ringleader.) Peke can imagine that the man preys exclusively on the elderly. It's so easy, and the elderly never press the police very hard; the elderly respect the system. Accept, resign themselves to the loss, collect the insurance. Remind themselves that they haven't been physically injured or even threatened. This criminal, this thief, probably counts on all that, and it works, and that infuriates Peke anew. Fans the flame.

And something else. Something else tucked into his rage and frustration that he knows he can't separate out. An extra texture to the crime, to his victimization, that he pushes away, that he is not yet ready to confront. *The uniformed men. The empty house.* His rage, he knows, covers it over and consumes it, for now. A rage that he knows is beyond this event. A rage that is visceral and primal. *The uniformed men. The empty house.*

Their plan had been to drive across the country, he and Rose. Take it slow. See America. Visit friends along the way whom they hadn't seen in years. Neither had ever driven across America. They were classic coastal dwellers, and they wished to finally erase their myopic coastal arrogance. Their clothes for the trip were packed into two suitcases in the Mercedes trunk.

They delay their departure while they sort things out. He gets them a room at a pretty little inn in town where they always wanted but never had occasion to stay. He makes appointments with the insurance adjusters, talks to his lawyer, files the first claims, begins to order and gather the few truly necessary replacement documents—the most recent bank and brokerage statements, another copy of the title to their new Santa Barbara home. He thinks about the contents of his desk drawers. Papers. Insurance policies. Monthly bank and brokerage statements. Stock buy and sell slips.

Nothing irreplaceable, he thinks. In truth, there aren't so many truly essential documents. Some phone calls, some explanations, and it will all be reissued. The wake of the disaster is more orderly and less stressful than he would have thought, and he can't help but think that is something the thief relies on as well.

Waiting at the house to meet with the two insurance adjusters, to take them step by step through the events, as they politely but insistently requested that he do, Peke is surprised to find the life of the house continuing in his absence. The grounds attended to, per the closing contract. (The new owners are returning from a five-year posting in Asia and will not take occupancy for another month.) He notices that mail keeps coming. Not the first-class mail, which is being forwarded, but everything else. The junk mail. Flyers, solicitations, credit card offers, TO CURRENT RESIDENT. And all the catalogs. Catalogs of physical objects. Of items, of things. A pictorial index of the known domestic universe. Beds and tables and chairs and hassocks and ottomans and lamps, candies and chocolates, tools and toys and boats. As if the Fates know what has just occurred and have dispatched catalogs filled with convenient and immediate replacements. Curtains and clothes and bathroom towels and linens and robes. What convenient temptation, and how perfectly timed. American commerce at its finest and most clever. He can simply reorder his existence. Dial 800, speak to flat-toned, pleasant Midwesterners, and reorder his life.

Dreams delivered to your doorstep. Consummately American, these catalogs, he'd always felt. The object as imagery, imagery as object, the distinction utterly blurred. Here was all any immigrant ever needed to see. Catalogs of objects, still entering his former wooden fortress of objects, sliding in deftly under the door, Trojan horse–like, glossy and perfect-bound.

He thumbs idly through an electronics catalog filled with gadgetry, trying to recall what purchase, if any, would have brought a catalog like this into the house. Maybe the security system; he thinks about the house's protection, its elaborate, multizoned alarm system, which he and Rose installed and then steadfastly kept unarmed. But it would have made no difference on the day of the move, Peke knows, when all the doors were thrown open, as it happened, welcoming the thieves, letting them shop—spend the day shopping, as it were.

He wanders around. The house is identically empty to their first and last night in it. But of course, that emptiness now has a completely different quality. The same wide-planked maple and cherry floors. The same panoramas of woodland beyond the windows. The same loved evergreens and deciduous trees and prize plantings doted on individually through the seasons like children. But a new memory now lies atop all the others, smothering them. The memory of plunder, of loss. Of the uniformed men's earnest and smiling faces. Smiling like carnival barkers.

The uniformed men. The empty house. The images push at him resiliently. He tamps them down, focuses intently on the here and now.

His desk drawer. His papers. He tries to picture them. Is he forgetting anything? That depends, he realizes, on whether he has truly grown forgetful. Perhaps in his new forgetfulness he'll even forget about this insult. Or perhaps this event will stir him from his forgetfulness. His lack of material concern, of material attentiveness, could hurt him now, particularly with the insurance companies. He and Rose could have itemized the things in the house, like the insurance companies always suggest. His wife might very well recall more than he, though he has begun to see that she isn't necessarily much better at remembering. And if he can see that in her, then isn't that a good sign about his own alertness?

His lack of materialism. Not keeping account. It concerns him as he waits for the adjusters. But only a little.

Is he forgetting anything? He doesn't think so. He hasn't had to truly worry about anything in so long.

The fact is, he's been good at forgetting. And he knows that while some of his forgetting is certainly biological, an inevitable consequence of aging, he also knows that some of it is another sort of forgetting. A habit, a practice of forgetting. Purposeful and protective and useful. Forgetting as healing, as balm. Forgetting ancient events that this event seems nonetheless determined to call up. He has never needed to distinguish between the two kinds of forgetting—the natural and the adaptive. They have contributed to each other, flowed into each other easily. He senses—fears—that that is about to change.

In the end, he doesn't know whether it has crept up into his consciousness or if it has been there all the time, while some part of him has vainly tried to suppress it. Suppress the parallels, which have loomed up, increasingly insistent. He realizes that this might be what Rose's silence is actually about. Embarrassment. Discomfort. At recognizing the parallels, too, even from the little she knows of them. Seeing them before he did. Remaining silent, not wanting to make it worse. She fears, perhaps, that it is too much for him to handle, to take in. That it is too much for him to accept.

The uniformed men. The empty house. It has happened to him before. As bizarre, as unpredictable, as unaccountable as what has just occurred is, it has occurred before. On another continent. In another life. He has tried to cut off the association, tried to bury it in the thick dirt and deep distance of the past. But it rises, powerful and insuppressible. An event poised fragilely between memory and actuality. Between the mind's eye and the witness's uncomprehending gaze.

The uniformed men. The empty house. It has happened to him before.

>>>>

The adjusters pull up. Get out of their nondescript sedan formally, funereally, though they're both cherubically young.

"Stanley Peke?" the closer one asks, squinting at the figure seated on the slate front steps.

Peke nods curtly.

The accounting soon begins. Walking through the empty house, room by room, to let each room trigger his remembering. Going through the items again in his mind, individually—just as he had watched the items that day as the movers loaded them into the truck. But this time, the cataloging is only in memory. This time, there is only each object's ghost form.

L aFarge doesn't mind all the lifting. He used to lift equipment in a rock band—keyboards, amplifiers—so it's second nature. Got him off the streets of the Bronx, after his graffiti stage, that band did. This is like being in a rock band. The four guys. The guys you're close to, you work with, you argue with, and then make up with. He misses the band and the music, but here the work is steady, the pay is good, and the only rule is you have to shut up about it. The lifting doesn't bother him. You get to know the secrets of leverage and angles. It's an art. You can do it even if you aren't an especially big guy. And you get to see the country. Fancy places you never knew existed. Fancy homes. Rich people. Crisscrossing this great land. It's an education. He has Nick to thank.

Nick probably wouldn't have liked seeing him talking to the rich old man, LaFarge knows. Probably wouldn't like it at all. Nick probably would be nervous. But LaFarge felt bad for the guy, rich or not. LaFarge knows it isn't really hurting these people. They're insured and all. They get over it. But he feels bad anyway.

They are at a rest stop, having a quick breakfast. Sitting on and standing around the rear gate of the truck with donut wrappers in their laps, a steady wind blowing off the interstate at them, carrying on it, even this early, that familiar oppressive highway hum.

The aimless discussion backs innocently, inadvertently into it. "I don't know," says LaFarge. "Seems awfully harsh. To even take their pictures . . ."

He knows as soon as he says it that it's a mistake. A big one.

Nick looks at him, instantly annoyed. Instantly transformed. "Oh, that doesn't work for you?"

LaFarge turns meek, goes silent. He says nothing more, but it's already too late. He's gone too far. He's touched a nerve. Nick is already stewing, going molten. His anger like bile, once risen, unsettlable.

"OK, then, we won't take the pictures," Nick says coolly, his sarcasm hardly masking his anger. His anger at being questioned, being challenged.

He tosses the remains of his raisin bagel into the Dumpster alongside them—*you've ruined my breakfast*—lifts the back gate of the truck, disappears into it.

Emerges with a carton.

Standing on the gate of the truck, above them, he heaves it into the huge green Dumpster.

"There. We're not taking the pictures."

>>>

A half hour later, after driving in silence:

"You take the pictures because you need to take everything," Nick says patiently, with exaggerated calm, as if explaining to a child. "Because you need it to be total annihilation. Total defeat. You don't want them getting any ideas about mercy from you. You want to create the impression of professionalism"—the implication clearly *with guys like you, LaFarge, it will be only an impression*—"so they know what they're dealing with."

The others stay silent. Listening.

"What's the point of taking everything if you're not going to take everything?"

They roll into the compound at night. 150 acres, dirt cheap—*dirt cheap*, in this case, having literal meaning. Paid for with cash, a form of payment that out here didn't seem to raise an eyebrow. It's about the ugliest 150 acres imaginable—scrub, dirt, pools of rusty standing water. But it's his. And it works. And this is only storage anyway. This is business. His life is in Vegas and Miami Beach and twice a year in Rio. Trysts with the comically proportioned, cartoon-chested Viola. Her body offers constant reminders and visual assurance that it can never be a relationship. That this can never be anything more than a consumerist arrangement. Which gives him a sense of control that he needs. She's a package on a shelf—a high, special shelf, out of the reach of others, he pretends—a package to take down, comport with, and replace back on the high shelf when finished. It is well suited to a loner. A loner with cash.

The crew knows about Viola. They don't know about Armando, and they don't have to.

Another difference that made his foster parents nervous, that made him nervous: a difference that wasn't merely his intelligence.

But fine objects have always aroused him. And Viola and Armando, they're both fine objects themselves. In both cases, it's an arrangement. He doesn't question it too much. That's the meaning of the term *arrangement*—no questions.

Viola. Armando. It's a reflection of his living outside the rules. That's what he tells himself. That's all he tells himself.

>>>

It has always concerned Nick a little that they are out here with the nuts. With the white separatists and the millennial fire-and-brimstone crowd and anti-IRS warriors and Aryan militias and ultra-Christians and Armageddonists. But what can you do? This is where his activities are the least suspicious. This is where his privacy will be respected. (Although he's started to have the feeling all these personal-privacy hermits and land-rights extremists and off-the-grid kooks might in fact be nosier than anybody else, but they won't act on whatever they might know or figure out.) This is where you can pull a semi in and out, and though people might talk, locals might mutter, they'll keep it to themselves, if it ever comes to the involvement of any authority.

The cults—they always have these ramshackle compounds, don't they? The guys who burn themselves up and go down firing and make suicide pacts and treat their children to poison juices. Is he in a cult, too? A cult of things, of objects? He's obsessive. He might be just as obsessive as they are. Just as crazy. But his is no cult of death. His is a cult of survival.

>>>

The welcome, sudden silence after the day-and-night drone of the engine. The fresh air after the close, musty stench of the truck's cab. The immense, star-soaked Montana night sky after the frustrating clots of traffic, the glaring illumination of highways and cities. Nick watches as Chiv, LaFarge, and Al go, wordlessly, familiarly, straight toward the farmhouse. He stands outside a moment, listening, while they crank up the spectacular stereo in the crummy, beat-up living room and splinter the stillness. Chairs and couches you can barely stomach sitting in. They are lighting up and stretching back. Cigarettes. Marijuana. Someone will start a midnight spaghetti dinner.

In a few minutes, Nick walks in with a carton under his arm. He goes past the mild celebration, the ritual winding-down, into his office. Flips on the office lights, closes the door behind him.

The Dell computer sitting on the Biedermeier table. The elegant Knoll office chair.

Rows of antiques catalogs. Rows of reference books. American eighteenth-century furniture. Ming dynasty porcelain. Postimpressionist paintings. All the Sotheby's and Christie's collection announcements, delivered biweekly to a post office box. He's fairly expert at this point. He laughs sometimes that it's the office of a fag. That he's a street tough in a fag business. Or maybe a fag in a street tough's business. He stands outside easy categories. In their blurry margins. That's partly why he remains a loner. But remaining a loner is part of his success, he knows.

The guys will unload in the morning. No rush. He'll begin to contact buyers. And only eventually—slowly—to fence. First store everything for a while, in case some police department does initially check with known fences, which is all they can practically do.

He will wait until the little bits of his trail go fairly cool, if not icy cold.

>>>

He's brought in with him from the truck the carton containing the old man's desk drawer contents. At the house, Nick personally packed the contents of Peke's desk while taking mental notes.

He begins now to go through it more carefully, systematically. You never know what you'll find. Old stock certificates. Savings bonds. Safe-deposit box keys. He always starts with the desk contents. You never know.

Within minutes, he's come across a decorative little cardboard box—about two inches square, must have held cuff links or something. He opens the box, and there it is: a safe-deposit box key. Labeled with the box number, for Christ's sake. What a world these people live in. They know their own forgetfulness. They think they're invulnerable.

Little town like that. Maybe two, three local banks at most. So this presents an opportunity, of course. To go back for the contents. Unless the old man has already emptied it out. If he's alert enough. Sometimes the shock of an event like this stirs them to alertness. Stirs them at least momentarily out of the lethargy and complacency they've been living in. But an event like this can also confuse them, paralyze them. If the old man realizes and changes the lock? There's a chance of that. But there's also a chance—a good chance—he won't even think of it. These rich old people. He's learned a lot about them, doing this. And one thing he's learned, a lesson initially hard for him to take in, hard for him to accept, given the material meagerness, the tatters and scraps, of his own grim upbringing: a lot of them, they can't even keep track of what they own.

Nick's got Peke's signature in triplicate on the stack of bogus transportation documents. In the desk drawer, he's got plenty of Peke's IDs—Social Security card, passport, etc. If it were a big institution, a big city bank, he would have someone practice forging the signature, to match the signature card on file, which would get them into the safe-deposit box vault room. But this is a small town. Probably a small, old-fashioned, personal bank. They might know Peke personally. They might even be watching for Peke's name. In which case Nick's got another idea. A deft, beautiful idea.

It's safer, of course, not to go back. Not to risk it. But there's something in this old man. Something in the man's proud posture, his swollen chest. Some arrogance, some strength, something unshakable, that rubs at Nick. That rubbed at him a little all that moving day. That's rubbed at him a little the whole trip here. The mild, unplaceable European accent. As if the old man doesn't belong in America and has come here and taken Nick's things. As if, if he hadn't come here, these would be Nick's things. As if this is a little Manichaean universe of just the two of them, and he has taken up Nick's rightful possession of it and right place in it.

He holds up the old key. Brass, faded, and dull. Cut with the old-style round fob. Check the oldest bank. The first bank. They'd lived in that town forty years, didn't he hear the old man say, and undoubtedly people like that don't change banks a lot. He may have forgotten entirely about the safe-deposit box. After all, here's the key in the corner of a drawer. Likely it's worth the risk, worth the effort. The old man's memory is shaky. And if he changes the lock, so be it.

This one, Nick is going to hit again. Wipe out completely. Pluck the last feathers of the proud peacock.

He continues carefully through the carton of desk drawer contents, but it's like staying down in the mine when you've already had a strike. In his head, Nick is already heading back East.

5

The adjusters gone, Peke closes the door of their home for the final time in forty years, slips the key for the last time into the lock, and at that moment—only then—thinks of the other key. The key in the corner of his desk drawer. The key to their safe-deposit box.

His heart clutches a little. He can picture it in the very corner of the right desk drawer, under the papers. He can picture it there, in its little box. Shiny, a brass invitation . . .

How can he have forgotten? But the answer is obvious. Because he is seventy-two. Because what's in the safe-deposit box hasn't been thought about by either of them for years. Because the annual charge for the box is simply deducted from one of the monthly bank statements that he barely checks anyway.

In a moment, though, he is calm again. Not alarmed. It's easy enough for Peke to have the box's lock changed. It's late afternoon; the bank is closed now. He can take care of it first thing in the morning. It seems unlikely that the thief will even come across the key.

The prudent thing will be to change the lock. The safe thing. Peke thinks for a moment about this.

If he did find the key, would a creature like this thief actually return for the items in the safe-deposit box? It seems preposterous. Clearly, the thief's scam calls for planning and care, and to come back to the scene of the crime would be outside the plan, unnecessarily risky. Nevertheless, the key is there, and Peke can't remember for sure, but he has the nagging sense that he actually Scotch-taped the box number to the key at some point, years ago, so that he wouldn't forget it. There are only a couple of main banks in town, so it isn't out of the question that the thief could locate the safe-deposit box.

Peke sits for the last time on the front steps of his former home. He forces himself to watch that day—moving day—again, carefully, in his mind's eye. To listen again. To observe again the care, the thoroughness, the precision of the operation. All of which he appreciated as he watched them work. All of which now have a different meaning, now seen in a different light. The calculation. The mechanical coldness of the short, broad man's smile.

Yes. The thoroughness, the completeness, seem somehow, for this man, part of the point. Maybe for this man it is a necessary annihilation. Maybe it's merely the perverse satisfaction of a job well done. He remembers men like that. He remembers that particular character trait, having observed it a long time ago.

Thoroughness, completeness. Admirable qualities in your employees, your colleagues—except when those qualities stand for something else, hostile and unresolved. Something more than thoroughness and completeness. Some effort to prove something, to combat some inner messiness, to deny some inner sense of incompletion. Yes, Peke could see how a man like this might actually return. Come back to finish the job.

To be sure, the odds are vastly against it, but just to be safe, change the lock. That is what any cautious, just-victimized, seventy-two-year-old man would do.

He has brought the stack of catalogs outside with him. He was going to take them back to the inn, to Rose, not knowing what else to do with them, exactly. He had set them down on the flagstone step next to him, while he fiddled with locking the door. Now, sitting on the cool steps of the flagstone landing, he begins to thumb through the stack, until he reaches the electronics catalog once again. He opens it, thumbs through, then begins to squint closely . . .

His seventy-two-year-old heart ticks a little faster.

And in counterpoint to his quickened heartbeat, Peke feels a momentary calm. The day seems suddenly supernally quiet, the wind and birds caught in a momentary pause, as he squints at the electronics catalog—its communication and information gadgetry, its security devices, its pages of protective paranoia—in the fading afternoon light . . .

>>>

The Pekes' safe-deposit box is at a local bank called First County. It's a small town. Peke knows the bank president from local charity functions. "Earl? Stan Peke."

"Yes, Stan, hello." Then a shift in tone. The formal, appropriate condolence, and within it, an authentic one, too. "So sorry to hear what happened, Stan. Jesus. What a world." *So the news has made its way around*, thinks Peke. *Well, really, how could it not?*

"Well, thank you. I appreciate that." His slow, authoritative tones. People always seemed to believe him. To accept his authority. To defer. That was good. A small usefulness of his past in the present. There was good reason to believe him. "Listen, the reason I'm calling. We've got a safe-deposit box over there at First County. And the key . . ."

"You've lost your key," Earl cuts in, hearing the first note of a familiar refrain. "You need a new one . . ." Earl's spry, neighborly eagerness to be helpful.

"The key was in my desk," Peke explains, "and everything in the desk was stolen . . ."

"Oh, OK, then. You need a new box *and* key. Just to be safe. You never know these days. I'll waive all the usual ID requirements for you; I'll see to that, you know, in light of what happened, and not having your documentation, I'm guessing . . ."

Peke goes a little slower now. Says it pleasantly, but as though he doesn't plan to say it again. "Yes, I'd like another key. That'd be nice of you, Earl." Now very slowly. "But no, see, I want to keep the same safe-deposit box."

"But . . ."

"I still want the stolen key to work."

"But . . . they could get into it," Earl says bluntly, not understanding. He sounds disturbed, distraught, as if it could be his own loss. "They could go through your effects, Stan, and they could figure out where that key goes. It's a long shot, but they could. I'm assuming you wrote down the number of the box somewhere— most people do—and isn't it possible they could come across that?" The fantasy of the thief's return, growing in the cautious banker, gaining in vividness, an increasing momentum of colorful alarm. "Don't you see, Stan, if they know what box it is, and if one of them can learn to copy your signature and uses your desk contents to put together some ID . . ." He calms down a degree. "I guess I could alert the employees to anyone using your name. But that's hardly foolproof or secure, Stan . . . I don't know." He pauses. "Christ, we're a local bank. Can't we just change the box?" Peke can tell that Earl is concerned Peke doesn't quite understand the nature of the danger. That Peke's not putting two and two together. Indicating

Earl's doubt about Peke's mental capacity. Probably now guessing at his long-standing customer's age. *Early seventies? So he could be a little senile, a little irrational.* Not unlike the thief, Peke realizes, with his false concern that the Pekes had a place to sleep that night. Only cleverly gathering the information.

"I understand," says Peke, assuring him, then repeating the odd request once more, just so it's clear to the banker. "I want a new key, but I want to keep the old box. I promise you, Earl, I understand."

P eke knows already.
It will be the watch.

A man's gold watch. From some Monaco estate sale, the money going to charity. Too gaudy to wear.

Practically speaking, the police won't—can't—simply station a man at the bank. The thief's return is too unlikely. Merely the paranoia, the vivid fantasy, of an old man recently violated, the police would say. And—assuming it is not paranoia—even if the thief does return, it could be weeks. Months. And an officer stationed there might prove useless anyway. Because someone this smart wouldn't come himself. He'd find a way to send a well-dressed woman. Or an old man. Someone inconspicuous. Couldn't Peke's signature be easily forged? Or could the thief find some other way to circumvent the old-fashioned bank's old-fashioned security? The more Peke thinks of Earl's initial alarm, the more Peke doesn't doubt the vulnerability. If he has the key and knows the box number, won't he be able to work out the rest? But the thief's return is hardly enough of a prospect to have the bank watched, or to make a special case of Peke's safe-deposit box, or to change the bank's safe-deposit box arrangements.

But the gold watch. This thief—whoever, wherever he is— probably can't display most of the items. The furniture. The paintings. They're fenced, undoubtedly, or kept privately, personally, perhaps in some kind of hidden, supersecure Shangri-la.

Yet the watch could be worn. It's gaudy enough. And this guy— whoever he is—he's like a crow, isn't he? Loves objects. Shiny things. It's one proof of his success that he can safely display, probably. The one item, perhaps, that he can risk having out in public. A constant reminder on his wrist—a reminder to himself and to anyone close enough—of his own success.

Peke needs to be sure, though, that he is not gravitating to it merely for its symbolic perfection. Time stopped, time collapsed, time upended, time repeating. Earlier time and later time, merging now, inseparable. Time circling on itself, lapping and overlapping, its hands dancing with one another on the watch face. No, this needs to be a practical choice. But it is, he decides. The symbolism is incidental.

The watch is perfect.

>>>

"This will be a long process," says the young insurance man morosely to Peke over the phone. "A claim like this, police reports, the research—I wish it could be simpler, faster, but," he says resolutely, "it won't be."

Peke nods. He knew as much. That's how insurance is set up. All possible process, all possible delay. If you're old enough, they probably hope you won't live long enough to see the settlement. At which point they can play new games with your estate.

There is, on the other hand, a certain lightness to owning nothing, he is quickly discovering. To living without objects. Without any possessions to weigh you down, to take care of. So much of their lives had become custodial, menial, in a way—luxuriously menial. Taking care of financial matters, attending to the grounds, lining up the service people—the tree people, the landscape people, the pond people, the cleaning people, the plumber for the old pipes, the painters, the electrician. That is all gone. Lifted. Which was, of course, a large part of the reason for moving in the first place. The absence of objects serves only to accentuate, to verify, the decision to sell and move.

Yes, there is a lightness. This thief, whoever he is, has returned Peke and Rose to a lighter, simpler time. Maybe he should thank him, Peke thinks for a moment. But only cynically. Because the lightness, the simplicity, is just a by-product. Of a rapacious violation. A lawless Mongol plunder.

The objects, the possessions, had measured the progress of their life in some way. This seemed true, in at least a superficial sense, for their friends and neighbors, for much of their social class. Their possessions marked the progress of their life not in a pure volume of accumulation—which in itself was somewhat embarrassing, foolish-looking, potentially imprisoning (one could be a slave to the abundance of one's own possessions). But the possessions measured progress in the way in which certain objects stood for certain stages in one's life, in one's evolving taste. Objects commemorated certain events—a painting for a birthday, a necklace for a celebration. Objects reminded one of enthusiasms—a favorite golf iron, a ratty sweater, a son's old catcher's mitt and mask, a stuffed animal that slept for years next to one's daughter. They signified what had mattered to you, and what mattered still. For Peke, that had particularly been the case. And that means of measurement was gone.

The symmetry occurs to Peke. The perfect, clean symmetry. That he who had everything now has nothing. And this thief—this thief who would otherwise have nothing, Peke presumes—now has everything. There is something big, pure, about it.

And for Stanley Peke, there is a special reverberation to it. An extra harmonic. Arriving in New York Harbor on a trunk steamer at the end of the war with literally nothing. Not just the proverbial nothing in his pockets, as he has joked latterly at elegant dinner parties in chandeliered rooms, but less than that, because in fact he had no pockets. Holes in both pockets of his only pair of pants, pockets that, as a nine-year-old boy, he couldn't foresee needing to hold anything in anyway—so onboard the trunk steamer he'd borrowed a knife to cut out the extra pocket fabric, and with the needle and thread and the assistance of a woman in the middle bunk of the strangely musty women's cabin, he had sewn knee patches with it, which he needed far more. He can still feel those pocketless pants when he tries to. The cold New York air reaching in to his bony white thighs. New York winter wind off the Hudson, entering through the pocket holes, finding his white skin. He has gone back to those streets with Rose, in winter, as it happened, pointing out all the places while the heat of the big black Mercedes poured out of the vents onto him and his wife, the big efficient heat of their big efficient German car. The enemy's car. (People seem puzzled about it sometimes, his having two Mercedes, but to him it's simple: he enjoys occupying the enemy's car—being at the wheel of, in control of, their prize creation. As if he has taken it. As if he is a thief.) The heat and the Berlioz symphony pouring into the passenger cabin, tumbling over the light tan, buttery leather and swirling around them, a personal, warm, supple atmosphere.

The freezing wind whipping outside was in fact rendered completely silent, inconsequential, by the Mercedes's double-thick window glass. He had pointed at his past through the windows with a mildly arthritic, liver-marked hand, pointed as if through a protective membrane, as if through a shield, as if through time . . .

He started with nothing, and has now been returned to nothing. As if the thief is some perverse incarnation of the Fates, howling down at him cruelly, whispering to him through this incident. But this thief is not the Fates. This thief is a thief. Preying on the old.

Stanislaw Shmuel Pecoskowitz. Another existence, which this clever thief has summoned back. Something that a thief has inadvertently returned to its owner. Should Peke thank him for that, too, as for the sudden sense of lightness?

Of course, they were going to live more simply anyway. They had spoken to some nice people at Sotheby's, some educated, diffident men and women who ran the relevant collections. They had mutually decided on a schedule for sales to begin, for tax reasons, about a year after setting up in Santa Barbara. They were going to live more simply—but on their own terms. Not on the terms of a thief. The proceeds would go to charities. Not to this . . . this clever, sneaky little animal.

Yes, it is just things, primarily. Just objects. But for him, for a survivor, they mean something more. The objects have a purpose beyond themselves—beyond their *quiddity*, as philosophers call it: the merely literal properties of the things themselves. He is doubtful, suspicious, of this extra layer of meaning but at the same time can't deny that he feels it. This connection of the objects to him, and him to them.

Perhaps it's simple. They furnish proof. It's evidence. Proof of life. Proof of *his* life.

And for him there is something even beyond that. Something that transcends his personal involvement. It has to do with wrongness in the abstract. Sheer wrongness and violation—and the opportunity to address it. An opportunity that, as a survivor, as a victim of history, he hasn't had before.

The opportunity to address a wrong. But he doesn't experience it as a moral imperative. A moral imperative would involve choice, and this is somehow beyond choice. Somehow beyond his will. In fact, he feels powerless to act otherwise.

The uniformed men. The empty house.

It is not even worth thinking about, in a way. Although it is uniquely tied up, he knows, with being a survivor—with how he experiences his human responsibilities as a survivor. It's impossible to describe or understand or pin down. No, it's not a moral imperative for Peke, but it's an imperative nonetheless. It is deeper, more basic, more primal, than moral.

He needs his things back.

Nick has a cup of coffee at Freedom Café, at the dirt crossroads of Rural Routes 102 and 33.

In a surrounding, unvarying universe of mud and dust and crusty dirt, of rutted tarmac and thick woods and rusty pickup trucks and bitter wind and harsh sky, Freedom Café, it seems, is true north. Locus and epicenter.

A wooden counter. Cracked linoleum tables. Inexplicable crater-like holes in the ceiling. An ancient refrigerator and griddle top, recipient of a cursory weekly wipe. All of it in proud, defiant violation, Nick is sure, of every building, fire, safety, food, and beverage code of the state of Montana.

Any time of day or evening, he's noticed, there's a smattering of the militia types in here. You can pick them out easily, because they're always sporting some degree of paramilitary garb. Sometimes head-to-toe camouflage, sometimes just an armband or a military utility belt beneath their rancher's jacket or dirty parka, sometimes just a DON'T TREAD ON ME collar pin. He doesn't like their smug, proofless pride, their meaningless swagger. But he contributes to their crazy cause. Slips cash into a plain envelope, gives it to the counterman, who obviously passes it on to an appropriate party, because of the modest, wordless head nods he gets. He gives what must be—here amid the dirt and scrub—a notable amount of money.

Nothing is ever said about it. Not much besides a head nod of acknowledgment ever passes between him and any of them. But Nick, with his mean-streets mentality, considers it protection. The dirt and scrub, the acres of dense brush and infinity of trees, are an alien landscape to a kid who grew up on cracked macadam, jumping in and out of abandoned buildings, sprinting gleefully through a paved-over universe. You never know what will happen out here. What will come. And he knows it's a good investment. Although nothing has ever been said, he knows these nuts can't wait to defend him. Are just itchy to show him their appreciation someday. To show him what they're made of. Come Armageddon.

These characters make him nervous. So do the local skinheads, who are louder and more boisterous and have at best a loose, looping connection to any philosophy or point of view. But he recognizes this is where he belongs. He bought his Dobermans from a skinhead who raises and trains them out of his trailer. This is the home of lawlessness. It's where lawlessness is the unofficial law. This is what's happened to the Wild West, he supposes. This is where it's gone. So this is where he's gone with it.

Peke picks up the new key from Earl, exchanges a few sunny pleasantries, and is led personally by Earl to the lovely red-carpeted foyer that is the entrance to the safe-deposit box vault room. Here Earl leaves him with a deferential smile. The VIP treatment, small-town version. Relaxed. Informal.

Peke walks straight to the box—Earl has looked up what number it is, but Peke thinks he might have remembered anyway by his sense of its position on the far wall. Damn it. So why did he bother to record it in his bottom desk drawer?

Well, this is all precautionary, so far-fetched anyway. The thief probably won't have the cleverness for this. Or might have more cleverness than this and stay away.

But a crow is drawn to sparkle—some instinct in Peke suspects such a bird, such a flight.

Peke opens the lock, pulls out the drawer.

Some bearer bonds, old stock certificates, a copy of a superseded will. He's forgotten about half this stuff. And nestled among the papers, clumped and curled, several pieces of jewelry too heavy and impractical and gaudy to wear.

What should he leave in here, as a lure? Only a little of it? Then the thief might suspect that Peke—or somebody—was on to him, and might withdraw. Might not take the bait.

Or does Peke risk leaving all of it, letting the thief feel overwhelmed by his good fortune, letting him try to stuff his pockets? Unfortunately, the more that is in the metal box—the more camouflage, the more distraction—the better the chance that what he's thinking will work. It's best, unfortunately, to leave it all.

He knows at least this about the thief: the thief will take it all. Whatever is in there. A thief who cleans out a home down to its bare walls, down to its dust, is a thief who empties out a safe-deposit box.

So Peke removes, for now, only the gaudy gold watch. Puts it in his pocket. Closes the drawer. Feels nothing in particular, he notices, about the contents. About the objects. He is onto something bigger now.

Itzhak had been a jeweler's apprentice when the war began. Here in town, he has a little local store. He's a different nationality from Peke. A very different background, a very different person. But they are nevertheless bound. As far as Peke knows, since Myra Goldtharp's passing, they are the only two survivors in town. The survivors' club. Exclusive. Lifetime membership. The dues are high.

Itzhak has had the little store for fifty years. It says so in the window. He has not become an industrialist or a philanthropist. But he has had a success. He has had a life.

Peke stands in the cool shop, amid the glass display cases lined with dramatically lit objects. Bowls and vases of porcelain and cut glass. Necklaces and bracelets and rings, mantel clocks and heirloom watches.

As if somehow knowing, as if without even being informed by the shopgirl or by his daughter, Itzhak emerges from the back.

Seeing each other inevitably summons the past for both of them. It's all they can mean to each other. Peke lived in the fancy section. Itzhak has his store and lives very simply, Peke knows. They are different stories from the same war. A war with fewer and fewer stories.

"I'm sorry to hear," says Itzhak. His accent still prominent after all these years here, while Peke's is almost gone.

"Thank you."

If anyone knows, Itzhak knows. How it is everything, a thing like this. And how at the same time, it is nothing.

"What brings you?" Itzhak says.

"What else? I have a jewelry job for you." He hears a slight return of his own accent, as if reengaged by Itzhak's. The slight harshness, the slight clipped challenge in his words. He takes out the gold watch. "My watch."

"What is it?"

"Can I show you in back?" Peke says. Clearly meaning privately.

Itzhak nods, leads him.

It is a dark, cramped little alley of a room. Broken clock faces; springs and gears and coils; dusty, chaotic, untended, particularly compared with the rest of the neat little shop. Time indeed seems stopped here. A fairy-tale workshop out of another era, and Peke can feel that it is Itzhak's alone—that the pretty shopgirl and Itzhak's daughter come only to the doorway, never step in, as if fearing they will be lost in time.

Itzhak frowns, looking at the watch. "But it seems to be working."

Peke takes a small, clear, unopened package from his jacket pocket. "But not with this."

Itzhak squints at the no-nonsense black lettering on the small, clear packaging. Beneath the plastic is a small sensor, half the diameter of a dime, about as thin.

Peke ordered it from the electronics catalog. He dialed the 800 number and spoke to the pleasant, midwestern woman operator.

A section of the catalog features security devices. Tiny cameras. Tracking and homing devices. Antibugging equipment. Seeing-through-walls surveillance. He's never gone in for any of these devices. He has insurance. It's America. He has felt safe, and with the devices, he would not have felt as safe.

"I want you to put that into the watch. Can you do that?"

Itzhak looks and nods with barely a delay.

"How long will the sensor run?"

Itzhak's low, inflectionless voice. The accent so thick it's slurry. "If I attach it to the watchworks, it should run when the watch does. But who's to say, exactly? It's a little bit experimental, yes?"

Itzhak opens the tiny package.

While Peke, standing next to him, simultaneously opens the somewhat larger package that came with it. An antenna on a small black box. Like a palm-size transistor radio.

As he watches Itzhak work, pushing and poking at different angles with the tiny jeweler's tools, he can see the little green row of numbers on Itzhak's inner forearm. Smudged, but still there. You can have them removed nowadays, easily, but what would be the point now for Itzhak? He may want to look at the numbers, be aware of them. Peke has no numbers. Escaped the numbers. Had an entirely different experience. His survival bears no physical evidence like Itzhak's. His survival is invisible.

Peke thinks how astonishing it is that Itzhak can come here and carry on the same craft in the same way—a world and a half century away. Still a jeweler. Picking up where he left off. Whereas Peke has had to remake himself entirely. Become a new person. Peke from

Pecoskowitz. The world has inverted, turned inside out, ignited within the crucible of history and emerged transformed and unrecognizable, and yet Itzhak is still standing at his jeweler's table. How is that possible?

He watches Itzhak work, and it takes only a minute, but in an idle, waiting minute a lot of thinking can get done.

Itzhak inevitably makes Peke consider his own assimilation. An assimilated American Jew. An identity, he thinks resentfully, as profoundly and unfairly reductive as any previous European one. Assimilating completely, into the dreams, the values, the spirit of the place, losing himself in it, abandoning himself to the new as much as Itzhak does not.

Once Itzhak is done with the minute work, Peke switches on the black, palm-size device to test it.

There is immediately a consistent little beep. The tiny setup screen flashes GPS—GLOBAL POSITIONING SYSTEM for a quick moment, before a grid of coordinates appears. He and Itzhak look at each other.

No, a thief is unlikely to equate an old man like Peke, an old Jew like Pecoskowitz, with the vanguard in electronic surveillance. But Peke is himself a product of the unpredictable, a subject of the incongruent, and he therefore knows its power.

"What do I owe you?"

Itzhak slaps away the question like an annoying insect buzzing around his head. You owe me nothing.

And Itzhak never asks why. Because, Peke knows, he can perhaps imagine. And something they both know—something that informs both of their existences so deeply that they never need speak of it, and never would: anything now is inconsequential, is mere coda, to before.

"I'll just set the time . . . ," says Itzhak, the final step, indicating he's finished.

"No," instructs Peke sharply. "Leave the time wrong. And don't wind it any more. I want it to run down."

Itzhak leaves the hands alone, regards the rare watch another moment, before passing it wordlessly back to Peke.

>>>

Peke knows that the tiny device represents much more to him than a chance to find this thief. He has known that since the moment he saw it in the electronics catalog, when he felt it immediately sidling up to his soul.

Global positioning. It's symbolic of being found.

It's a powerful talisman, an electronic amulet, for one who was once so lost. One who was once a seven-year-old waif, a child wandering the earth . . .

Peke feels a stirring in himself—a momentary uplift—a brief, blind optimism that the world actually progresses, that man's knowledge, his science, his efforts, make life better, make it good . . .

Now, you could be located anywhere on that earth's surface . . . Now, no one is lost . . .

A watch, thinks Peke. *Tick, tock, tick, tock.* Every moment relentlessly marked. And with this special watch, marked in time and space.

He still recognizes how unlikely the scenario is. Absurd, farfetched. This is something he's doing merely for himself, to fashion some response, to be doing *something* in preparation, in defense. And the watch is appropriate for that, too, he realizes. Its slow ticking. Its limitless patience. Its countdown quality. All appropriate to a rendezvous. One that will probably never come.

Tick, tock, tick, tock.

S o entertain me," Nick says to the blandly handsome man and the pale-skinned, oval-faced woman who have just slid together into Nick's booth in a dimly lit working-class bar in Yonkers, a town at the forgotten blue-collar edge of Westchester. "Let me see. Entertain me," he says, without a smile, so they understand he has no interest in entertainment.

It has come together smoothly up to now. Not surprisingly, Nick knows quite a few experts on keys and locks. One of them told him, simply from the vintage of the key, what year the issuing bank went into business. That made it easy. First County it is.

He has hired Constantine to case the bank for a couple of days. Constantine—neat, silent, morose, accurate. A human tomb, with the knack of invisibility. To make sure no one is watching the safe-deposit boxes. To check on bank procedures and make sure they stay in place. Casing it to make sure no one else is casing it. Being careful. These rich old guys. They're rich for a reason, after all. And the old man might very well at some point remember that his key is in his desk drawer, the safe-deposit box number taped on it.

Per Nick's specific instructions, Constantine has in turn hired the man and woman in the dark booth with Nick now. Nick wouldn't go into the bank himself, of course. That would be foolish.

It is, after all, a small town. And the old guy—if he's still around—would certainly remember what Nick looks like. He might be ingrained by now in the old man's angry memory.

Per Nick's instructions to Constantine, the man and woman rented a safe-deposit box together at First County a week ago. It's a small-town bank—the new rented box and the old man's box aren't far from each other, as it happens. It's such a small-town bank, according to Constantine, some longtime customers still go unaccompanied to their boxes. The signature cards with the box numbers are kept in a Rolodex outside the entrance to the vault room. The way it's been for decades, no doubt.

When the man and woman now opposite Nick rented their box, they signed the signature card together. As husband and wife. Making themselves immediately less suspicious, and giving themselves twice the time to get a good look at the signature card itself. Its card stock. Its layout. Its typefaces. To confirm each other's perceptions of it. In order to help Constantine make a duplicate of the signature card over the next few days—an exact duplicate, with only one small, important detail different. A different box number printed on it. Stanley Peke's box number.

"Go ahead. Let's see," Nick says now in the booth in the bar—humorless, insistent—and the man obediently reaches into his pocket and takes out a deck of playing cards.

Nick has even checked the house once more, just to be sure. The Mercedes sedan wasn't in the garage. He half expected to see a Volvo station wagon or a minivan, young kids in the yard, a new life, turnover, but found the house still empty. In any case, no first-class mail in the mailbox. The Pekes seem to be long gone. Santa Barbara, didn't the old man say?

The man shuffles the playing cards expertly. Here in the dark, stifling bar, Nick feels the air from the cards as the man shoots them showily from one hand to the other.

It will take place, in fact, before anyone even enters the vault room. When a half-attentive small-town bank employee pulls out their signature card, and while they are all engaged in the process of signing names and verifying signatures, they will—again, the advantage of two of them—cause the signature card to innocently drop and, retrieving it, will replace it with the duplicate signature card, identical to their own, except for Peke's box number on it. Signatures verified, the employee will then ask for their safe-deposit key. They will hand Peke's key to the employee. The employee will bring them Peke's box.

In the dark bar, the man holds up a card, buries it in the pack, takes it out of his shirt pocket a moment later. He shows another card, fans the deck to show it's no longer there, pulls the card out from under the booth's table.

"So, what do you do?" asks Nick.

"Small after-dinner shows. Adult parties. Business functions. Local Rotarian stuff."

"But not around here," Nick confirms.

"Never around here," says the magician.

It should be nothing. The simplest switch—either beneath the Rolodex table or even as they are signing. The most rudimentary sleight of hand. An ace for an ace. Compared with an attentive, eager after-dinner crowd looking for their secrets, a distracted small-town bank employee not expecting magic should be a simple audience.

The man holds up the king of hearts. Drops it on the floor next to the booth. Bends down, picks it up, and turns it over. It is the king of diamonds.

Nick nods with satisfaction. It's very Nick. It's in Nick's style. Utterly simple. Low-tech. Try as he does, Nick can't resist a smile.

And hey, if they can't pull it off, if they smell something wrong, they always back off. They don't have to go through with it.

They do some piece of business at their legitimate box and exit the bank. But they've been hired specifically for their manipulative dexterity. And they know there's significant reward for their performance. They'll decide when they get in there.

>>>>

Nick stands across the street from First County, thinking it all through one last time. He wants to be sure he's considered everything. He watches a well-dressed, lucky-looking yuppie couple head up the steps and through the bank's big, twin white doors. The young couple, he notices, seem carefree, cheerful. For their exuberance, their attentiveness to each other, they could be crossing a threshold. Even from across the street, they appear untouched by hardship. He's always felt resentful of people like that. They bring out his bitterness, stir his ire.

He's been as careful as he can. So when his yuppie-looking couple enters the bank, heading to their new safe-deposit box, there's no reason to stand there anymore. Nick heads down the street.

Time for them to deal their one-card hand.

>>>>

An hour later, as agreed, they meet Nick at a different bar in Yonkers. He searches their faces as they sit down. They look to him and smile—the blandly handsome man, the oval-faced woman—and a feeling of power and satisfaction flushes through Nick. It worked. Christ! It fucking worked. So the old man didn't remember, apparently. Did not even think of it. Some were that rich: they forgot about their safe-deposit boxes. It took their children to remind them.

In the parking lot behind the bar, the man and woman transfer the contents casually from their pockets into an empty manila envelope Nick has for the occasion. They know to hold nothing back, these yuppie magicians. It isn't even a question in Nick's mind. The old brass key that Nick mailed to Constantine, the man hands back to Nick separately. Nick gives the man a small white envelope of cash.

Alone in the rental car, Nick spills the manila envelope contents onto the passenger seat. A few faded, folded bonds, perhaps redeemable, perhaps worthless now—he'll have to see. A thick gold bracelet. A ruby necklace and ornate matching earrings.

And look at this. Glittering in the sun streaming through the windshield. You don't see them like this anymore. Hands and numbers composed of tiny diamonds, rubies, and emeralds, perimeter crusted with gold. Some small, defunct, and elite German maker. One of a kind. It needs to be set. Has been sitting there for years, undoubtedly. Time. Time inside a safe-deposit box, waiting to tick again.

He sets it by his own cheap Timex. Winds the ruby stem carefully. With satisfaction sees the second hand begin to move. Time. Time released. Time to let the good times roll.

10

In an intensely floral, aggressively cheerful room (immense green and yellow swells of curtains, bedspreads and blankets and armchair and hassock, a riot of matching bloom), in a steep-dormered inn near the Delaware Water Gap, Stanley Peke and his wife are awakened from an afternoon nap by a small but insistent cell phone–like beeping emanating from his side of the bed.

"*Turnitoff . . . ,*" Rose mumbles irritably from beneath her pillow, assuming it's the clock radio set by a previous guest, as she rolls over and adjusts the pillow on her head for a few more minutes of rest. It's a reaction to what has happened, he knows, this need of hers for extra sleep. Her unconscious physiological defense. A way of pushing events away.

Peke gets up, feels around for the little, black beeping device buried in the bottom of the suitcase of new clothes, takes it out and into the bathroom with him. He closes the bathroom door, turns on the light, squints at its tiny buttons, and unfolds the paper directions next to it. He sets the directions down on the edge of the sink. His hands are trembling—with excitement, with disbelief—an extension, a manifestation, of the trembling in his chest, in his being.

He presses the zoom out button and is somewhat startled to see the digital display of a portion of Westchester County. Look at that. I-95 is marked. A little blinking dot right on it. He is trembling, but here in the harsh, sudden bathroom light, he can't help smiling either. Global positioning. Many cars come with it standard now. His friends have shown it to him excitedly on afternoon outings on their boats. Palm-size devices mounted alongside their sonar that simply and accurately position you in the universe. It must have been a short step, technically, to separating the two functions, to dividing them into twin packages: the tiny sensor that locates where you are, and the little screen and dials that explicitly display that information. Keep track of your kids. Of your cheating wife. The paranoiac's home companion.

Technology is the opposite of mystery. Technology is the end of mystery. Puts the lie to mystery. Makes everything explicit.

He feels suddenly youthful. Like a fresh-faced boy, bent over a toy, jittery with excitement, excitement uncontainable.

The thief has come for the safe-deposit contents. Peke can't believe it. It is some dark connection between them, some perverse sympathy of mind, some synchronous, watch-like ticking and clicking in unison.

The thief has come for it. It is Peke's good fortune and ill fortune rolled into one.

>>>

"Maybe we should get going," he proposes, moving her shoulder gently back and forth fifteen minutes later. "Skip the museum. Try to make Pittsburgh."

"Why the rush?" But even in her mild protest, he can hear her acquiescence.

He smiles. "Our American tour continues." An upbeat explanation they both know is rich in the unsaid.

They are finally setting off on their delayed cross-country trip. He has no plan, exactly. But he has purpose. He has motion. A country is waiting. And a vague, unshaped rendezvous.

S tanley Peke drives with few possessions, no firm itinerary, no responsibilities. Severed from the conventions of his previous life. Unburdened of everything—except a leaden sense of mission. He would feel truly free at this moment, he thinks, except for that.

He is aware of how he must appear to the cars that pass him, to the cars that he passes. Like the desirable result of America's promise. The magazine version of its comfortably retired and healthy senior citizens. Clothes new, button-down shirt and slacks and cardigan in tasteful tones of brown and gray, creases crisp, thinned white hair cut and combed neatly. His wrinkled but still pretty white-haired bride next to him, in a pale-peach blouse and blue skirt with a bright, new scarf—her attire sensible but with flair. Respectable and appropriate, but smart and alive. They will never be sweatsuit seniors, he and Rose. Despite the convenience, the thoughtless ease, it just isn't in them. Set in among the wrinkles, her blue eyes still sparkle. Twin jewels admired for a lifetime. Like a final fashion touch.

They are setting out across America. Like twenty-two-year-olds, fresh from school or just sprung from some dispiriting job, free now, on an adventure, exploring their unknown homeland. Except that he is seventy-two and she is seventy. This trip—this venture across

America—is a trip on which a twenty-two-year-old would feel possibility, boundlessness, a sense of new beginning. Peke feels it, too, but also feels a sense of ending. How can he feel both beginning and ending? Feel both so acutely, riding along together companionably, like he and Rose? It is no surprise to him. His life has been filled with such ironic extremes. With a double helping of experience. Twin lifetimes, collapsing into each other, each breathing down the other's neck.

On the Pennsylvania Turnpike, he turns to her.

"You wonder where we're going."

She looks out the window, not saying anything. *Yes, of course I'm wondering.*

He knows how she feels. He's always known. Like she is one of his possessions. It is how he treats her—even in his wonderful, attentive, seamlessly caring way. An object. A possession. It's a survivor mentality he can't escape or surmount. A characteristic bluntness derived from the bluntness of his experiences. A possession, too, because he had no others. Arrived with no others. And she seems to accept it. To understand. She has taken it as part of the bargain, along with what she perceives as his strength, his confidence, his seriousness, his solicitousness. She has understood the bargain, and that was something vital and essential he saw in her from the beginning.

She was always his possession. They both understood that. And now she is his last possession. His only possession.

They cross America. An America he has always felt safe in. At home in. An America he has felt a similar possession of, ownership of. Wide bands of interstate, like asphalt carpet runners just rolled out in infinite multilane welcome. And the countless colors and models and variety of the automobiles that cross them, their radios emanating a hundred songs and opinions—American choice, American prowess, and personal freedom, on simple and prominent display. Taillight brigades slipping smoothly beneath the westering sky. Democratic America. Standing next to one another, lined up silently, obediently, and respectfully at rest-stop urinals.

There are two pasts for Stanley Peke, in a continual, sinuous dance of veils with each other. The past that is primped and shaped for familial and marital consumption, and the past that remains— like a watch in a safe-deposit box—locked away, unavailable, even to him. He has never spoken very much with her—not even her— about certain details. That was clearly part of the bargain with him, too, like accepting the sense of being his possession. Part of their understanding from the beginning. Once, when he drove her around his first American neighborhood, it was with the hope it would satisfy her, subdue further curiosity, fulfill his husbandly duty. As for the time before his arrival here, he's made only a passing reference here or there, with the understanding that anything further, any deeper revelation or exploration, will come from him at some more opportune time. Yet it never has. After fifty years, she is still waiting, he knows. Oh, she has a good sense of it, he's sure— from her reading, from history, from his passing references, from his personality. But she is still waiting to hear it from him.

"We are going to find our things," he says.

"But they don't matter," she responds, flatly, without pause.

"But they do matter," he says as flatly back. The familiar ping-pong of a half century of marriage.

"Then you'll have to tell me why." All this while watching out the windows, not looking at each other. That, he has thought, is maybe the greatest freedom, the deepest genius, of automotive design. Intimacy, because you are not looking at each other. Perspective as you talk.

But he doesn't know what to say to her. He doesn't know how to phrase any of it, how to even begin to unwrap it. Here is a chance to explain, but he doesn't know how to tell her—yet he knows exactly why. Because it defies the shape, stretches the bounds, of the survivor's story. And more than that, because it is unfinished. Because it continues—furtively, sickly, perversely—in his head, and in the bedroom's blackness around him at night. No, he still can't tell her. This kind of story, you can't adequately tell until it is finished. So he is left alone with the story's newly insistent fragments as the landscape slides by.

〉〉〉

On both sides of the highway, Pennsylvania's steeply raked hills display broad swaths of forest. Surprisingly dense and unbroken and pristine, he thinks, for a main artery in the eastern United States. Only occasionally, a gas station plaza—its meaningless flags and pennants waving colorfully, vaguely carnivalesque—flies bright and fleeting by their windows, disappears evanescent, as the landscape melts into slanting green woods again.

"I know you had nothing," Rose says, and after a pause, "I know it has to do with that."

And unsaid: *I can't know any more than that, because in all these years of marriage, after three children and a life together, you have never told it to me fully. You mythologize yourself, you gain psychological advantage, by not telling it, and I know this about you by now, and I think you are at least honest enough with yourself to know this, too, about yourself: that you are very much about psychological advantage, and that's the main reason you don't tell it. Not the pain of the past. No longer the pain of the past. The pain must be gone by now—must have healed somewhat by now.*

He knows she feels all this, feels it and senses it all in her slight resentments, accumulated into a small and still-manageable mound after fifty years. He wishes—he only wishes—that that were the truth about his past. It should have healed. That would be the natural human course, the standard human response.

He is asking a lot now, he knows. Driving her into the unknown.

The device on the dashboard blinks occasionally, silently. She regards it with some inseparable mix of mild abhorrence and prim, formal interest.

"That's a tracking device of some sort, isn't it? From that ridiculous catalog. We're following somebody, aren't we?" she says. And, after only a slight pause, "Following it to our furniture."

She's always been an intelligent woman.

There is a long silence, which answers her definitively.

»»»

A survivor, he has thought, has no identity. To others, yes. Ultraidentity. Sacred identity. Worthy of hallowed whispers and respect, respectfully pointed out at a benefit, a gala, a charity function, all in smooth black tie. Look how far he's come. Imagine, from nothing to this. A survivor fills a chandeliered room—any room—with his brutal past. But to him, no, it doesn't work the same way. To him, he has no past.

So, to a survivor, other things must fill in for identity. Affiliations. Clubs and memberships. Responsibilities. Children. (Who are made too important—it is a hard burden for children to bear. He has observed the brutal toll on some survivors' children, has eventually seen the subtle toll on his own, but it is a toll he seems unable to mitigate. Mitigation would be to change who he is or what has happened, and that can't be done.)

A survivor is caught in a world of surfaces. Like his daughter as an awkward preteen girl, he thinks, curled up with a fashion magazine. Minutely observing a luscious world, imagining herself vividly in it, but separated from it: a world that played across the page without her. The survivor knows nothing but glossy surface. Lives in glossy surface. Because nothing else in the present can ever be as real.

He wants his possessions back. Because he wants back the part of his identity that his possessions helped to make.

His possessions are part of his assimilation. An assimilation he hasn't thought very deeply about, yet he senses now that it's gone. In part because its important trappings are gone. And he's tossed back. As if to begin again.

Peke. From Pecoskowitz. Not everything is what it seems, after all. The big, white, sparkling moving van. The crisp uniforms.

The American-sounding name. A bent-over, harmless old man.

No, not everything is what it seems.

>>>

Rose Peke is mesmerized by the occasional blink of the light on the device that Peke has set between the seats. It is as blindly mesmerizing as her husband in sum has proved to be. Just as steady, yet just as oblique. As obvious as it is mysterious. As charming as it is twinkling on its surface. Its hardwiring, its purpose, less ascertainable, less knowable. He is like that blink of light. Charming but formal. Modest but insistent. Simple but transfixing. And like him, it leaves little choice, it seems, but to follow.

And she has followed him as blindly, as trustingly, as he is following the blinking light. Because he is like a beacon, a lighthouse, against the wild shoals of her emotions, her longings, her ambitions.

Nowadays, of course, it's unfashionable, incorrect, to follow a man like that. Back then, it was considered virtuous, and today it is considered weak. But even then, even in that world of half a century ago that largely accepted it, her sophisticated friends, her cultured parents, her colleagues at the architecture magazine were surprised. So independent a woman. With so independent a spirit. How could she?

No one understood that it was a choice. Eyes wide open. Because her fierce independence, the independence that she prided herself on, seemed to be nothing, withered and pale, compared with his. In truth, she has found that she does not need a full accounting of his life. Of what has happened to him. It is obvious from his capacities. From his resolve. She has gone along with his life, partly in wonder, partly to observe, to see how far his independence can go. The facts, the tragedies of his life before, he has never offered, but she has never pressed for them. And oddly—ironically—it is nevertheless *their* secret. The secret that they share. The secret that, in fact, she doesn't know anything about, when everyone of course assumes she does.

The secret that is still a gulf of mystery, that they have tacitly agreed to leave intact. For her to look across the canyon at him with that terrifying gulf between them. And find him—in that unknowing, in that distance—continually attractive. Alluring as the distance—as the far side of the canyon across the gulf—always is.

"It's a long ride. Perhaps this is the time to tell you what happened to me," he says. A little miracle of mind reading that ceases to seem miraculous—that indeed they have each started to expect—after fifty years of marriage.

She smiles. "You must feel pretty guilty about dragging me along. Because you feel the need to offer something substantial in return." Her eyes narrow slightly in thought, and then their edges turn up in mild amusement. "And as of right now, that's the only gift you can give me. The only thing you still own, isn't it?" She looks out. "But give it when you really want to. Not when you're offering it because you're in a corner."

She smirks. He sees her expression and smirks in return. In each of their expressions is some indivisible quotient of annoyance and affection. Both of them melt slightly into smiles—thin, conspiratorial—in recognizing it.

Of course, there was always one other thing: something not evident or explicable to her cultured parents or sophisticated friends. Something that should have been obvious to them, in their sophistication, but perhaps was not. Something so obvious to her. How he looked at her. And how she could see in that look what she meant to him. How to this survivor of unspeakable events, she was everything. How there was nothing and no one else. How despite all their possessions, their friends, their children, their lives, there seemed for him to be nothing else but her. Even after all this time, he still regarded her that way sometimes. As if there were no other matter, no other protoplasm in the universe. Blinkered, bottomless, utter desire. Beyond words, beyond description. But now, of course, they were headed off to find those same possessions she was sure had no comparative meaning to him. Making her question what had so long seemed unquestionable. Making her challenge the one unchallengeable assumption of her married lifetime.

The interstellar display of evening lights has flicked on. They drive on in silence until her question. "Will they stop somewhere?"

"At this point, it's just a he, I think," Stanley tells her. "He's not going to stay the night anywhere, I'll bet," he says. "He'll drive all night, into the next day."

"Do you know where he's going?"

He shakes his head no. "Somewhere sparse. Somewhere they attract no attention. That's my guess. He might stop for food and certainly gas, but that's all. But we'll stay the night somewhere. The signal should remain."

A concession she knows is mainly for her. She knows he could drive all night. He has the stamina. Even at seventy-two. He is a half step slower these days, but he is magically healthy, blessed with an almost animal vigor. In the rare menial task when he needs it—lifting luggage, shifting furniture—he still has much of his bull-like strength. He exudes a life force that makes some of their increasingly frail friends jealous, she sees. His energy can seem, well, inhuman. An apt description, if you strip *inhuman* of its negative connotation, that is.

>>>

At the Four Seasons in Cleveland, the valet takes the Mercedes. There is a midwestern ease, a slow, informal pulse, to the bellmen and the desk staff that is at odds with the majesty and hauteur of the lobby as the Pekes check in. They have called ahead to some old friends, a retired oncologist from the Cleveland Clinic and his wife, whom they first met on a Caribbean vacation years before. *Yes, we're driving cross-country. Once before we croak.* In their phone conversations to set up a dinner, the theft never comes up.

They meet at La Fontanelle, Cleveland's finest French restaurant.

The Mercers smile broadly as they approach the Pekes, seem nearly giddy, as if with the unmediated glee of having won a contest and now striding up to collect the prize. All four of them are dressed with like smartness for the occasion, the men in crisp navy blazers and bright ties, the women in simple but sophisticated dresses, with print scarves and shawls. The Mercers have, Peke can sense, new spring in their step, new energy, on seeing their old Caribbean pals, and he feels some of this energy, too, though he knows it is only the Mercers' energy momentarily reflected in him.

"Hello, hello, hello"—an awkward but affectionate pas de quatre, an effervescent round of handshakes and hugs and arms across backs. Peke sees Rose's joy of connection—a temporary break from the pressures of events, from her loneliness amid them. Full decorum is restored only as they are led to their table.

The restaurant achieves its strived-for Europeanness—a Europeanness that, paradoxically, seems to become more pronounced, Peke sees, more strived for in certain settings, the farther into America they go. A regal, formal, forced elegance: crystal chandeliers suspended from high ceilings, a thick leather folio of wines to choose from, even the dining chairs correct in proportion, immediate in comfort, rife with civility. It is a Europe he never knew, of course. A Europe that was taken away from him when he was still a boy. A Europe that, he can see, exists in American dreams as it exists in his own. Does this in fact make him more of an American? Sharing this wistful fantasy of Europe? It is another misty irony in his double lifetime. *One life collapsing into another.*

"So. The continental crossing," says Dr. Bob Mercer, grandly, safely.

Stanley Peke nods with a smile.

"Well, welcome to Cleveburg. A place to raise families. Flat, virtuous, unironic. A place not to think too much. Which makes it as American as you can get."

"Oh, now, Bob," his wife, Emily, reprimands teasingly.

First, children, of course. Children and grandchildren. The requisite but exultant exchange of information. Jack is in the film business in Los Angeles, an editor of documentaries, has two darling little girls, says Emily Mercer. Our daughter Sarah is out there, too, says Rose; she's a lawyer specializing in the oil industry, deals a lot with the Saudis. Our other daughter, Anne, is an internist in New York, with three boys, God bless her. And Daniel, of course, took over the business. Very solid. He has a boy and a girl. Names and ages. Each offspring getting his or her due. Hitching a ride on the forward progress of their children's lives—their own lives don't describe a similar forward arc of news anymore. In their own lives, the news is now *made* to happen—planned and purchased. Overseas trips, concerts, charity dances. Lives that have had their turn now take their turn observing other lives.

There is, in their grandparent stories, their modest anecdotes, a palpable sense of completion. Dr. Mercer adds to it more specifically. "I retired late last year," he tells the Pekes.

"Forty years in oncology at the Cleveland Clinic," Emily pipes in.

"Forty years of saving people," says Rose graciously.

"And not saving them," Bob adds, not gloomy or reflective, but rather for the record.

"Bob is working in a free clinic downtown now. Donates his services."

"The local golf courses are quite pleased about that," Mercer jokes. "The grass is back."

"He couldn't just retire. Couldn't go cold turkey," says Emily.

"Like Stan did," observes Rose.

Which merits Bob's unalloyed curiosity. "You, what . . . just stopped one day?" asks Bob. "That amazes me. I mean, what do you do with your time?" An unblinking midwestern bluntness that Peke likes.

"Exist," says Peke, more humorously than cryptically. "And that's good enough for me." Knowing they will accept that. That a survivor's answers are given wide berth, are allowed to make sense. He's seen enough for one lifetime. Just wants to relax. Enjoy the little things, the creature comforts, the leisure he never had. The Mercers are assembling some version of that, no doubt.

He elaborates slightly, only out of regard for them. "Read. Garden. Think." *Brood.* He shrugs. "I look in on the business occasionally." A chemical business that produces a line of high-grade bonding materials that the automotive and aerospace industries use in manufacturing. "My son, Daniel, runs it now, so I can still pop in and snoop around. Daniel puts up with me politely. I still know most of the employees. When they know you're a survivor, everyone's very polite, of course. Even your own son." After the world has been so impolite. He smiles. "I have to say, Daniel's got it running smoothly. At this point, honestly, it doesn't seem to need me *or* him. Things work in America," he says with a twinkle. "You go use a toilet five miles into the woods in a national park, and it works."

"Almost everything," counters Bob, with intentionally dark implication. "We haven't talked to you since the Trade Towers." The oncologist is conversant with death. Is a mortality professional, is comfortable discussing it, has labored in its portals all his professional life. "We were obviously less directly affected by it here. How was it?" he asks Peke, assuming, it seems, that a comfortable reacquaintance has sufficiently taken place.

It is a question that, Peke has noticed, their out-of-town visitors to Westchester have begun to ask as well. Acceptable, almost required, dinner conversation. Nearly impolite if you *don't* ask. Though usually a subject drifted to, and not summoned so directly.

"How was it?" Peke adjusts his seat. "It was kids," he says, getting to what for him is the pertinent point. "Our kids' generation. Working fathers with young families. Even a few our own kids knew." It's all still inconceivable, he can sense, to his neighbors, to his family, to that magnificent city. He can still see that inconceivability—the immense brute block of the unimaginable—in his neighbors' eyes. But it's not inconceivable to him. A catastrophe, yes, but catastrophes can become as familiar as sunlight.

"Not all kids." Mercer looks at Peke. "Stan, did you know there were several Holocaust survivors in those buildings? Survivors of the camps?" It is for the first time a searching, direct look. A look in which their wives and the elegant restaurant are momentarily gone, and the two men are somehow alone.

"Yes." Peke nods, says flatly, "I did know that."

To survive the base depredations of one continent; to inhabit the noble heights of another. To daily occupy soaring symbols of commerce and productivity and human achievement. To ascend to heaven in the morning and back to Earth each night, to travel freely between Earth and clouds, to look down from the sky every day at the famously welcoming harbor that in fact welcomed you—and then to have that daily heaven, that epic statement of human capacity, fall away beneath you. Toxic fumes descending from the ceiling . . . trapped with hundreds of others . . . unable to breathe . . . the perverse echo, the ancient feverish black repeating dream, unexpectedly enacted in serene offices high in the air. Would you think, in your fraught final moments, that fate had singled you out, that fate had taken special notice of you for this treatment? Or would you think, conversely, that fate had taken no notice of you at all?

"They survived, thank God," says Robert. "They weren't among the dead."

"They survived." Peke raises his eyebrows and gently corrects him. "But, Robert, my old friend, they *were* among the dead."

To be a survivor, Robert, means you emerged from among the dead.

Now, only after wine, the recent domestic calamity is described. The heads of their dining companions shake in disbelief, hang in sympathy. But the Mercers bring their inborn midwestern optimism to bear. It's only things. That's why there's insurance. *You still have all this* is the conclusion of the evening, the subtle, reassuring point of the retired oncologist. *Meals like this. Evenings like this. Friends like us.* Which is true. Indisputable. The oncologist has lived around death, and now, retired—with a few hours a week treating the coughs and infections of the wide-eyed children of uninsured young mothers, telling the kids knock-knock jokes to put them at ease—

he is determined to live around life and is determined that his friend should do the same.

Dining sumptuously in Cleveland. Heading cross-country in their Mercedes.

It hardly seems a ride toward destiny.

But Peke feels—knows—it is. Is it the ultimate fool's errand, attempting to seize one's fate? Or is trying to seize one's fate the ultimate human act?

There is no sense of mission in his selection of a chateaubriand. In his approval of a mid-seventies Bordeaux. But he knows. Feels it in his bones.

He looks at his two friends from Cleveland—and at warmly lit restaurants, proudly elegant hotel lobbies, pristine hotel rooms—as if for the last time. And realizes—with a shock of recognition—that is always how he looks at them. A summary look, like a squint into dying light. The only way to look he's ever known.

Vegas. Three in the morning.

Nick and his Viola are in a high-roller room.

Nick has driven from Montana. That morning into that night, slipping across the sometimes verdantly thick, sometimes dusty carpet of America like a scuttling bug. And here he is. In the city that is home to all the world's Nicks. Home to anyone who chooses it. If you recognize it as home, then it is yours.

Vegas, three in the morning. The ultimate hiding place, and the ultimate playing place. Therelessness, perfectly constructed, perfectly understood. Anonymity refined to a sterling point.

This is the only possible place for him.

Maybe Miami.

The hotel room is mirrored, cut off, isolated, a sanctuary smothered in audio to filter out Vegas's anonymous noise. Temporal and aural suspension. It's an isolation tank in reverse—all the hedonistic pleasures and recreations poured together at once.

They lie there. Intercourse is the business at hand for a short and somewhat formal first segment of the night. A piquant appetizer. And with Viola's hard, tan body and outsize balloon breasts, it is pleasurably cartoony. Comically perfect and unreal. Amusement-park stuff: bright-colored flags waving gaily, hyperdental big white smiles. Viola used to ride rodeo—hence the flat stomach, the muscled biceps and calves—and then a girlfriend introduced all this to her, and she moved from horses to men. The superbreasts came later, celebratory, part of calling Vegas home.

He observes it as he performs it, and though there are reliable but modest pleasures in it, he finds that he wants this portion of the festivities over with. His thoughts drift to Armando as he thrusts, as he lies there afterward, and he must repeatedly tether himself back to the scene.

"You see this watch?" Nick says to her. He reaches behind him, picks it up from the night table, dangles it above her white teeth. "This is what a Rolex wants to be. Wishes it could be. This is what a Rolex dreams of at night."

"What is it?" she asks, the pupil lying naked with her hoary teacher.

"Bildetmeyer. German. So rare, there's no way to put a price on it. How 'bout that?" He giggles a little at the concept. He feels a relaxed postcoital glory. A temporary lightness. "I want you to have it. It's yours."

"Nicky." Cooing but nervous—*What does this mean? What does this change?*

"Go ahead. Put it on."

She pauses. Clearly a man's watch. So it will be clear someone gave it to her. As a statement of some sort. *She made time stand still. Made time go backward. She was that good.* Something like that.

"Soon as I leave town, you could hock it and go anywhere in the world you want to," Nick says with a sly smile, full of wolf teeth.

"Would you come find me?" she asks.

He doesn't answer. They look at the watch now together as she holds it up against her tan wrist. "Take it," says Nick.

"Really?"

"Yes."

"You mean . . . it's mine?"

"Yours."

"Really?"

"Really." Nodding with solemnity.

She closes the strap. Clasps it. Turns the watch in the suite's gently set lighting, admiring it.

"Mine," she says, checking once more, reassuring herself.

"Yours."

She smiles. Something seems to settle in her, to relax and soften almost physically. Her prostitute's elaborate defenses seem momentarily breached.

Women. Women and their objects. They are simple creatures, aren't they?

>>>

Early in the morning, Viola still curled in sleep, Nick, fully dressed, steps quietly around to the table on her side of the bed.

He picks up the watch, puts it back on his own wrist.

He peels ten hundreds from his wallet, places them exactly where the watch was.

She needs to be reminded of what the relationship is. He needs to remind himself.

He'd like to leave it. He meant to. But he just can't.

Anyway, she's had the brief pleasure of ownership. The magical moment of possession. So now it reverts to him.

He glides down in the silent elevator, is released into the empty lobby still fragrant with contrails of last night's teeming humanity. He strides out into the Vegas dawn, the air heating up already, the changeless sun already preparing to scorch the streets again.

The Bildetmeyer is back on his wrist. And despite the long, tiring, reckless, drunken, and chemical night, he finds that he immediately feels better.

13

At night, when Peke checks the device, there is western movement, far ahead of their own. He pushes the little buttons, the crude digital map comes up. LAS VEGAS, it reads. His heart sinks. Tourists stacked room on room, strolling in bright-colored flocks down bright-lit boulevards at night, crowded gleefully into the casinos. He'll never find the thief in Las Vegas. The little light's insistent blink will be meaningless there. And could that be where the Pekes' belongings are, anyway? In some warehouse? Some nondescript self-storage facility among dozens in that booming city?

He is puzzling this out, thinking maybe, like the occasional tourist, he'll get lucky in Vegas.

But in the morning he checks again, and the digital map has changed, indicating a direction north-northeast.

The watch. Its tiny, steady *tick-tock*, thinks Peke.

Tick, tock, tick, tock.

They see old friends in Chicago. Attend *La Bohème*. Stay in the Four Seasons again. Luxury and comfort become even more so when they're predictable: an aphorism of American life, he thinks. He might record such observations of his trip in a little spiral notebook, if he were another kind of older American.

Yes, yes, we're making our way to Santa Barbara. Stan's never seen the country. His adoptive land. Never had the time.

Well, you've got to do it once before you die.

Oh, we are. We are.

You've got to do it once before you die. The startling choice of words like a mocking missive from the Fates. The conventional, unthinking quip from their friend, an engineering professor, is suddenly a dark little joke, placed in the man's mouth, reaching an audience of only Peke.

Inevitably, he returns to the question: Are they worth this? His belongings? He thinks of the objects—the Biedermeier chairs, the Oriental rugs, the Andalusian settee. Considered separately, they have nothing to do with one another. They are from across epochs, from wildly divergent locales and aesthetics and temperaments. Separately, they are trifles. Tchotchkes. Junk in the back of a truck, random and unrelated.

But taken together, they create a home, comprise an environment. And more than that, they are a missive, a single message—of culture and civilization. Of mankind at peace. Mankind at play. Mankind creating. Mankind imagining. The best of man, his most primitive and noble impulses, in fact: making himself a home, a safe harbor against the elements, against harm. All man's possessions are just this impulse, aren't they, filtered through civilization—simply the impulse for a home.

Yet he knows this is only a version of an explanation that he is framing for himself. He knows it has little to do with the objects themselves. It is the principle of the thing. One cannot disrupt another life. There has to be a consequence.

It is hard for him to sift out whether it is the long, deep injustice of his own early life that makes him take up this cause. That gives him no choice.

And a shadow thought—itchy, uncomfortable—accompanies all these others: Aren't they really the same? This thief and he? Desiring, needing, the same objects? Yes, he earned them by obeying society's rules, while his antagonist won them through a clever manipulation of those rules, but don't they have the same hunger? Isn't it only their means that are different, while their end is the same? But while Peke can entertain that thought, while he can allow it, it is not enough to make him adjust his route. It is not enough to make him turn the Mercedes south, point it toward the easy bliss of Santa Barbara.

Sometimes, in a flash here or there, it appears simple: in a life robbed of justice, he intends to see some done.

And where justice leaves off and revenge begins? He knows that is impossible for him to say. He knows that his past has left him no natural experience with justice, and so he has no reliable perspective from which to understand.

After Chicago, the country opens up slowly, steadily, to the elemental. To sky and land, to swaths of color, to immensity. As if the Mercedes is being poured from a bottleneck of urban density out into vastness and shapelessness, out into inexplicable space and plenty.

The bright busyness of western Illinois—gargantuan suburban malls glistening beside the interstate, anchor stores like mother ships in a universe of consumerism—gives way over hours, as if in a gradual shaving away, a more and more scrupulous scraping off of the busyness, to the fields and farms of central Iowa. Farmland, every inch of it eagerly sprouting, it seems, rows of greens and grains of such majesty and magnitude and nearly comical endlessness that Peke is certain America could feed the world—could feed the universe—just given the geopolitical chance.

The populace recedes, grows measurably less present—like a cast of midwestern millions making a gracious, prearranged exit with a bow.

An automobile passing the other way becomes a minor event. The accents of the hosts and callers on local talk radio grow flatter and more measured, as even as the land itself. The voices, and their words, become simpler, devoid of unnecessary expression—auditorily featureless, an aural equivalent of the topography. Eventually, Peke turns the radio off and they ride in silence. He listens to the hollow rubber thrum of the tires on the macadam, a low, industrious, unaltering note. The double yellow lines brighten where a municipality has proudly repainted and in the next county go faded and sorry again. As there is a reduction of sensory input, there is a reduction to one's thoughts, too, Peke notices. They seem to become elemental as well. The sameness and predictability of the road and view reduce the sense of question in him. Reduce interior discussion to barely a murmur. He is soon following the lines and the road as unthinkingly as he is following the blinking of the black device. He fights sleep, yawns and shakes away the yawn, blinks himself into alertness—like any older American on a long drive. But the other septuagenarian cross-country drivers—the ones he sees occasionally, stretching at a rest stop, picking up a coffee—undoubtedly travel to the warming vision of an old college roommate, or a raucous class reunion, or a favorite grandchild at the other end of the drive. Or perhaps only the image of a quiet guest room over the garage. Or of a magnificent sixteenth hole. Where he has only his unknown destination, his blind rendezvous. Its hundred possible outcomes combine and collapse in his mind into a blurry blankness, though every outcome features the thief. The thief Peke thought was only a uniformed foreman, so his physical image remains blurry, too.

Even after all these years, he finds he still has the extra perspective, the extra appreciation, of a foreigner in America. Yet he also feels the homeland pride, the sense of custody and connection, of being an American. A European American, an American European: he is having it both ways or inhabits some no-man's-land in between.

And these sun-soaked, shimmering vistas. These picturesque farmhouses. This epic sky. Does it all shimmer like this because it is in some sense more real, more meaningful to him than to the next elderly traveler—who takes it for granted, who has known only this? Or does it shimmer this way because it is *unreal*—a fantasy, a borrowed view, a vision through glass that can be snatched away? Does his fractured past, a world and lifetime away, render this landscape more real? Or less? It fascinates him that he cannot really know.

West of Chicago, they switch their style: they begin to stay in motels and bed-and-breakfasts. After the Four Seasons, the motels and B and Bs seem not so much a comedown as an adventure. To get the flavor, the whiff, of authentic America. (Though Rose doesn't ask explicitly, she also senses it is now time to be less recognizable. Now time to blend in, in order to watch.)

He had expected to experience immensity, and yet, with the hours ticking by, there's an increasing sense of smallness. A manageability. Maybe it's the big, insulating Mercedes. Maybe it's the focused insistence of the little, black blinking device. The hours tick by, the landscape remains unchanged. But this now makes it seem small and knowable to him, rather than the reverse. Perhaps it's his age: the huge clumps of time folding in on themselves, time that moved so slowly as a child, streaming along unrecognizably now. Perhaps it's his hidden purpose, which holds him focused, unopen. Perhaps it's the sum of his past experience, which leaves no room for new experience.

The pretense of a tour has fast evaporated. "We should be seeing caves. Looking at statues," Rose says with forced jolliness. "We should be stopping at sights with postcard stands. We should be holding our guide books up to shield our eyes in the sun. Turning up our noses at cheap souvenirs, then buying them at the last second," she says, accepting that it will never happen, that this is a different cross-country trip they're making, but half meaning it, too. Half crying out for normalcy, for the foolish things, the standard activities and memories of older American couples.

He thinks about the device's chancy battery connection, the extra draw on the watch's power. The longer the device must deliver its signal, the more time there is for something to go wrong. It should be fine, according to its printed instructions, according to Itzhak's somber nods, but Peke can't be sure, and so it remains a small nodus of anxiety, tapping at him, keeping him moving.

Outside of Huron, South Dakota, in the light of early evening, they see a neon sign for the Stanley Motel, and Rose is gleefully insistent. The sharply pebbled driveway announces their arrival like the roll of a snare drum.

The motel's whitewashed brick facade, its industrial carpeting over cement flooring, are sadly immaculate, as if this stark cleanliness is the only goal and purpose of its managers' lives. Low, squat, thick, and solid, the building seems explicitly constructed to withstand the climate's severity, and to have no aesthetic consideration beyond that. In the fading daylight, they see how the land stretches flat and featureless behind the motel—the sky and horizon their focal points by default, by the absence of any other. A squat, clean, spare motel, no frills and no nonsense: the spiritual descendant of the sod houses that once dotted the prairie, standing alone against the elements.

They eat at the diner across the street, choose meat loaf and three-bean salad delivered by a waitress close to three hundred pounds, whose weariness is as abundant as she is. Yet she speaks with a high-pitched cheerfulness so unlikely from within that weary mass, her voice seems eerie and disembodied. Peke carefully calculates and recalculates the tip to be appropriately generous but not outrageous, to create satisfaction but not insult.

"At least Mount Rushmore," Rose says from her side of the lumpy queen-size bed, staring at the cottage-cheese ceiling.

"It'll be too far to the south of us," Peke tells her.

"We're crossing South Dakota, and we're not going to see Rushmore?" she says, hoping to make it sound ludicrous.

"Graven images. It's against my religion," he jokes. "Big stone heads . . . like the self-commemorations of pharaohs."

"Valuing the individual," she counters—challenging both his doubtful point and his jokey spirit. "The primacy of the individual."

"Sure. Standing in a line of hundreds at the park entrance for an hour. The primacy of the individual."

"Where's your democratic spirit? Washington, Jefferson, Lincoln, Roosevelt." As if the names alone are argument enough.

"Making gods of public servants? Hardly the democratic spirit. Their heads carved sixty feet high, set five hundred feet up—you think that's the legacy they wanted? Perfect for Stalin or Mao. Which should tell you what these fellows would have thought of it." He feels, beneath his argument, something more significant pawing at him. There is a kind of obscenity to this glorification of the individual juxtaposed against the numberless and nameless, the only ones who would remember them lying alongside them.

"The Avenue of Flags. Fifty-six states and territories. The Presidential Trail. The Shrine of Democracy." She is joking now, tossing out terms from her handful of lobby brochures. She knows she has lost. She never expected to win. "Stanley Peke, are you an American, or aren't you?"

They both know it is a question larger than her joke. He is. He isn't. He is a firm believer. He kisses the soil, weeps in gratitude. And yet he doubts it all. Looks on his adopted land with narrow-eyed suspicion. Watches closely for the next human disaster. Inevitable as a storm.

He hears, beneath their exchange, their annoyance with each other. He knows her frustration with his inflexibility and willfulness. He feels his irritation at her teasing, her disrespectful, mocking challenge. They both hear attributes they know will not change in their lifetimes, and perhaps this gives them special resonance. At their age, the argument is never the argument. There is always a meaning beneath it. A half century into marriage, this much they understand. They just don't know exactly what the meaning is.

Yes, Rose thinks, lying there in the motel room's preternatural quiet and dark. *Yes, godlike.* Stone, inflexible, immutable. Mutely heroic. Unknowable and inalterable . . . blindly admired and out of reach. And a mountainside of frustration. Frustration that rises into the sky. She doesn't need the Rushmore visit, she realizes. She has Stanley.

Her doubts are no greater, no less, her questions no more or less answered, than when she stood at their wedding in a Manhattan hotel lobby almost fifty years ago. It was an assertively nondenominational event: a justice of the peace; a two-minute ceremony. And yet: he had the place swimming in flowers. Towering arrangements. Wrapping the columns. Overflowing from the window boxes. Garlanding the banisters and balustrades. He'd located a swing band in the seediest bowels of downtown, whose black female vocalist was a phenomenon. The night rode a crest of their friends' high spirits undimmed and undiminished into morning. And the point was clear. Creating their own life. Making their own choices. Her proud, wealthy, fifth-generation Congregationalist parents stood demurely by, masking their disappointment behind brave smiles. It was a spectacular, high-spirited night, but more than that, it was fully, inarguably, inviolately theirs. And who was this man standing next to her in the lobby, smiling warmly and securely on the dais, this man swinging her on the dance floor, laughing helplessly? This handsome man, self-assured, powerful, infinitely patient, unpredictably brusque? Who was he, exactly? But she understood, then and there, even as the justice of the peace spoke: He was who he would be. He was the future—his, hers, theirs. And he was as clearly committed to that future as to her. So she accepted not knowing, experienced her questions as part of an energy: swirling and spinning like the newly married couple on the dance floor.

Now she was not so blithe. Not so sure. A half century had inevitably provided, if not answers, exactly, then a *sense* of answers, circuitous and indirect. Which made the remaining questions feel starker and the questioner more exposed.

>>>>

Driving west through South Dakota, amid the startling sparseness, the Mercedes is becoming more and more conspicuous, claiming too much attention. For significant stretches, it is the only car to be seen, which makes it more noticeable than Peke would like. Peke sees a farmer point to it from his dusty pickup.

Selling it, though, will be conspicuous, too. Out here, its own provenance might follow it—that old man with the accent in the expensive Mercedes. He is tempted to simply leave it in the lot of a bed-and-breakfast one morning—check out at the front desk, come out into the sunshine, call a cab to take them to a car dealership, simply pretend the Mercedes isn't there. But that would attract undue attention, too: *a man just left his Mercedes one morning.*

West of Pierre, they drive along the strip of car dealerships, flags and banners waving in the Western breeze in a proud and antic display of local spirit, standing firm against the windswept barren plains.

Peke pulls into a Ford dealership, parks the Mercedes right at the door. He and Rose enter politely, respectfully, as if into the hushed foyer of a funeral home.

"It's starting to give me trouble," he explains to the salesman. "I'm seventy-two. I'm too old for car trouble. I want to drive out of here in a Ford." *There's an American sentiment for you, Rose*, he thinks with some amusement. *Is that American enough for you?*

"You want to go from that Mercedes to a Ford?" A prairie frankness. The salesman doesn't bother to hide his confusion. His bland startlement and obvious disapproval.

"A used Ford," adds Peke, even less comprehensibly. The salesman nods, not knowing what else to do. "A used but reliable Taurus, for example," Peke explains. "Except we don't like the new body style." Pretending some forethought to this seeming impulsiveness.

They check the Blue Book for a price on the Mercedes. While the salesman and the manager test-drive the Mercedes down the dealership strip and back, Peke and Rose stand out front, watching them, wordless, hands shielding eyes from the bright sun in a Western pose, as if counting cattle. The manager returns, jots a credit for the Blue Book amount on a slip of paper from his shirt pocket, hands it to Peke. It all happens quickly—with the wordless, unspoken efficiency of what Peke imagines as an American frontier transaction. A settler's quick trade with the Indians. They are clearly afraid of Peke changing his mind.

With the salesman's help, Peke picks out a gray gunboat of a Ford Fairlane.

The salesman moves their luggage into the Ford for them, and they thank him. The manager scribbles out a check for the difference. Mercedes minus Fairlane. There is more tight-lipped, nearly wordless outpost trading, until there is a handshake. Peke will deposit the check quickly, hoping they will speculate only briefly, conclude Peke's reversal of fortune, and think nothing more about it after that.

>>>

"We have millions of dollars in the market, don't we?" she queries him calmly, staring out the window, the scenery of the American West rushing at them, running down the side panels of the strange car like liquid. *Millions in CDs in the bank*, she thinks, holding her gaze steady, almost haughtily. *Our homeowners' policies have never had a claim before this. We could replace almost everything in a blink, without batting an eye, without missing a beat. Get anything we need or want.*

She knows he knows it. Saying it aloud won't make the point any more obvious or compelling to him. So she shifts her thoughts away, addresses something higher.

"You're not putting us at risk, I hope."

Because it's not worth risk. We still have time ahead of us, years to be happy, to enjoy our children, the tribe of our grandchildren that grows as steadily as those enumerated Bible tribes.

But I can't tell if you care about any of that at all.

I'm your last possession. Your last chattel. Even if I am just chattel to you, don't risk losing me.

This unsaid, too.

"I won't put us at risk," he says. As if he has calmly and accurately read every thought in her staunchly expressionless face. "I promise. If it comes down to that, I'll back away. We'll just go on to Santa Barbara."

At any moment, of course, any moment he chooses, he could decide to ignore the insistent little beep and flash. The tiny blinking red dot. At any moment, he could shut off the device. At any mile in the two thousand miles so far, he could have turned the wheel, changed course, headed the car toward the gorgeous simplicities of Southern California, continued their lives.

But he cannot. And if it were even slightly possible at the outset to abandon his plan, it is unthinkable now. The insistent little red dot is like a heartbeat. Hypnotic. Not just an electronic pulse— it is somehow *his* pulse. He cannot abandon it, because he would be abandoning himself.

He could stop this chase anytime. Except that he can't.

A seventy-two-year-old man who has lived several lives already, who has balanced on the ledge of life, who has been curled into the heart of the planet's fiercest mid-twentieth-century insanities, doesn't have that much to give up, it seems to him. A few dinners. A few conventional family celebrations and milestones. An endless stream of the morning paper, one day's edition largely indistinguishable from the next. A few cycles of seasons, which come at him now with such demoralizing speed, it might be easier giving those up anyway. But he has to keep in mind that she doesn't understand this. He has to make allowances. His perspective may be skewed. On the other hand, she has to understand that the willingness to risk was how he has gotten anywhere. How they have any of this. That in a way, risk is all he knows. He will try to rein it in. Out of deference to her. He will not let her lie awake unnecessarily. What would that accomplish? But he can make no guarantees.

Seventy-two. How much more is there?

He has lived his life. No one is more thankful for that than he. But now, after all, he has had that life. And here is a last opportunity. When he thought he was done with opportunity, in the land of opportunity, here's another. How can he pass it by?

14

G reat Falls, Montana. A sea of sky. An ocean of land. Elemental and raw and open. A stunning inverse of the way he
arrived here—amid endless water that still haunts him in only
distant, fractured memories of his passage. The close gray sky that
hung above the crowded, creaking, groaning steel vessel. The vast
blue sky now above the steel craft that floats over the waves of the
road in soft, plush American-car style. The slap of water against the
hull, the whistle of Western wind against the car windows. There is
in him a sense of coming full circle. But still, making a crossing.

He pushes the buttons of the GPS display once more. They're
within a few hundred miles of where the signal settled a day or so
ago. Stopped its movement.

Great Falls. He pulls the Ford off at a scenic overlook. They get
out and stretch. The snowcapped mountains are so distant, so out
of scale, they seem to exist in another dimension, to be lit by a different light. One feels, staring at them, a sense of personal glory and
yet of inconsequence. He listens. There is a kind of sacred silence
here. He has noticed this silence, growing in tone, enlarging somehow, as they travel west. A silence that is sacred, but common and
natural, too. A grand quiet that is repeated on a human level in the
acutely limited exchange of words that is the local style—in diners,

at rest stops, in convenience stores, at motel registration desks. He was always more comfortable not speaking. Silence is far preferable. Maybe this is where he always belonged. Maybe he was meant to be a Westerner. He feels an affinity for it. He smiles.

Great Falls, Montana. This is a land he could have been happy in, he senses. Here is his chance to look in on other lives, lives not lived.

He checks them into a bed-and-breakfast. It is much less quaint than their previous B and Bs, sparer and plainer. Thin white towels, simple bureau, simple bed, no embroidered curtains, just a single pull shade. He tries on a cowboy hat in the shop next door, likes it, buys it. Finds boots a few doors farther down. Pays cash for both. More the norm out here. Comes back upstairs, all smiles, to his wife. Looks in the mirror at an American of a certain type, of a certain age. A rancher. A Westerner. Grain prices and hog futures. His accent so mild it's heard now only in a slight stilting of speech, his Europeanness revealed (and only to a sophisticated observer) by his dark-eyed, watchful gaze, his habit of separateness. His middle-European features, his slightly prominent ears and proud nose, his outsider identity, all disappearing under the brim of that hat. Disappearing, it occurs to him, at long last.

After sixty years of trying to fit in, he thinks with amusement, all it took was one of these hats.

He puts it on the hat rack behind the door. A hat rack! My, my.

And really, what is this seventy-two-year-old Jew doing in the land of outlaws? In the land of last stands?

Making one.

"National Moving and Storage."

"Annelle," the voice says.

"Nick," she responds, automatic, curt. Nick can feel her anxiety from here. Her hostility. Her dread on hearing his voice.

It's a small, careful selection of frightened women on insulting clerk's salaries who work in the back offices of a handful of moving companies. Annelle. Dora. Sara-Jean. Cultivated carefully over time, with a modest but reliable stream of cash. Nick, like the steady husband none of them has, the silent, sturdy provider, and that seems to serve some classic need, to tap something primal in this subspecies of woman.

"You miss me, Annelle?"

No response. As he would expect. Her silence, her resentment, signal that all is well in the relationship. She hates needing the money. She needs the money.

"I'll call you after five, Nick." Easy to decipher: *I can't talk now. I'll have your names for you by then. Your prospects.* Nick knows she'll call. She needs the money. She knows the consequences.

It's simple, what they have to do. Everything is computerized in these places, and the computers are always on. They look at a screen, scroll and troll, tell him what it says. Call him from a pay phone—not from the office, not from home (though in 95 percent of the cases, that would probably be just fine)—and give him names, addresses, and pickup times. Simple. A twelve-year-old can do it, and earn money for dope.

Moving-company offices are casual, congenial, blue-collar places. Employees tend to gossip about clients anyway—sweet old lady, husband just died. *Man, Annelle, you should have seen this place!*

And then the simple counterbalance, the safety check to his system. Virtually every one of the moves is interstate. Moving to Florida, California, Arizona, New Mexico, coastal Georgia or South Carolina, from the Northeast or Midwest. Interstate manifests have to be filled out and filed with certain state offices in advance. A trucking company has to file its plan. And as part of that plan, there has to be an estimation of cargo value. It's simple: his contacts in the interstate trucking offices call him when they see a high-value estimate. (The trucking companies don't lowball the numbers, because they pass this cost, like all others, on to the customer and mark it up. They love coming across a genuinely high-value move and have a financial incentive to duly record it for the authorities.)

These guys are state employees. Like Annelle and Dora and Sara-Jean, they need the cash. Trucking is dirty. Mobbed up far back into its history. His contacts have grown up in that culture. To some degree, they seem to feel they *should* be calling him with the figures. As if it were part of their job description. His white envelopes of appreciation, they count on as part of their annual income.

One of them initially thought Nick was an undercover cop, keeping tabs on suspiciously high cargo values, investigating if there might be something illicit, something stolen, being moved. Nick got a good laugh out of that one.

That's how he checks the moving-company information. And the moving companies are how he checks his interstate information. And they all know he cross-checks—he's made that clear. It's how he keeps everybody honest. If that's the word.

He ends up with a short list, and on it is exactly what he wants: a widow in Austin, about to be moved to San Francisco. (Good after the drop-off in Albuquerque, where he's found a dealer to take the rare china.) A little web research, local newspapers online, tell him more: husband, chief executive of a natural-gas company, dead of a heart attack.

Moving day currently scheduled for July 23.

Actually, Mrs. Warren, that's gonna be July 22.

Eager Beaver Movers. One Step Ahead Transportation. All kinds of names and slogans suggest themselves.

>>>>

A used Ford Fairlane drives north, deeper into Montana. An older couple is inside. Fishing rods. A fishing trip. Americans on vacation.

They have taken a cabin on the Kootenai River, which rushes sparkling and magnificent alongside them as they follow the turns toward the rural address. The morning sun dapples the river's surface stunningly, squintingly bright. The river is furiously loud. Powerfully peaceful. A place, he can see already, of serenity and contemplation. Soon they are on the dirt driveway, which runs along the river like a joyous dog.

As they head up the long driveway—at least a mile—he looks around him. He is far out here. You can't get any farther out.

And as he drives, it comes back to him from a distance, from a misty dot on the horizon. He doesn't say anything to Rose, but the association is like a storm suddenly dark and gathered, like a sudden clap of thunder overhead.

These woods. These trees. Gnarled, wild, twisted specimens. Dense, prickly underbrush.

It makes sense for the line of latitude, he thinks. For the geography. For the temperature and climate.

It looks exactly like the woods of Poland.

He is seventy-two years old.

He is seven.

He and Rose pull the old Ford into the little dirt lot in front of the grocery store.

Inside, they nod to the proprietor. Put milk, juice, eggs into the cart. The proprietor is about Peke's age and seems to assume communion and permission from that fact.

"Understand you doin' some fishin'?" he asks. "Up at the McCane cabin?"

No secrets here, thinks Peke. Despite the silences as vast as the vistas. Despite the respectful distances.

Peke nods. Smiles pleasantly. "That's right." He's reluctant to say much more. Reluctant to reveal his mild accent, which brings silent speculation, he suspects, to this kind of American. Discussion after he's gone.

"Beautiful up there," says the proprietor.

"Oh, it is," says Rose, stepping in for Peke. *We are nice. We are just nice older people fishing.*

"How'd you ever find it?" the proprietor inquires.

"We were headed west," she says. "We wanted to stop and fish. A realtor over in Spinesville had the listing," she tells him, reasonably, unmysterious. The proprietor nods.

There's no one else in the grocery store, but in the dirt parking lot, as they're loading the groceries into the car, Peke sees a number of pickup trucks. A couple of motorcycles.

He squints at the establishment on the other side of the dirt lot.

FREEDOM CAFÉ. Hand-lettered. Red and blue letters brushed on a plywood sheet quickly, unevenly. Free of the constraints of conventional lettering, he sees. Free of the cost of a sign. Almost childlike.

He ambles across the bright, dusty lot to it. Drawn to its authenticity, its Americanness.

An old man emerges through the rickety wooden front door, taking the trash around to the back. The apron he's wearing is covered with grease. Peke can't help notice he's about Peke's age and happens to look like him. Same short haircut. Same white hair. Same permanent squint. But there, presumably, the similarity ends. A dishwasher, a hired hand, at a Montana eatery. Bent over with the heavy trash, and with a lifetime of backwoods labor. The kind of American life with which Peke has no intersection.

Up the two low, mud-crusted wooden steps. Through that rickety wooden door, which, with a loud languorous insolent squeak— a squeak as lazy as the morning—announces his entrance.

It takes a moment for Peke's eyes to adjust to the darkness inside.

Three skinheads are at a table. Open vests on naked torsos. Each one's skin a mix of careless sunburn and eerily translucent paleness. Sitting with beers. Beers in the morning.

All of them look up at Peke.

One of the skinheads has a green swastika tattooed between his eyebrows.

Another has a larger green swastika on his beefy white bicep.

Peke stares at the swastikas for a moment. Unable not to.

Swastikas. Here in Freedom Café.

It's too much of a surprise to him. It's too much unexpected meaning. He has not seen it out in the world, adorning a human being, in a long, long time. He looks a moment too long.

"Whatcha starin' at?" says the skinhead with the swastika between his eyebrows. In the local accent—flat, expressionless—his mellifluous, calm local voice at odds with his fierce appearance.

Peke blinks, as if to blink away a dream.

The seventy-two-year-old man turns. As if obediently. As if in submission.

But in fact to preserve his stealth. His mission. His dignity.

No longer looking at the skinheads directly—as if not daring to—he nods acknowledgment to them. What kind of acknowledgment, he has no clear idea.

He silently turns, steps carefully away. In a relieved moment, he finds himself back out in the dusty lot.

The skinheads smile to one another, sip their beers with renewed satisfaction.

Sorry-ass old man. Fuckin' A.

names as he makes his way up the hierarchy. He closes the window, shutting out the sound of the rushing water to hear better. He has waited until Rose is out for her walk.

In a few minutes, he gets him at last. "Daniel," he says.

"Dad." Peke can hear the note of a child's surprise, even though modulated, smoothed over, in the voice of an adult. And with it, instantly, the accompanying note of caution, of protective reserve. It pains him. But it is at least familiar pain.

"How are you? *Where* are you?" his son asks.

"Fishing in Montana," says Peke.

"Fishing in Montana," his son repeats, not knowing how else to respond, or what to say after it.

"I bought a cowboy hat and boots," says Peke.

"You didn't."

"Oh, I did."

"Well, you two enjoy yourselves," says Daniel. "You deserve it."

"I have a favor to ask," says Peke suddenly.

He knows the statement will be met with dumbstruck silence. He is famous among his children for never asking for anything. For never in their childhood revealing any need, or ambition, or wish, or dream.

"Your eighteen-wheelers," Stanley says to his son.

"Go ahead," says Daniel. As if challenging him to come up with it. Come up with anything.

The eighteen-wheelers are something new—part of the loading-dock upgrade and general expansion of the business that Daniel engineered.

"You can spare one?" says Peke.

A pause. Though Peke senses it is only a pause to guess at why—not whether. "Of course," says Daniel.

"And a crew?"

Another pause. "Sure. A crew."

He knows what Daniel is thinking. That it is already clear his father wants no questions about this. Is he afraid that if Daniel knows more, he might turn him down? Derail his wild plan? *Dad, you're crazy* . . .

So he is asking of Daniel something new between them. He is asking, from two thousand miles away, for a deep and instant trust, a sudden companionship in a sudden foxhole, that they've never known before. Maybe, thinks Peke, simply because they've never had a reason to know it before.

"And I want Grady to head the crew."

"Grady," says Daniel warily, his discomfort rising, his anxiety awakened.

"Grady, Daniel. Tell Grady I need him."

Because his is the only brand of fatherhood they've ever known, Peke's children have experienced it not as sadness, or distance, or frustration, but rather as a kind of benign absence. Absence despite presence, because their father has always been there for them. They've always detected a fierce protectiveness of them that conveyed love but wasn't love. Love itself—simple, unconditional—was not in the equation.

Neither Daniel nor his two sisters have ever felt a full connection with their father. But for Daniel, the one who took over the business, and the only son, it has been a more mystifying and painful relationship. Daniel had eagerly anticipated—given the atmosphere of mute circumspection he grew up with at home—that he would finally discover more about his father down at the plant. That there, among other men, his father would be looser, freer, reveal more of himself. That working alongside him, Daniel would get to know at least some piece of him.

But his father was, if anything, even more distant at work. And though his connection to any of his family was meager, Daniel remained the one whom—paradoxically—he seemed to connect with least. (With his sister Anne, his adorable, brilliant, secure, walk-on-water doctor sister, it was different. There was always a gleam in their father's eye. Stanley glowed in her presence, as she glowed in his. Though Daniel knew it was something his sister didn't understand any better than the rest of them.)

Nevertheless, they worked together, desk touching desk, in the years when Daniel learned the business. And in the years since his father's retirement, Daniel had succeeded in growing the business— smoothly and surely taking it to the next level beyond his father's management of it. It had been Daniel who'd opened the distribution center, who'd built up a genuine Western presence, expanded the loading dock, and established a delivery fleet. He had thought all this success would win his father over in some way and might finally bring connection. His father, looking in from time to time, curious, merely nodded noncommittally as Daniel caught him up on the latest developments. He left it entirely to Daniel. To a fault.

Daniel had his own children now, and had learned that he was one of those fathers for whom his children were everything. He loved them vastly and unreasonably and would always wonder if this was in reaction to being his father's son—or was it simply who he was, anthropologically or chemically? Having his own children had softened the pain, but increased the mystery, of his relationship with Stanley. He wasn't singled out for harsh treatment, after all. His father treated everyone equally. Was unfailingly fair. Which was painful for a son who wanted more than equal or fair.

Grady had been with them from the beginning. Even when Grady began, Daniel had somehow known to be careful around him. Even as a boy visiting with his father, he had picked up something, sensed something, about Grady.

And now, very specifically, very sternly, this request. These stipulations.

"You just say when and where," says Daniel. His offer a declaration, an affirmation.

"I'll call," says Peke. "But when I call, they can come right away?"

"Day or night," says Daniel. "What, to Montana?"

"Yes, to Montana. I don't know when, exactly. Soon."

"A truck is ready, Dad. My best crew."

He deserves to know, Peke feels. *He deserves an explanation.* "I'm getting my things back, Daniel."

"I assumed."

"You can't say anything to anyone."

"I assumed that, too."

"And you can't come."

There is a pause. Frustration, annoyance, pain. "All right."

Daniel doesn't say be careful. Doesn't say don't do anything foolish. Doesn't say any of the things a son or daughter would otherwise say. They are useless sentiments with a man like Stanley Peke.

"You call, and it's there," says Daniel summarily.

"I know I'm difficult," says Peke. "That I'm distant. I know the burden I can be."

Two thousand miles away, Daniel Peke is astonished to hear it so suddenly like that. From his father, it practically qualifies as a speech. He can only respond smoothly, conciliatorily, from his adult outer shell. "Well . . . it's all right, Dad . . ." Brushing the moment away. Prisoner to their strained and disconnected history. He's been ambushed by the truth, sideswiped by the moment. Nonetheless, there it is. Recognition, confirmation, that it is not merely his own failure, dark and silent and invisible in his father's long shadow.

And to say it so suddenly like that . . . It is instantly obvious to

Daniel that some act that impels a personal accounting—something final—is taking place.

So is now the time to intervene? To disobey his father? To see what, exactly, is going on? To finally reverse the roles and protect his father from himself? But one thing Daniel has come to understand, working beside him: his father's self-reliance is his very being. His self-reliance *is* his self. Alone, in some sense, is the only way Stanley Peke can be.

The arms that carried Peke, the big hands that passed him, the rough palms that pushed him into a trunk with holes punched underneath to breathe, from the woods of Cracow, to attic, to attic, finally to a boat. The powerful arms, the big hands, of nameless, faceless adults who saved him. Those who despised him, he knew their faces, their smells, their nicknames, their habits, he dreamed of them even as he dodged them. But those who loved him so selflessly, he never knew, he cannot picture.

From subsisting on scraps in Cracow trash cans to surviving with a child's wolf wiles in the woods outside the city to the thick, close sounds and smells of that trunk.

Peke is startled, remembering the trunk. The smooth wood inside, some lone craftsman with old-world values finishing the interior with pride, knowing all the while that a trunk was for storage and it was unlikely that anyone would ever know of the craftsman's extra efforts. Except, as it turned out, the little boy shoved into it, hidden in it. How he ran his fingers, repeatedly, incessantly, down the smooth wood, its darkly burled pattern barely visible by the light from the narrow breathing holes placed low, nearly invisibly, along the back side of the trunk. Is this where a dangerous obsession with possessions, with things, came from? Because a physical object had saved him? Or is this just more searching, his casting about for explanation?

And now his own son responds like those nameless, faceless saviors.

In a moment, Peke finds the ancient phone's black receiver in its cradle and finds his own eyes wet with a gush of gratitude.

The cabin is comfortable. Beautiful. There are pictures throughout of the Western family who owns it. Photos on the mantel. Local items, local artisans' crafts, chosen with care. Soft, deep couches and settees where grandparents can jostle and tease with grandchildren. Upstairs bedrooms with scuffed walls where grandchildren can tussle and jump. The snowy old television that bespeaks life without it. Life lived outside. Life with fresh air and no rules.

Someone else's things. Someone else's life. *How strange to inhabit someone else's life,* thinks Rose. To wander through someone else's rooms. They take on a new interest, a new fascination and meaning and tone, she finds, when you no longer have rooms of your own.

She moves through these rooms, and waits, while her husband sees through this silent task of his. As he heads out on his silent, unacknowledged missions, as he makes his furtive phone calls out of her earshot, as he wordlessly and continuously asks her forbearance.

In the years of the manufacturing plant, he never discussed his work much at home. Rarely revealed even the shape or tenor of his day. But that silence became a comfortable one. A certainty in itself, a silence to nestle into securely and predictably each evening. While this, she knows, is a silence born of danger. Fraught with it, she is sure.

She can stop him. She can demand that he stop. Demand, threaten, insist, stamp her feet, issue an ultimatum. And perhaps he would respect that demand, and perhaps he wouldn't. But she is unwilling to do that. Threats and ultimatums are not what Rose and Stanley have been about. Interrupting what is truly important to one or the other, what truly matters to one or the other—for whatever private or unfathomable reason—is not what their marriage is about. Their marriage is not built on interruption.

So she is consigned, for the moment, to the role of the waiting wife. Her husband is in the middle of a project. Not repairing a toilet, or a window shade, or a garage-door opener, but trying to repair their life. It's a dangerous project—dangerous in direct proportion to the degree he tries to pretend otherwise. After fifty years of marriage, she knows his techniques, and she knows at least that.

So she cooks. Reads. Patiently and brilliantly resurrects the owners' garden.

It is easier for him, she thinks. He at least has some control on this transcontinental errand. He at least has reins to hold. While standing in another family's cabin in another part of her country, she has nothing.

Maybe even less than that. Because a new question has been pushing at her, one that she has in turn been forcing away from herself—it is too powerful, too much to bring close. With the longer stretches of their silences, the new degree of their isolation, with what seems in him a deeper sense of brooding as they have traveled farther west, closer and closer to some unknown eventuality, she has wondered: Does she even have Stanley?

Marriage to Stanley Pecoskowitz has always incurred a cost in aloneness, in distance. But fate is lately laying on extra penalties.

The loss of their things. Yes, she is shocked. She will always be shocked by it, in some sense. But her relative silence about the event is not from that. It is from an inherent paradox that she finds difficult to digest. On the face of it, it's not a paradox; it's reasonable: while she knows and genuinely believes that it all means nothing—all this stuff—she nevertheless wants it all back. Of course. That's fine. But then it immediately deepens for her, into a paradox both of existence and of feeling, that hangs over her, ceaselessly, at every moment:

You have your life, but you don't anymore.

It is this realm between, this inhabiting of uncertainty—having your life, but not having it—that she knows her husband is expert in. Armed with few specifics, few details, she nevertheless senses that Stanley Peke knows his way here. That no one is as experienced in these shadows as Stanley Peke. So she lets him lead. And she follows.

To live in someone else's life for a few days—it is a reminder of what your own life once meant. Could mean again. And that, in the end, is the dangling leaf of hope—shimmering in the immense Western light, turning in the cool breeze, clinging firmly and miraculously to its branch—that holds her here.

Peke sits fishing. The light dances fiercely, dazzling, on the river. A postcard scene. A princely realm. Warm bright sun but cool dry breeze. A horizon to infinity in an unbroken blue. The day goes through him with its beauty. Fills him with its peace. *Fishing* is a fancy word for waiting—functionalized waiting. Which is perfect, because he is waiting on more than fish.

He casts his line, remains motionless, until he feels the sure, unmistakable tug, and reels it in. He watches the silver fish wiggle with an energy, a life force, that must be respected, before throwing it back.

He casts his line identically again into the loud peace of the rushing river.

A black bug crawls along the ground by his leg. It burrows in the dirt busily.

A Western bug—he doesn't know what it is. Fat, though. Purposeful. Some kind of beetle, maybe. He watches it work.

Seven years old, living in the woods. The memory loosening in him, made to loosen by a conspiracy of circumstances, by layers of imagery revivified and close by—these brushy woods, the chill breeze, the empty land and sky. And, not least, by standing at a closed gate, wondering what is up that dirt road.

He watches the bug.

Suddenly he scoops it up in one hand, blocks its escape with the other.

He looks at it. Watches it scoot frantically around on his broad, ancient, creviced palm, looking for a path, an exit.

Then, impulsively, he slaps the black bug into his mouth, bites down a few times, hears and feels the unmistakable crunch in his jaw, then swallows.

Stanley Peke, epicure and connoisseur. Stanley Peke of four-star restaurants, of genteel chefs bowing at the table, of sommeliers standing obediently at the ready, a respectful two steps behind his chair. Stanley Peke of precious wines from special reserves, brought up from the corners of deep cellars.

As he suspected. As he remembered. Not bad at all.

The woods, the thicket, the dirt fields outside Cracow. All come rushing back in the taste of the bug. That is connoisseurship, after all. Sense memory bound to taste, rushing back with each bite. In Cracow, Abel taught him how to test the trash can food first—how to hold it in his mouth, what to taste for, to know it was OK to eat, before swallowing.

He is unchanged. It is still him. He is still the boy. The wily survivor.

He feels it welling up. A ball of rage, packed tight, pulsing. A dense fury, dense enough to have its own gravitational pull, like a geological body in space, the gravity assigning it direction and purpose. The rage harbored, intact, since seven, Peke is suddenly aware. Since seven. *Contain it. Contain it. Don't descend to them.*

His creeping forgetfulness has been only situational, he realizes. Nothing organic. Here in the fresh Montana air, he is focused. Alert.

He has been drifting, somnolent, with no need to think. The slow slide of complacency. Preparing to die. Now he is thrown back to an earlier time. When he was—at every moment—relentlessly preparing to live.

He picks up the fishing line again, methodically casts it again, feels the pleasure of its gentle tug, of its modest weight and momentum in air, the *plink* and settle into the sun-dappled river.

He waits.

Contain it.

He waits.

Another widow—this one via Annelle. A Florida job. Gold Coast matron, moving in with her family in the DC suburbs. Easy. Why not? They'll make the Albuquerque delivery, do the Austin gig, then turn the white truck east.

To time it correctly means a couple of days and nights in Miami. Like shore leave for LaFarge, Chiv, and Al while Nick scouts it. And then, if it checks out, if the information is good, if the routes are safe, do the job on Thursday.

And after returning from it, a little break. Drive to Billings, fly to Seattle, on to Rio and Armando. To the hot breeze and the hot breath, to bury himself in hedonism, hide from himself in

Armando's simple self-absorption. Armando. The love of a beautiful thing. His torso. His tan. It is nothing more or less than that. No need to understand it further. Armando. The love of a beautiful thing.

Soon, the huge white truck rolls out the gate.

On the move. The white, gleaming monster—an eight-hundred-horsepower, twenty-ton Grendel—heading off to gorge again on the infinite promise of America.

18

Peke stands again in the dusty silence, outside the rickety metal gate. The harsh red blinking hasn't altered in days.

He looks down into the dirt by his feet. He smiles.

New deep tire treads. Fresh. The tire treads are running the opposite way now. Going out.

His heart beats harder beneath the big, featureless Montana sky. His body fills with a kind of glory. A vindication. An aliveness.

An old Ford Fairlane moves crisply on the road into town. Out here, its speed, the urgency to its movement, translates into nothing unusual to observe. There are no respected speed limits. Speed is your inalienable right.

At an intersection in town, Peke drives in over the gravel and pulls up to the pay phone on the outside wall of the filling station. One street up from Freedom Café. He dials. He says his name several times into the receiver, as his call makes its way again up the hierarchy. Moments of suspension. A series of clicks. Until Daniel's voice is once again at the other end.

Peke utters the three words he has patiently waited days to say.

"Send the truck," he says.

19

There is an old man standing alone on a dirt road in Montana, squinting at a closed rusted metal gate in front of him.

Is he wandering? Is he lost? Those in a passing car might think so and stop. But it is unlikely that a car will pass by. It's too remote. There's no reason to be out here.

A white plastic supermarket bag is clutched in each of the old man's hands. Perhaps he's collecting cans by the side of the road.

Minutes before, he pulled his Ford off the road into the high brush several hundred yards past the gate and shut off the engine. As he walked away from the car, he looked back to be sure it wasn't visible from the road, submerged in high brush and high weeds and grasses like a sunken ship.

Now Peke looks at the gate, as if he has come upon it unexpectedly. He stares at it a moment.

Then he pulls the gate aside, his face muscles clenching slightly against its loud, rusty, swinging squeak, and begins to walk up the path of dirt road. He walks up the middle of the road, an old man alone, slightly swinging the white plastic supermarket bags.

He can't ask the truck to enter the property without his looking first. Without his being sure. He's asking something far out of the ordinary, after all. He must take responsibility.

The woods and brush open onto a clearing.

An old farmhouse. A couple of trailers—vintage-looking—on cement blocks. A couple of late-model pickup trucks. And behind them a hundred yards, a huge storage barn—an unpretty, efficient farm building—utilitarian and immense.

He does not have much chance to take it all in.

Two sleek, snapping black dogs are racing furiously, flat out, toward him, across the weed-and-dirt field. Big mutts, but with plenty of Doberman in them. Waiting for this moment all their dog lives.

In that angry, whirling moment of their approach—barking, snarling, choking on their own enthusiasm, he knows now what he suspected. Why there is no fencing. Why the gate can be swung open. Why there is no other protection system. Because it's this. Protection, Montana-style.

And he has a quick, vivid, instant, blackened vision of the other dogs. The officers' dogs. The dogs he learned from.

The dogs are closing in . . . almost to him . . . preparing to leap. Their Doberman sleekness makes them bullets of black. Preparing to leap . . . but not yet committed to the attack. He sees them looking, judging, examining, processing angles and smells and sounds and sights and sensations in their dog brains.

Dogs trained haphazardly, no doubt. Dogs taught with a casual love of violence. Trained to attack, trained into aggression out here, but almost certainly not having, in this wilderness, anyone to actually attack.

At this moment, Peke, letting out a furious, piercing scream, runs straight at the dogs, just as they run at him.

It is not a human sound, nor a human behavior at all. Not something they have seen in a human.

One dog falters for a moment.

Peke focuses on that one. Roars at it. Then abruptly stops his roaring to stare at it. Staring at them both now.

Both dogs have stopped.

I have seen much worse than you. You're nothing. Nothing. You know that, don't you, in your little dog hearts? It is etched in his face, obvious in his stance, full in his own heart.

In theirs, too, apparently.

Because now they circle warily. Snarl. Growl.

Peke circles, too. Snarls. Growls.

Then Peke begins laughing. Howling hysterically. Raucous human laughter. A sound, a happy sound, they undoubtedly know.

They bow their necks, paw the dirt in confusion.

He looks in their eyes. Looks all the way into their black eyes like they are equals. Stares into their souls. And they seem to know it. As if they have met one of their own. A kindred being.

One dog whimpers for a moment in puzzlement.

Then, in a sort of culmination of his staring, Peke empties the two supermarket bags. From each bag, an immense slab of Idaho beef falls to the ground.

They look stunned for a moment at the meat. Then leap to it, each dog settling down onto its haunches and going to work, shredding and feasting.

He watches both intently.

A minute or so into the meal, one of the dogs looks up at Peke dumbly. Sated. Satisfied. And something more than that.

The dog blinks repeatedly.

Now the other dog is blinking, too.

Before either can finish its feast, they have rolled to their sides, slumbering.

In the woods of Poland, they made the compound from mushrooms and bark. Here in America, it was simpler. He knows what medications to buy at the pharmacy to grind up together. Ingredients he has disguised with a much broader pharmacy shopping list.

These are descendants, spiritual cousins, of the officer dogs—those shadow-colored hell-beasts.

Descendants that were bred mean. But not mean enough.

>>>

"Hello?" he calls out, as flatly American as he can.

He walks up to the farmhouse. "Hello?" His voice made minuscule, swallowed up in the landscape. "Hello?"

Is someone feeding the dogs? Or are they living off the wildlife that is bound to be plentiful within the borders of the big property? It's an important point, because it leads to the next question: How long until the thieves return?

"Hello?"

No response.

Surely the commotion of the dogs would have brought someone out. Or barricaded them in. Let them prepare. "Hello?"

He crosses the dusty front yard, climbs the gray steps to the front porch, stands on the small farmhouse porch a moment, the floor planks painted gray. He tries the front door, already knowing. Locked. He looks in the front-door window. A living room with large stereo speakers, a big-screen television, a beaten-up couch and shredded rug, and not much else. Temporary. Transitory. A room of men passing time. He can't see the cases of beer, both full and empty, but imagines they're there.

He steps down off the gray-planked porch.

The wind. The sun. An old man in a wide-brimmed Western hat, wandering alone. He has entered an American landscape. He is in a painting.

He walks around the side of the farmhouse, then the hundred yards or so back to the barn. He sees that truck tire tracks—lots of tire tracks—crisscross everywhere.

But the truck is not here. He feels himself relax a little. Hears his own breathing become steadier with relief.

He stands in front of the big barn. Looks up at the ancient, wide planks of its vast skin. "Hello? Anybody here? Anybody?" His voice vibrates oddly against the flank of the enormous building.

He steps up to the barn's side door, pulls at it. Solid. Locked.

He looks at the keyhole of the heavy door's handle.

Again looks up the side of the giant barn. There's a ridge of slatted opening at the crease of the tin roof and sides. To let the hot air inside escape. Nothing more.

He looks again at the keyhole in the door handle.

Peke heads now to the back of the farmhouse. Walks through the dust and dry dirt, up the steps of the exposed landing, presses his face against one of the glass panes of the farmhouse's back door.

He sees no wires crossing the glass inside. No wires running along the door frame, at least not visible from here.

Peke steps off the landing, stoops, and picks up a rock about the size of a fist.

He steps back up onto the landing, looks once more, then covers his fist with the sleeve of his barn coat, and taps the rock firmly through the door's lowest pane of glass. Three quick punches clear the pane out.

He waits. Waits to hear something. Anything. An alarm. Another dog. A shout from someone roused from a nap.

Nothing.

He reaches his wrist in carefully to the inside door handle, turns it. The back door opens into the kitchen.

Peke glides through the ancient room, its black-and-white tile floor heavily cracked, its cabinets deeply scarred, thin and slapdash to begin with, hanging crooked, having suffered fists and blows and recklessness. He passes through the living room with the big television and stereo speakers. He can feel it is a world of men—transitory, haphazard, rough—a barracks, stale and ramshackle. A house in such contrast with his own, where everything was considered, thought out, to add to the warmth, to the sense of peace and charm. Peke moves lightly, invisible, ghostly. He steps into the office, hardly pausing, settles down at the oddly ornate desk as if it were his own.

Picture books, price guides, auction catalogs, fill two walls. Catalog consumerism gone beyond itself in this farmhouse hideout, a dark inversion of the cheerful missives of American plenty that flooded his mailbox.

The computer sits on a metal stand to the left. He stares at its mute green screen. He is tempted to start it. But no. Not now.

He opens the desk's top drawer. Black ledgers, spiral-ringed notebooks. He leafs idly through the top ones randomly, discovers immediately that they are neatly kept lists, itemizations of objects.

He sits there. A thief at a thief's desk.

He opens a second drawer. He sees Rose's necklace immediately. Finds the two ruby earrings next to it, hers also. He puts them into the velvet sack still in there with them, stuffs the sack into his front pants pocket.

He finds next to the sack—not so surprisingly—his own safe-deposit box key.

He stuffs that into his pants pocket, too.

It occurs to him: it is a precisely parallel action. A swift, perfect justice. Finding the safe-deposit box key in the thief's desk, after the thief found it in Peke's. He's rifling through the thief's desk as the thief rifled through his.

He pulls a couple more drawers, soon finds the old bonds, the old wills, and, in a quick inventory in his head, realizes he has everything. Everything, that is, except what he came inside hoping to find.

He rises from the desk, heads to the back door. But he stops first at another doorway—almost involuntarily—when he sees it is a bedroom. Better furnished, more serene, more finished, than the brusque, dilapidated, untended other rooms he has hurried through. It has the feel of a sanctuary in the chaotic, ramshackle ranch house.

He looks inside and is momentarily disoriented by seeing it at the bedside. Gaudy, gold, sparkling in the low light.

The watch. Peke knows that the thief, though he might cherish it, can't wear it on a job. It's too distinctive. Not what the foreman of a moving crew would be wearing. It's why the red light has continued to blink, unchanging, these last few days, frustrating Peke, testing his patience.

The watch that guided Peke here.

If the thief had kept it on, of course, Peke would still know his whereabouts. It would take some of the tenseness, some of the risk, away right now. He presumes they're away on another job. But he has no idea how far away or for how long, nor even exactly when they left. It creates a low-grade, continual anxiety to Peke's presence here. A thief doesn't belong in your house, but you certainly don't belong in a thief's. If the thief would at some point put the watch back on, Peke thinks, it might still have its uses.

Wouldn't it now be too suspicious to leave the watch here and take back everything else that was his?

He could pry open its back, leave it open-backed on the desk—show the thief how it was done. Show him how he was followed and found.

Or he could leave it here by the bed, and the thief might presume Peke simply did not see it, if everything else was gone.

Peke picks up the watch, looks at it one last time, sets it down on the bedside table exactly as it was before. His gift to the thief.

He is nervous, jumpy, being in here. He's suddenly aware of needing to relieve himself. He steps carefully into the bathroom. It's a narrow L, he sees. As he urinates, he inspects the toiletries on the low plastic shelf to the side of the toilet. It is neat, well organized, like the bedroom. He thinks, for the first time, with surprise, about the possibilities of the thief's sexual orientation. His wife is fascinated by the family cabin they are staying in. By the family's life. Peke is as fascinated by this den of thieves. By the thief's life.

He still has not found what he is looking for. He exits the bathroom and scans the beat-up, worn-down farmhouse interior once more, futilely, and turns to leave.

Then smiles. Because it's in the act of leaving that he sees it. Right where he should have looked first. A small key ring hanging on a nail by the door. It might as well have been labeled BARN or SHED. Peke obviously doesn't see as well as he once did, but he sees well enough.

First, though, to a small moving job that, unfortunately, can't wait for Daniel's crew. That has to be done before they get here.

There is a wheelbarrow upside down, ten yards away from the back door. He rights it, wheels it briskly across the muddy field to the comatose dogs. He turns the wheelbarrow on its side against one dog's torso, pushes the animal against the wheelbarrow's edge, and rights the wheelbarrow with the dog in it. The sleek, fierce animal is surprisingly light in the wheelbarrow. There is a dog pen around the side of the house. He wheels it up to the dog pen, opens the gate, wheels it in.

He dumps the sleeping dog gently onto the dirt inside.

He had expected the effort to wear him out, but he feels invigorated. Feels reserves of energy.

He repeats the process for the second dog.

For all their snarling, outsize fury, he's surprised again by the lightness. As if docility makes them lighter.

When both are in the pen, their forms still splayed out, oblivious, he pulls their rusty water trough inside the pen with them, careful not to spill any liquid. They'll have water. They'll be OK. He shuts the sturdy pen door. Checks it to assure that it will stay shut.

Peke stands at the door of the barn, the key ring glistening in the sun, and tries the few keys systematically, until one turns in the lock.

He pulls down the handle, pushes open the heavy door, ducks into the darkness.

It takes a few moments for his seventy-two-year-old eyes to adjust from the bright, brutal Montana daylight to the low light inside—light coming mainly in a sharp path from the door he's just opened.

When he can see, he looks around him.

Paintings stacked out from the walls. Some still in their expensive gilt frames, others simply pinned against unpainted wooden ones. Beautiful, ornate pieces of furniture piled high: desks, highboys, dressers, chests of drawers, Chinese vases, rolled Oriental and Turkish rugs, Mediterranean amphorae. A warehouse agglomeration of art and civilization, heaped high, here in a barn on an overgrown lot in the Montana woods. European craftsmen, salon painters, artisans from across centuries, in their final home in the off-the-grid American backwoods. In a benighted gallery. In an unknown museum.

He sees the outline of the inside of the locked overhead doors toward the far end of the barn. He moves toward them. As he gets closer to them, they loom up surprisingly large. Twin, mammoth entrances.

And there, piled just inside the doors, are the Pekes' belongings.

Even the Mercedes convertible is there, tucked to the side.

He steps over, looks more closely at it. Runs his eyes sternly, appraisingly, down its flanks. Unbruised. None the worse for wear.

He steps to the overhead door of the left bay garage, throws the lock, struggles a little at first, then succeeds, in lifting the huge door.

The furniture, the cartons of books and china, the bright flanks and chrome of the Mercedes convertible—all their belongings—are pierced and bathed by the light of day.

20

The truck pulls grandly onto the compound grounds. Big, white, new, gleaming brightly. Twenty tons of warrior-savior, at the beck and call of the mottled septuagenarian standing small in front of the barn.

As it happens, painted white. As it happens, roughly matching the truck that took his belongings. Once again—like finding his safe-deposit key in the thief's desk—an elegant symmetry of fate. Justice as if mathematically balanced and precise.

He has Grady's cell phone number, called early this morning from the cabin one more time before they went out of cell range. They had just passed the Idaho border. They had explicit directions from him. He even drove the final hour of it himself several days before, gathering landmarks, just to be sure. Coming straight into the compound, he figures, is how they'll arouse the least suspicion. A truck pulling in, a truck pulling out, like always, he is sure. Certainly no one will think anything as the truck pulls past the cross-roads. Pulls by Freedom Café.

Through the truck's cab window—broad and flat, like a movie screen—Grady, the driver, big and muscled, sees an old man in a Western hat, standing out in the Western barrenness and scrub, gesturing the immense vehicle toward him.

In a symphony of hisses and squeaks, of sharp turns and air brakes—the grand concluding notes of its cross-country song—the truck backs into position outside the barn.

Grady hops down from the cab, looks around at the oddness of the scene. A kind of bright desolation. He wears a closely contained but still evident air of amusement at where he suddenly finds himself after two days in the saddle, blasting westward.

"Why, hello, Stanley Peke," he says, the slightest bit of Irish brogue still in the uttering of his old boss's name, his blue eyes smiling brightly. Peke sees the familiar scar down Grady's right cheek—a barroom scar, he's always been sure. He knows this isn't just any crew. It's a crew that's ready, just in case. Grady. There are such various immigrant experiences, thinks Peke.

If the crew with Grady doesn't always have such a paramilitary quality to them, they have effectively assumed it here. They ask no questions, proudly make it clear they will not ask questions, will respond only to whatever the need is. They're alert, Peke notices, not immense men, but beneath their T-shirts, not men to tangle with. The crew remains silent, as if to further abet the powerful, seamless impression of a dream. Of a calm, sure, smooth unreality in the truck's arrival.

They are the men in the white hats, Peke thinks, riding into a Western town to save him. The opposite, the mirror image, of the thief and his crew. He notices the symmetry. Another symmetry. Like his being in the thief's office.

Peke shows them. "Everything in this pile. Everything here. It's mine."

Grady nods. "And where's it going?"

Peke hands him the address on a scrap of paper: *3901 Pacific View, Santa Barbara, California.*

Grady nods again.

But before beginning the task at hand, before marshaling his men to it, he regards Peke with a sudden expression of loyalty and reverence and curiosity that Peke can't quite decipher. Grady's half smile is on the verge of words but is containing them. A look that half warns: *I will ask one question, one relevant question, and that is all.*

"And where are *they?*"

"Taking someone else's," says Peke—with a vehemence, a disgust, he did not expect to feel. It surprises him, there inside the barn. It satisfies him, too.

»»»

If Peke went to the local Montana police, he can imagine what would happen.

They would raid it, yes. They would have the glory of breaking the burglary ring, of recovering the merchandise.

But after that, he would become a witness, needing to fly back here continually, or even east, to where the original theft took place, to be deposed, to testify—it would consume his privacy, his time, his life.

And his belongings—they would become state's evidence, exhibit A. It could be months of argument and appeals before he and Rose got them back. The valuables more damaged by months as state's evidence, probably, than in the careful thieves' hands.

Returned to him finally, perhaps years later.

That's how these things work, he knows. He is seventy-two. He doesn't have that kind of time.

And maybe it wouldn't result in a conviction anyway. Maybe it could be argued away, or there would be a backroom compromise struck, a deal made, as there often is, where justice is the last matter, the last item on the agenda. Maybe it would be lost in legal argument, in point and counterpoint. Maybe it's harder to get a conviction on interstate transportation, for instance. Multiple jurisdictions.

Maybe the thief even knows all this, relies on it. Maybe it's part of his plan.

The loss of Peke's privacy. The loss of his time.

To be a hero. To be of service. In bringing a chancy justice.

He watches them carrying the items from the barn. No. This is much better.

To help with the loading would be foolish vanity on his part, counterproductive. Yes, he is a strong and healthy seventy-two, possessed of a rude, raw physical health that is a genetic accident and gift. It is the envy of his wife and friends, he can see, this basic robustness, that always shines through his aches and pains. But he senses Grady and the crew don't want him lifting alongside them. It mildly reduces and insults their heroics. Isn't really useful, anyway. But it feels foolish to just stand here, watching. So what will he do while they work?

Peke finds himself wandering the property.

It is scraggly, brushy, dusty, and undistinguished. Untended woods and field, undifferentiated weeds and undergrowth. Without the haphazard fencing, there would be no sense of borders at all.

In a few minutes along a narrow path, where the woods open unexpectedly into a field, he comes upon it: an immense mountain of trash. They must simply pile it up out here, not bothering with any formal disposal. The property is large enough to accommodate its own trash site. But as Peke ambles closer, looks up at it—maybe twenty feet high—he can analyze its contents better, more specifically. It is filled with cast-off household dishes and furniture and toys and games and televisions and electronics, all clearly from other lives like his own.

Some scraps of food—melon rinds, eggshells—lie scattered a few yards away from the mountain's perimeter, probably dragged around gleefully by local feasting wildlife. But that's the minor part of it. It's mostly hard goods, in various states of destruction and unrecognition.

A particularly American pile of detritus, Peke thinks. Brightly colored packaging, retaining its resolutely cheerful color after season upon season in the rain and snow. A pile of absurd variety, of ridiculous plenty.

It occurs to him that this is where much of it ends up anyway, in a pile like this. That despite his arguably brave and high-principled rescue operation, despite any subsequent return to normalcy, when he and Rose pass on, their children will take a few items to which they assign personal meaning, and the rest of it will make its eventual way, either over weeks or over years, to a place like this—a legal one, but one that looks much the same.

He feels that simple realization like a weight on him. Amid the exhilaration and excitement of retrieving his belongings, a sudden weight of brooding. It's almost enough to make him go back, tell them to unload the truck again, back out empty, call it off. This is where it will end up for the thief, too. Their odd communion. Meaninglessness piled high.

Only now does he notice the books in among the items. Hardcovers, paperbacks, which, like so much of the rest of it, must have no value to the thieves. Books, cartons of books, among the broken chairs, the drawerless upturned desks, the half beds.

How could he not think of it? Maybe because it is so distant in time and place. Maybe because he was resisting the memory. It is as if the pile has been accumulated, assembled out here in a field like those other fields, by the woods like those other woods, exclusively to pierce him.

How could he *not* think of it? They would come at night, in the wee hours, he and the other boys, to the smoldering piles at Cracow's eastern edge. To scavenge what they could. Using the immense pile itself as camouflage, remaining unseen by the guards by keeping the pile between the guards and themselves, like a game, while they picked over the items, took what they could carry at a run, what they could trade, what they could fit inside their torn coats. The guards were old and unalert, when there were any there at all.

It continues to pierce him. Because at first there were the other boys, a wild pack of them, swift and dancing night creatures with the power and confidence of their numerousness and anonymity, but in the end, it was only Abel and he.

The items piled high. The stuff of life. Life, history, existence, piled up and burned. The piles were both practical and symbolic. *Your lives are done. Piled up here in front of you. And the small, technical, leftover detail of your aliveness—we'll attend to that soon.* An efficiency, the pile, but an efficiency meant to humiliate.

He looks up, and Grady is standing next to him. "We're ready. You want to check it all?"

Peke shakes his head no.

"Beautiful Mercedes there, sir, if you don't mind my saying."

Peke smiles. *It is, isn't it?*

"We'll be at 3901 Pacific View Tuesday morning," says Grady brightly.

"We'll be there to let you in," Peke replies.

They smile briefly, diffidently at each other. It's proving easier than either of them expected.

"I'll close the gate after you," says Peke.

Grady frowns, clearly uncomfortable with Peke's staying behind. "I don't know if that's such a good idea. These people will be back."

Peke pats him lightly on the shoulder, never dropping his gentle smile. He can play old and wise when he needs to. "I'll only be a few minutes behind you. It's OK."

Peke watches the truck pull out. White and gleaming against

the landscape, its surfaces playing games of light with the afternoon Montana sun.

He walks one last time into the big wooden barn.

The outside light is cast at an angle against the old Mercedes convertible, tucked into the side of the garage bay.

He opens the door. Settles into the richly familiar driver's seat. Inserts the spare Mercedes key that is still on his own key ring.

The car coughs twice and turns over. He pushes a button on the burled-walnut dashboard. The top lowers, smoothly mechanical.

He pulls his car carefully out of the barn, into the sun.

It has been so easy. So fluid, so smooth. So quiet, so dreamlike. An old man casually strolling the enemy's lair. He is suspicious of how easy. But he is suspicious of everything. Maybe it is simple at last. Maybe there is a balance here. That in a life in which what should have been easy was so brutally hard, it is time for what should be hard to be easy.

>>>

A rich, bald old man drives past Freedom Café in a vintage Mercedes with the top down.

The three skinheads sitting in the cafe look out and notice.

Out here at the crossroads of Freedom Café, it rates as an unusual event. You don't see that kind of thing. It is only a moment. A dream.

There is something loosely disconcerting, something annoying, about it.

One of the skinheads thinks vaguely of an old man who wandered into the cafe a few days ago. But that guy had a cowboy hat.

The big white Mid-South Partners truck pulls past the gate, past the pickups and trailers, past the farmhouse, across the mud fields, and around to the overhead doors at the far end of the barn. Home. Transitory, dust-crusted, roughly kept, but home. Forty-two hours after the fact, Nick is still stewing about the poor Miami Beach taste of the widow. Eccentric modern furniture, too distinctive, too difficult to move. But there were some paintings. *Christ—all that money, all that leisure time, and no taste*, thinks Nick. *No taste.*

Nick hears the dogs barking but doesn't see them. They usually come greet the truck, scrabble and dance excitedly around its tires as it pulls in. Maybe they're around the other side of the barn, chasing something in the woods.

LaFarge hops out of the truck and trots over to the overhead doors to unlock them while Nick maneuvers the truck around, backing it into position. It was a tiring, all-night drive. He's thinking they can unload later in the day, leave it all in the truck for now, break open the beers, pop on the stereo. Although it's hard to gather everyone back to the job after a few hours of drinking, after they've been off the clock.

He hasn't yet moved out the previous goods. Still too early. He'll have them put this load in next to them. Once dealers are found, it'll be more efficient anyway to deliver the marketable parts of the loads together.

"Hey, Nick?"

"Hey what?"

LaFarge stands looking up at the cab with a stricken expression on his face. Like he's done something horrible. Fucked up big.

"Some of our stuff . . ."

"What about it?" says Nick irritably.

LaFarge can barely believe it even as he says it. "It ain't here."

Nick stands looking at the empty space just inside the huge barn's garage bays.

He paces the dirt-pack floor. Looks down, stares, as if waiting for the goods to reappear.

Someone's found him. He's deep in these goddamn woods, where he lives with no one and nothing, exists like some grumpy fairy-tale character, like some miserly ogre or banished warlock, yet he's been found.

He feels the invasion. He feels the violation. He is aware of the irony, that this is precisely how his victims must feel, but his thinking for the moment is occupied by more practical concerns than irony. Data; information; implications; revenge. Irony is shoved far to the side.

He thinks first of the locals, of the crazy neo-Nazis he's coexisted uneasily with, the nuts in the woods, seeing him go in and out with his truck, unable to resist anymore, sneaking in to share the spoils. His fury rises. They're fools. He'll find them.

He soon sees, though—his overorderly, overclerical mind almost immediately notices—that the only items taken are items from the last job. Nothing else touched. In another couple of weeks, depending on buyers, the items would have been intermingled. But they weren't yet.

The neo-Nazis would have cherry-picked, grabbed only what intrigued them. Or ransacked it, leaving a trail of mess. One or the other. But this is neither.

He looks again more closely, considers. Other quick theories and visions—of petty pilferers and local teenage adventurers and reckless hayseeds—drop away.

It's only the items from the last job.

Including, he now sees—feeling its absence like a physical emptiness inside him—the silver Mercedes.

It's as if—carefully, considerately—the owner has come and retrieved his things. That old man with the accent.

Nick feels his stomach clenching. He's aware of a throb at his temples. He feels his brain winding tight, seizing like a broken machine.

That old man.

It would explain things, except for the fact that it seems impossible. From two thousand miles away? How would the old man have found them? Could the truck have been followed? Nick would have noticed. He was looking. He is always looking out for being followed. He could not have been followed day and night across two thousand miles by an old man.

Did it happen when he went back to the safe-deposit box? That seems more likely. But he hired locals, was so cautious. He can't imagine that he was even seen. He was never in the bank himself, and if seen, then—again—certainly not followed. Not—again—across two thousand miles. He would have noticed—

careful Nick. Alert, aware, spending his professional life looking in the rearview mirror.

He is instantly and sickly aware that if he has been found like this, then very possibly the police have been informed, have maybe taken a look already, and have been patiently, watchfully waiting for his return.

In which case they will be swooping in, noisy and overstaffed and overarmed and overarrogant, any moment now.

But all is quiet. They do not.

And if the old man were going to contact the police, he would not have taken his things back like this. If the police were involved, this is not how it would go—one person's possessions retrieved, others left. The police require evidence. Procedure. Equal treatment of the victimized.

No, he realizes, at least for now, there seems to be no police involvement. The police have not been called. *Did not call the cops.* He tucks that away.

As he begins to accept that it might actually be that old man, he gets angrier. Angrier that the old man has somehow pulled this off. The clenching in his stomach spreads, becomes a heat surging through his body like a chemical, like a medicine gone bad, sitting hot in the bottle too long.

He's alone in the barn. The others huddle outside—they know to move away when Nick is angry.

Nick moves slowly out of the barn, still stunned, confused—the anger still spiraling upward.

He notices only now that the dogs are in the pen. The pen is closed. How did he do that? How did the old man get them in there?

As Nick opens the door of the dog pen, his dogs come bounding out, released, freed, jumping around him, exultant.

He kicks the first one in the jaw. It yelps and recoils.

He kicks the second in the side, before it can move away in confusion, in instinctive defense.

"What the fuck good are you?" He goes to kick them again, but they are faster than he is; they steer clear, scurrying away across the field.

He runs at them, tries to land a few more kicks, but they manage to stay a few steps ahead of him, adeptly avoiding him until he stalks the other way.

If he has to be with them to give the attack command, what the fuck is the point?

Nick inspects the garage-door mechanisms. The side-door lock. The career thief reconstructing how he was robbed. Bringing an expert's perspective.

Nothing damaged.

He sees car tracks in the dirt. The Mercedes tracks.

He stalks up the farmhouse's back steps, sees the broken pane.

He toes the broken glass off the wooden landing.

Entering, looks at the key ring on the nail by the door. It's there, where he always leaves it. But returned there, he is sure, by the old man. The old man who saw the key ring and knew. Keys to the kingdom. Maybe even thinking, *You found my brass key. Now I've found yours.*

Sullenly, wordlessly, Nick heads for his office.

Sits down at his desk.

Opens the second drawer.

Of course.

The jewelry is gone.

Nick feels it. The old man sitting here. The fury rises in Nick, a fresh wave of it, washing over him.

He pounds his fist on the desk. Spins in his chair and yanks open a file drawer behind him. Riffles through it frantically, until he stops at a folder. He stares at the folder a moment, before pulling it out and opening it.

The old man's signature has been ripped off the top sheet. Nick took it to make copies, sending the copies of the signature to the safe-deposit box actors, for them to practice from.

But the rest of the fake pink form is still there, with the address: 3901 Pacific View, Santa Barbara.

Is the old man really taking his things there? Is he that arrogant? But he is arrogant enough, after all, to come collect his things deep in the Montana woods.

Will he now try to hide from Nick? No—he will go on with his life, certain, probably, that Nick wouldn't risk an escalation of events. Wouldn't tangle with someone so clearly and completely onto Nick. Someone crazy and determined enough to cross the country, to somehow find his way here, in order to retrieve his things. Or maybe the old man figures Nick has already tossed the original delivery address. But even if Nick didn't have it, he could probably still get the destination address from Dolly, his moving-company contact, to confirm it—that's where the Pekes' name came from. It's probably still in Dolly's computer. The old man must have guessed at Nick's having some mechanism, some system, like that. Or maybe the old man simply figures Nick would never jeopardize his whole enterprise by coming after one old man, one particularly stubborn mark.

In which case, the old man—pretty good at figuring, apparently—has finally figured wrong. Smart old man. Stupid old man.

You can't just come in here and steal my things, thinks Nick.

I'm gonna get my things back.

Nick sits inside Freedom Café. The three skinheads are seated around him.

He's asked if he can join them, speaking to them directly for the first time, and they sense that this has significance, that this is an occasion. Nick senses they've been itching to know what it is he's doing with that big white truck on that property out there. Maybe they've even come by, aimlessly curious, but have seen the gate, heard the dogs, and thought better of it, though it's probably only fed their curiosity.

Nick's been thinking about the old man, and that gracious, tasteful house, and that accent that Nick heard in the few sentences he exchanged with the old man.

That accent. That beautiful house.

You don't want to leave anything, he's explained to his crew, punctuating the lesson by tossing the carton of pictures into the green Dumpster. You want to take everything. You need the annihilation to be total, so they know what they are dealing with. So they're not tempted to tangle.

He has explained, demonstrated all that to his guys, and look what happened.

He's been thinking about it all night. Thinking about the old man's show of friendliness. Thinking about his own crew—Chiv, Al, LaFarge. The trick with them is, they're real movers. They look like they are, feel like they are. They have a simplicity of spirit about them not to arouse any suspicion. They make the marks feel relaxed. In part, he knows, because they're not, at heart, mean guys. Nick knows very well that he is the mean one.

For this, he needs a little more meanness than his guys have.

"I'm Nick, by the way."

"Dustin," says one of the skinheads.

"Lee."

"Pork," says the third, with a hard, hungry body, and an expression that says, *Don't ask*.

All curt, militaristic.

This could work.

He sits with the skinheads and tells them exactly what he does. Tells these peculiar, dangerously disconnected near-strangers exactly how he makes his living. How he bought the farm. Tells them about the operation. All about it. They are rapt, fascinated, drinking it in, their eyes lit like children's at Christmas, twinkling in the light of the tree. Visions of sugarplums. Nick tells them so that they trust him.

Nick sits and talks to them and looks at them with their swastikas on biceps and between Dustin's eyebrows, like Manson. Early twenties, all of them, he's guessing. He looks at them in their identical open leather vests, with their fierce conformity to one another. He has always known that despite their wild appearance, the skinheads out here are ultrarightists, Aryan-nation supremacists. While they all sit over a morning beer, then two, then three, getting comfortable, getting to know each other, he draws them out a little in their views, casually points to a few headlines on the front page of the Great Falls papers in the wire newsstand by the door, and he hears enough guarded jokes and sneering asides—about faggots and towel-heads and sand niggers and slants—to know they are subtly testing him, too. Poking around at the edges of his own intolerance. They're the backwoods-Montana, American-pop version of Hitler Youth. With the same militaristic bent. With, Nick assumes, the militaristic urge for a mission.

"So, listen," Nick says finally, honestly, "the reason I came over, the reason I wanted to talk to you"—he leans forward, comes finally to the point—"I've got a job for you to do." *You freedom fighters. You super-Americans.*

Their eyes light with a new charge of schoolboy eagerness. Nick is nauseous from the ease of it.

A Jew, Nick tells them. A Jew in California. A Jew in a Mercedes. As if the Mercedes part and the California part furnish irrefutable proof of the Jew part. He tells them what happened. How the Jew came and stole Nick's things.

Pork, Lee, are suddenly even more animated, shifting in their seats, excited. Hey, they saw him, driving. Shit, yeah, they were sitting right here. A half memory. As if they've seen the old Jew in their dreams. As if this is fate. As if their future has been put divinely and finally before their eyes by a higher, unknowable but ultimately righteous, force of justice.

They look at one another. As if they can't believe their good fortune. To be called to the Cause.

Dustin. Lee. Pork. It might be the beers, but Nick finds himself warming to them. Feels a connection to them. He recognizes in them his own sharp anger, his own impatience with the world. His own distastes, his own bitternesses. It's laughable, but he doesn't deny it. In some strange sense, they're his boys.

Nick hasn't the slightest idea if the old man is Jewish. Who knows? Who cares? But for the purposes of his new partnership, he certainly is. Big-time Jew.

And coming after his belongings like that. Finding where Nick is. Taking back only what is his. That niggling ledger-book accuracy. That sly justice. From everything Nick knows about him, seems like a Jew.

I t is a California morning—meaning perfect. The sun is bright, the sky a crystalline blue, suspended above a deeper blue and endless Pacific. A Pacific that suitably frames forever.

Peke is on the back deck, having his pulpy, fresh-squeezed orange juice and his bowl of granola, staring out at the ocean. Rose is not awake yet; typically, she will be another hour. They are already settling into their new patterns. Their last new patterns, he knows, the patterns that will in all likelihood take them into their final sicknesses—whatever those turn out to be—and gliding frictionless and light, he hopes, into the ends of their lives.

But the thought evaporates in the vision of the blue Pacific. In its unfathomable depth. In its rhythmic wash of eternity. It is God rendered in liquid and gases. Not merely evidence of Him. People misunderstand that. It *is* Him. That ocean. Peke doesn't know if that conception of God comes from a seven-year-old boy's untutored, wild deifications in the brutal winter woods of Poland—a protective mechanism of survival, an adaptive trick of mind. Or if it is—as he half suspects—actually a genetic inheritance, an ancient collective-unconscious connectedness that someday science will better grasp. He knows only that when he looks at the ocean—or the moon, or a redwood, or a leaf, or a stone—he feels he is literally looking at God. He's surprised others don't simply feel that. He knows he is like primitive man in that regard. Which is odd, ironic, given the majority of his life, a life of urbanity and sophistication and intricate judgments of art and politics. He is, has always been—in many more ways he sees as he grows older—a primitive.

They are settled into the house. As planned, much has gone into storage now. The new house is gracious, California contemporary, teaks and redwoods, proud beams and broad glass soaring.

They have spent time with some old friends, Manny and Sylvia Walsh, who preceded them here, have become closer to them lately, now that all of them seem to understand—unspoken—that they will spend the remainder of their lives with one another. They have already been to dinners and local theater with some of their new neighbors. They already command respect. They are already welcome, as they have been welcome everywhere, as worldly success makes one quickly welcome, as simple civility makes one welcome. It has taken almost no time. This is already their life. Educated, civilized retirees fit in instantly in Santa Barbara. Santa Barbara is for them.

Though he can't help thinking about Montana, of course. He debates whether to now inform the police, afraid that if he does, the story will get out somehow, the local press will somehow sniff out the appealing, irresistible tale of an old man retrieving his things from a master thief. He will be made into some representation of bravery or revenge, something abstract and unreal. The police, regardless, will not like that he acted alone, took matters into his own hands, no doubt illegally at several stages, and he will make them look bad and incompetent besides. At the least, he will have to testify, his wife will have to testify, it will be time-consuming, ugly. The police will be annoyed, and maybe more than that. He is willing to trust policemen as individuals, but not the police as an institution. He hasn't had fond experiences with institutions of authority.

But if he doesn't tell the police, will the thief come find him? He came back for the safe-deposit box, after all. Came back as if it were an item he'd simply forgotten, or an item he'd simply dropped, traveled back across the country to scoop it up. He is possessive, this thief. So will he come find Peke?

Peke eats his granola on the porch, the redwood decking beneath his slippered feet. From this high perch lording over the Pacific, commanding it, owning it, but thoroughly humbled by it, too. Once again, the vista sweeps away his darker thoughts, as if with a glittery, foamy wave.

He smiles, remembering the moment when he pulled their old Mercedes convertible up to the fishing cabin and Rose came out the screen door, onto the porch.

It felt like a date. Neither of them knowing exactly what to expect of the other.

A prince arriving in a carriage.

Bearing a gift. And no mere trinket. The gift of their past. The gift of their lives, retrieved.

"Get in," he said to Rose. Meaning, *Just get in—leave the bags in the cabin, leave everything else behind.*

It had been a moment that sparkled not for its time or place but for its feeling, for its instant lubrication of the soul. And he noticed soon after, and notices again now, how it was a moment balanced between possessing his things and being free of them, having them again and not having them. A moment poised between both victory and freedom, awash in the two.

Seeing him in the Mercedes, she knew, of course, that there'd been some sort of victory. She accepted that. It was enough to know. She really didn't need any further details, and he didn't feel any urge to supply them.

"The Ford?" she asked.

"Left it at the side of the road."

And they had driven west, into the setting sun, the top down, one with the Western highways, the wind noise around them mostly too loud to speak above, but what would they say anyway? What was the point of words amid the Western magnificence? They would not drive like this again. They had never been here before; they would not be here again. A sentiment one began to experience more regularly at this stage of life.

Back in their own Mercedes. Driving west, like any other Americans. Like any other older American couple. Meeting their belongings at their new home in Santa Barbara, California.

And now, on his redwood porch. Like any other American retiree.

Looking over the blue Pacific.

Thinking, for a foolishly serene, blissful moment—for a high, clean, cool moment, in the high, clean, cool air—that this can last.

The alarm screams at three in the morning.

Peke sits up as if shocked into sitting.

He has the circuit rigged to everything. Threaded like a string through the house. The two alarm engineers—oddball electronics-whiz kids who seemed by their pallor never to have stepped out into their native Southern California sun—at first resisted such a thorough residential system, then got absorbed by the challenge and eventually were proud of their handiwork. Dozens of sensors. Redundancy circuits. The latest electronics that—once again—could hardly be expected of a seventy-two-year-old survivor.

His heart and pulse thump so forcefully, it occurs to him sharply that a heart attack is probably a greater risk than the break-in itself.

In a few seconds he orients to the dark and the situation and swings his legs off the bed assertively to head to the stairs to see.

"No," says Rose, trying to hold him from behind, her hands surprisingly forceful around his forearm, trying to restrain him from getting off the bed.

"Yes," he says, pulling his arm away, in a way she knows there is no choice.

The alarm whines and moans insistently. Wails like a sack-clothed widow, sings its perfectly repetitive song of human disaster. He heads to the top of the stairs, pulse still pounding.

It's ringing at the police station, too, he knows. They'll be here in less than two minutes. They timed it—two friendly, suntanned officers did a practice run when he had them over to demonstrate and integrate the system. The Pekes live in the hills above town. The station house is down in the coastal flats. On the one hand, two minutes is pretty good. On the other hand, a lot can happen in two minutes.

He looks through the windows onto the street. The house is so much glass. Easy for a thief to see into. But easy for an owner to see out of, too.

From this angle, he does see something. Feet disappearing up the sidewalk. Gone. Like wildlife retreating. Human wildlife.

The police arrive in two minutes precisely.

This patrolman is deeply suntanned, too, despite the night shift. A movie cop. Peke sits in his robe, helps fill out the paperwork. Forms to be buried and forgotten, he's sure.

Whoever it is didn't get very far, thinks Peke with satisfaction. This time. But someone smart could use this as reconnaissance. Whoever it is now knows what they are up against.

Someone smart . . .

Is it him? Is he back?

"You *fuck*head." Nick curses Pork crisply, three blocks away, where they are panting for breath, diving into their rental car. Pork, who, listening to no one, motivated by nothing in particular, started to mess with a downstairs bathroom window.

Nick should have figured. He should have figured on foolish impulses, on kindergarten capacities, a childish lack of control.

They'd been difficult all the way. As difficult to listen to as Nick had known they would be. He'd known they would drive him crazy. But he didn't know how crazy. There was almost a capital crime outside the old man's new home. Nick killing Pork and his idiot Nazi friends. *Christ Al-fucking-mighty.* They have used up any well of affection he had for them. Their lack of impulse control is stirring his own.

They are back in the fleabag motel. Sitting in the dark by the algae-crusted pool, whose pool lights don't work—smoking, drinking, regrouping. He made them cover up and mask their swastikas. Made Dustin cake makeup over the one on his forehead. Too identifiable, too alarming, even in seedy, low-life Southern California. Now they merely look like thugs, and so they blend in. Nick smirks. That these guys can fit in. What a planet.

"He was expecting me," says Nick, finally, slowly exhaling.

The skinheads look at him. No comprehension in their eyes. Foot soldiers. Cannon fodder.

"That alarm system," Nick says. "Jesus Christ." By Pork's foolish and incompetent fussing at the window, Nick has at least learned something useful—that the alarm system is elaborate, thorough. But he knows his temporary partners don't understand.

He stares into the scummed, green pool water, the surface stirring, restless, troubled up in the night breeze. He had intended primarily to case the house. To check street routes. He had considered breaking in and taking a few choice items, straight theft, to frighten Peke, let the old man know that Nick knew where he was. A small theft, ominous and open-ended. Nick didn't want to risk more just yet. The old man knew where the farmhouse was, after all, and obviously called in some kind of help, and that's why Nick was thinking of only a little theft, theft as threat, and nothing more for now. He'd figured Pork and Dustin and Lee were up to that. And when and if they encountered the old man during it, Nick would have the skinheads to scare him. Maybe even rough him up. But after driving 1,200 miles with these idiots, Nick is impatient, annoyed, on edge. He feels his mind's cogs and wheels oiled by anger. He knows it's not his usual care and consideration. He's usually wary of his quick temper, but events are moving faster now, and he's going to move with them.

"There's only one item we can get out of there," says Nick, his general annoyance a lubricant now, his irritation rendered useful, as he adjusts their plan on the fly, accelerates his timetable. "The most valuable item in there." He starts to see it, to understand it himself, and thus to elaborate—first obliquely, but then the edges of his vision filling in. "There's only one item in there that gets out beyond the alarm's security perimeter. It penetrates the perimeter every day; it's there for the taking anytime. And it's the most valuable of all . . ." He is expansive now. Feeling the rounded, satisfying weight of the simplicity of the idea. He looks at them. "Him."

He sees it suddenly clearly now. The man's full value. The way to get it all back. Not some mere token of victory. All.

He leans forward. It is time for a lesson here at the low-rent, algae-infested poolside. "Hitler was wrong." He watches them shift uncomfortably at his assertion. They don't want to tangle with Nick on this. "He thought the Jews were worthless," he tells them. "But a Jew is worth a lot."

Their smiles of comprehension are painfully slow to arrive, but when they do, they seem sweeter.

It's all getting simple again, thinks Nick. That's good. Given his current company, simple is good.

I'm going with Melinda Carlson to Los Angeles tomorrow," says Rose. "We're going to see the new exhibit at the Getty and then shop. You'll be OK here alone?"

"Of course," says Peke. "You go." The warm Jewish inflections that he hears frequently in other Jewish voices and is occasionally surprised to detect in his own. Irony and warmth in sweet, inseparable accompaniment.

"It's OK with you?" she asks again. "I'll be back by dinner."

Paradoxically, this little trip of hers symbolizes their settlement here, he thinks. It symbolizes their new home. That this is now the place to go away from and come back to.

"Of course. You go," he says, warm insistence.

"Use your keys. Lock up behind you," she says.

Of course. Of course he will.

After she leaves the next morning, Peke finishes his breakfast, glancing through the *Journal*, watching the financial-news channel. He put his dishes in the sink, makes his way through the pile of mail, pays the bills. He waters the plants. They have a woman come in each day to clean, straighten up, and check on them. He writes her a note, takes the keys, locks up behind him, heads weightless outside into the California sunshine, stepping—he feels it no less each time—into a sunny dream.

The gardeners are there in the yard. Every morning. In the East, they would putter, chatter, plant, and trim laboriously, but out here it's a professional crew, sweeping through like a commando brigade with weapons blazing. Peke's Spanish is too rudimentary, too rusty, to connect with them. He nods and smiles apologetically. They smile and nod back energetically but blankly, the bridge across cultures too rickety, too far.

The Mercedes rolls out of the garage with its top down and is soon heading down the wide, clean boulevard past kindred Mercedes, models both classic and sleekly new. Here in Santa Barbara, his classic Mercedes belongs at last. Peke doesn't quite know whether its driver does, but he has a better chance here than elsewhere, at least.

He rolls into the post office to mail a birthday gift to a grandchild.

He gets gasoline. Self-serve. Gets out to pump it, to give himself something to do. Stops at the pharmacy. A new toothbrush. Some reprints of pictures of his grandkids. Gets a prescription refilled.

An old man's errands, he knows. Part of the cycle of an old man's day. Where the pleasure must be in the ability to do them at all.

He picks up the dry cleaning. He happened to see the ticket on the refrigerator.

He pulls into a sunny downtown lot. Puts the roof back up, because it feels strange to him to leave an open car, though he can see there are other convertibles left open in the lot around him.

He sits with a cappuccino in a shady café with a book. Winston Churchill, *Memoirs of the Second World War*. Reads a few pages. Puts it down. Watches the street life around him. Watches it at the remove from which he has always watched life.

Though he feels a distance from Montana's events, he feels a closeness to them, too. A pull toward them. It is odd, he knows, contradictory, given its remoteness in geography and circumstance, to still feel Montana so powerfully. The scare of the alarm two nights ago brought back the strong emotions of the theft in Westchester, but that was a different kind of invasion, after all. There is no real reason to think that the foiled break-in and Montana are at all related.

He walks back to the car, unlocks and opens the door, gets in.

As he settles into the driver's seat, he pulls the door to close it but can't. He looks over to the door to see what new mechanical problem the increasingly temperamental Mercedes is presenting, and he is suddenly face-to-face with the leering, puffy features of a shaved-headed youth, holding the door open.

Heartless unseeing eyes, and between the eyes, at the bridge of the youth's nose, inches from Peke's own eyes, a green swastika . . .

As if through some increased perception from the convergence of surprise and terror—or the convergence of past and present—Peke manages to take in the features, and the incendiary marking at their center, in a single visual swallow.

Then beefy white hands are pushing on his chest, shoving him deeper into the car. At the same time, Peke feels himself pulled brutally backward, by other hands under his arms, over the hand-brake and into the passenger seat, and then the beefy hand has ripped the key ring from Peke's own hand and the shaven-headed youth has spryly tucked himself in behind the wheel of the Mercedes, and by the time, a moment later, Peke is fully aware of another figure—at least one more—in the backseat behind the driver, they are in motion through the bright California parking lot.

He turns to reach for the passenger door handle.

But a hand comes down onto the door lock and holds it down. A short, wide, white hand, knuckles covered with hair. And a voice comes almost simultaneously from behind Peke's head, into his ear, enough above a whisper to immediately recognize it.

Brusque. The message concise, businesslike: "3901 Pacific View. Your address was still on the invoice."

The voice goes through him like a toxin. He feels a kind of general collapse within him.

It's him. It's the thief.

But when Peke tries to turn to look back, the hairy hands grab his head from behind and hold him facing forward, primitive, wordless instruction not to try that again. It is strange, in a life now largely without physical contact, to be touched so roughly, in so short a time, by so many strangers. This, oddly, is what occurs to him.

"Got us a Jew," says the brusque voice, addressing the other occupants now, indicating its leadership, its authority. "A Jew in a Mercedes. What more could you want than that?"

They drive all day and all night. They switch drivers. There is silence. Demon focus, demon purpose. Although Peke cannot look behind him, within a few minutes he realizes—from the breathing and shifting of bodies—that there are actually three of them squeezed into the backseat. The air-conditioning is blasting, but the Mercedes is hot and stuffy—dense with bodies, and dense with tension. The tension of avoiding notice by other cars. The tension of having elevated the stakes. A live prisoner. Kidnapping. They all have to adjust to the feeling of kidnapping.

Only two hours north of LA's frenzy, the Western highways are already empty. Interstate 5, through California desert, changes to Nevada in only a single, colorful road sign and the slightly different shade and sound of macadam, but not at all in the vast topography. They avoid the little traffic there is, the rare vehicle alongside them; they watch alertly for state troopers. But shaved heads in a Mercedes do not necessarily arouse suspicions in Southern California, thinks Peke, nor does a packed car on the road to Las Vegas.

He knows where they are going. He knew well before they turned north.

They are headed back to Montana.

>>>>

In the Nevada desert, Swastika Between the Eyes—still at the wheel—can contain himself no longer.

From the driver's seat, with no warning, he backhands Peke in the stomach. Peke gasps. Goes to swing in defense. But his arm is grabbed and held from the back, and he is pinned against his seat.

"Let's kill him," says the driver, with sudden childlike, unrestrained zeal.

"What's wrong with you?" a backseat voice counters. "Where's the fun in that?" They drive for a moment in a chaotic, unbalanced silence. "First, we have some laughs," proposes the same backseat voice. "Then we can kill him." The binary logic parsed out carefully, as if it is a complex sequence of events.

It would be mere bravado, but it's said cold, without affect. Devoid of human connection. Like kids pulling legs off a frog. Said in that flat, unplaceable, vaguely American accent. Southern, Texan, Californian, could be anywhere. Soft, easy, languid, relaxed tones—the accent of combat heroes. But talking about killing a seventy-two-year-old man.

They drive in silence. "He's old," another backseat voice ruminates. "He can't take much fun."

The thief, seated directly behind him, says nothing in all this, Peke notices. Despite the bits of discussion that jump surly and half-expressed between the others, Peke still senses the man seated behind him is in charge. Peke knows that this man understands that Peke is worth a lot. It seems he is allowing the bravado to vent—it's big talk, car talk—and at some point he will step in, take over, shut it down. Though it's possible, Peke supposes, that it's not mere car talk. What does the thief's silence signify?

"Idiots," says the brusque, businesslike voice behind him finally—weary, frustrated, explaining to children. "We tell his wife we'll return him once we get what we want." He can hear the thief breathing behind him. Ugly, heavy, animal breath. Breath heavy with experience, somehow. "Then . . . then we'll see," he says.

>>>

They're headed for Montana.

Hotbed of freedom. Land of the Free Men. Believers in, defenders of, a Higher Justice. Montana.

He gets a glimpse at the swastika between the eyebrows again.

They didn't catch him when he was seven.

But they have caught him now.

More than sixty years later.

More than sixty years borrowed; more than sixty years lived as if with something unknown, unseen, pursuing, something at his back. At least—at last—he can see what is pursuing him.

They have finally caught him.

And, oddly, there is some kind of resolution in that. Some sense of completion. A circle finally closing, fully forming. He knows at some level it is insane to feel that. And yet he feels it. There it is.

So much life. A family. The admiration, the respect, of others. A long interval of comfort, civilized life, and at least outward peace.

A dark little piece of him feels that he has stolen these sixty years. Pilfered them from a pile, tucked the years away under his tattered coat, like a seven-year-old boy, abashed, ashamed, living in the woods.

A dark little piece of him feels that somehow he had this coming.

The old man is silent.

Nick is, too, but feels there is some connection between the old man and him. That the others, the little neo-Nazi jerks, are interlopers, keeping the two of them from the fullness of that bond. That the Nazi jerks' fierce, bland provincialism serves only to highlight this connection between the two of them, throw it into dramatic relief.

Nick envisions a conversation between them. An exchange of ideas.

They travel in silence, through the American West, all their polar individual identities, their contrary lives and outlooks, merging temporarily beneath the American sky that harbors them all.

"I've gotta piss," says one of the backseat voices. "I'll just piss right here on the carpet." Peke hears the quick, arrogant whine of a zipper.

"Aww, man, you'll stink it up in here."

"What the fuck—it's his car."

"It's my car," says the brusque voice, quiet, low, sure. "And I'd rather you don't piss in my Mercedes." The authority clear—the consequences implied.

He is touring America again in his Mercedes, Peke thinks. He watches the changing sky, the great, dark, billowing clouds.

Occasionally, one or another of the young Nazis begins to speak about white Christian identity, Aryan superiority, obviously spewing some pamphlet or manifesto, but there is no fluency, no follow-up, no discourse. "We are the true descendants of Adam through Abel, and you are of the Mud Peoples," explaining it to Peke in a prairie-flat cadence. A tutorial, delivered like immutable fact, as if in a one-room Great Plains schoolhouse. "You're the issue of Satan's seed, of his forcing himself on Eve . . ." "We are the true Lost Tribe, the Chosen People, and the Jews are the usurpers of our rightful place. But your conspiracy is now discovered . . ." "You're Cain's chaos, the seed line of the sinister . . ." They are mangled half-thoughts without context. Mind burps. Elevating, accreting, over time, over the highway, into brimstone declarations to the wide, empty sky above them. Though one of the declarations sticks with Peke in its diametrical simplicity, its reductive absurdity: *You are the people of darkness, and we are the people of the light.* As if there must be some measure of truth lurking in its purity.

To Nick, these declarations from the skinheads are the same as silence, in a way—white noise, he thinks—and he's sure that if he is able to distance their inanities like that, push them away, the old man probably can, too.

"How'd you find me?" Nick finally asks casually, after a silence, with no acknowledgment of the preceding fanaticisms. As if he and Peke were old acquaintances.

"So you can avoid being found next time?" Peke counters sarcastically. His first words of the journey. The skinheads seem half startled, and fascinated, by the sound of his voice.

But Peke says nothing further. And doesn't answer Nick's question.

The man's calm, the man's serenity, is not helping his cause, thinks Nick. *Show some fear. Show some concern.*

They stop at a railroad crossing, one of the few stops they are forced to make in more than a thousand miles. They have to wait ten minutes for a freight train to go by. The skinheads get out of the car and urinate next to its open doors, allowing Peke to do the same, watching him. Only cattle observe them. Much of the freight train is cattle cars, the cattle packed tight together, braying, whinnying, but patient, too, their heads pressed against the bars by other cattle, their clear, limpid, brown saucer eyes looking out. It's a dose of Americana, thinks Nick, getting back in the car: a new-style cattle drive, on the ancient railway that opened up the American West.

But the scene sends Peke a different message, one whose echoes and reverberations overwhelm any redolence of Americana, of outdoor tradition, of big sky and freedom, which he, too, might otherwise have observed and absorbed. The cattle packed like that. He thinks about other trains, trains of people packed like these cattle, crossing open terrain beneath low, changeless sky, condensing hundreds, a thousand miles, into nothing, into meaninglessness, or else into a single meaning—making the mind turn those thousand boundless miles into a small, airless cell, into a hard nub of confinement.

He, of course, is in a Mercedes, his own Mercedes, packed with people—if you chose to call them that—headed into the woods.

And more than sixty years later than the terrified, confused passengers on those trains, he—in contrast—has history to help him imagine what fate might hold for him. He is terrified but not confused. He has history as his grim guide.

The police are with Rose, doing their soft-spoken Santa Barbara best to calm and console her while explaining again: for twenty-four hours, it can be only a Missing Persons. It can be only a report. They'll ask officers on the street to keep an eye out, of course, but no more formal action can be taken yet. She is frantic, but they are firm.

He's how old?

Seventy-two.

And in his own car?

Their doubts about this being anything serious are loud and unsubtle in their pointed questions.

It's a Missing Persons, they tell her again, as if the repetition will make it more acceptable to her. There's nothing we can do for twenty-four hours. Missing Persons. Nothing more. We just don't have the manpower.

She can tell what they think: that he is simply lost in his own car. Has forgotten where he is or what he's doing. Has neglected to call in. Or is simply unaware that she's already back from Los Angeles.

He's seventy-two, you say?

And how can she tell them the story about Montana and what happened there? It's not believable to begin with; plus, she has no corroborating details—he kept her away. She knows the address of the fishing shack, but nothing else. His chivalry, his habit of silence, his personality, all leave her in the dark.

Twenty-four hours might be too late.

"We'll look for the Mercedes," says the cop. "But, ma'am"—a reassuring Santa Barbara smile—"he's probably fine."

She looks at him hard. "He's probably not."

And she is sure—to her dismay—that she will be proved right.

I t is exactly as he predicted.

As if being held and treated exactly as he predicted is part of the punishment, increases it, becomes part of its effect.

As if they know that perfectly executing what he has imagined will make it more painful, more fearful, for him.

He imagined himself, saw himself, in the beaten-up living room of shredded sofas, taped to a chair.

He is in that living room, taped to a chair. The shredded sofas have been pulled away, creating a spare stage. An old man taped to a chair, the only thing on it.

It is as if they have read and utilized his imagination, having none of their own.

From the smallest one, Peke senses, if not exactly intelligence, then an evenness, a pausing and considering, that in the circumstances can dimly qualify as intelligence. Despite his smaller physical size, he is the one who is slow, brooding, deliberate.

The middle one is the jumpiest—has a sinewy, ceaseless energy, muscles in continual flex, seeking an outlet, looking for trouble. He is a natural mesomorph, blessed with a sculpted physical definition that would be beautiful if he were not so ugly.

From the biggest one, the beefy one, Peke senses evil. He smells it dripping off him, a high concentration of it, nearly chemical, emanating continually. He recognizes it. His civilized friends, his children, his neighbors, have trouble recognizing evil, identifying it, because they've never seen it in pure action in their modern, lawful, civilized lives. It is disguised, filtered, unclear. But he has had the unfortunate privilege of seeing it exercised openly, unmediated, uncalibrated. He knows it when he sees it. And in the big one, he sees it. Naturally, unfortunately, it is the big one. It probably explains his leadership, the pecking order based purely on brute strength and brute hatred, the prevailing social organization of their group. The only order of their tribe.

Perhaps he should be more careful not to show his disdain. His open disdain may only get him killed more quickly than even they might want. His disdain is one of the few weapons in his limited arsenal, in his thin quiver, and he will have to deploy it with the utmost care.

>>>

Their first moment of sport was the dogs. The dogs were yelping, howling at the back door, and the skinheads let them in, and the dogs rushed up to the chair, barking fiercely.

"See, they know," the beefy one joked with satisfaction. "They know he's a Jew. They want that Jew meat."

But the dogs rushed the chair, then sat and stopped barking. Stood panting, almost expectant.

Waiting dumbly, only Peke knew, for more of the sweet special meat he'd brought them before.

"Go on, get out," the beefy one burst out, annoyed with their sudden docility. He hustled them to the door. "Go on, get out. We got work to do in here."

〉〉〉

Peke assesses the thick silver windings of duct tape over his thighs, wrapping beneath the chair. The duct tape wound around his shins and around the chair's front legs. Across his stomach and around the chair's sturdy back. His wrists are bound tightly behind him. It is a union with, a marriage to, the simple wooden chair, a parasexual closeness. As if giving oneself to the position, to the needs, of the chair.

It was only a short time ago that he was in the driver's seat of his Mercedes. A prisoner of that seat, too, but a prisoner of a different kind. A prisoner to the blinking light of the tracking device—but a prisoner of his own choosing, in a seat of command.

Now it is this seat. Wooden, primitive, unforgiving. As primitive as the Mercedes's seat is advanced. As freely chosen as this seat is not. And here America does not rush gloriously across the windshield. Here is just a grim room, the same view, a reduction of elements. Nothing moving or shifting or changing.

He knows he must immediately begin the business of keeping himself alert. Keeping himself sane. He imagines that this is the Mercedes seat. That he is still driving his beautiful silver Mercedes convertible, his beautiful wife, Rose, beside him, crossing through the West, top down, hair blowing. It is an advantage to his imagination that he has logged so many recent hours, so many recent days, traveling like that. Such vivid, celebratory days, once the Mercedes convertible was retrieved. He pictures those days. He draws on that drive from Montana to Santa Barbara—an opposite drive, literally, figuratively—and in his mind he tries to recalibrate, reexperience, every remembered stretch of it. To erase, mile by mile, the imprisoning drive north with the liberating drive south.

To make this chair like the seat of his silver Mercedes. To make this, too, a seat of command. That is the goal.

He will beat this thief. He will survive them. That is what he does. Survive.

>>>>

The middle one flexes his bulky white biceps absently, incessantly. Not knowing what to do with all his stoked energy. Waiting to be told. Waiting to deploy it.

Peke has seen him looking at Peke's wrists—not glancing nervously, uncomfortably, like so many glances in the past fifty years, prepared to see something forbidden, pornographic, totemically powerful—but looking openly, expectantly, and somewhat disappointed.

"How do we know he's a Jew?" he says to the beefy one.

Ah, he wants to see the tattoo. He knows about the tattoo. Skinheads—they love tattoos. Even concentration camp tattoos. Maybe especially those. The authenticity of them. They aren't mere decoration; they *mean* something, a status the skinheads secretly wish for their own. A standard their own tattoos can't meet. Could there even be sardonic camaraderie? *Hey, look, I've got one, too*—the beefy one pointing to the swastika between his eyes. But Peke has no tattoo to offer them. No such authentication or perverse camaraderie. He is no mere survivor. He is an escape artist. Unmarked. Perhaps not even there.

He recognizes the moment, the stage they're at. It is that moment when they've caught the snake, cornered the critter, when they are observing it, examining its features closely, before they decide what to do with it, what tests to put it through, what entertaining end to plan for it.

He is seven. He is seven again. Except that at seven, he slipped through them, snuck by them, and at seventy-two, they have caught him.

In a different country. In a different place. But the same—the same insane hatreds, the same celebration of the perverse, the same motivating mélange of ignorance and greed and darkness.

He can tell that these shaven-domed, square-headed brutes have no idea what Nazism actually is or was. They have raided history's dusty shelves, grabbed a trinket, swiped it in the dark. They have perverted and distorted the ideology, one that was perverted and distorted to begin with. Another twist in it will hardly alter its appearance or effects. He regards them. In the human species, they are but dimmest reflections of one another, ancient Stanley Peke and these skinheads, Manichaean occupants of the globe of human experience. Surely God could concoct no greater variety in a single species. Surely that is the miracle and irony and puzzlement of mankind. But a piece of Stanley knows this is something he is telling himself—building this difference, this gulf between them—to prepare himself, in mind and soul, for the confrontation that he knows must come.

"Do you think I'm Jewish?" he asks, very quietly, dangling the question with an air of puzzlement. "Why? My accent? My money? The art on my walls? What makes you think I'm Jewish?" He lets his puzzlement grow into a look of outsize incredulity, exaggerated confoundment. "I'm a Congregationalist," he declares suddenly. It has conclusiveness. As if unchallengeable.

They regard him, unmoved. Their level of communication and comprehension will be, he sees, an extra, unintended torture, added to their intentional ones. An extra circle of hell.

He looks from one to the other expectantly.

"Nick said," says the middle one finally, distantly, after a short silence—as if compelled to respond.

Peke feels the click of the moment. It is the first time—however absently, however inadvertently—that they have addressed him with any directness. He seizes this strand of connection.

And the thief's name—Nick.

"What makes Nick say I am? Does he know me? Are we friends? Do we socialize?"

He looks at them. "And I don't have the tattoo, do I?" He shrugs. As if case closed.

It is only a shallow edge of doubt. They seem generally untroubled by this lack of evidence. But it is a beginning. He must begin. Jump in somewhere.

"I'm Dutch," he adds, to explain the accent. "And I'm Christian. Peke's a Dutch name. Don't you know anything? I'm Dutch." Congregationalist. Dutch. Christian. The versions of his life begin to fly.

A Jew.

Nick said.

The irony being, Peke knows almost nothing about Judaism. He has never had any formal religious training. He has never practiced it. He has no familiarity with the faith. On the rare occasions when he's been at a synagogue service—the social commitment of a bar mitzvah or a wedding, or taken by friends on the High Holidays—he has had no comprehension of what he is witnessing. It is as foreign to him as if he were a Catholic or Protestant observing the strange ancient ceremonies for the first time. Before his life as a feral child, he was present, as required, at a few ceremonies, and watched them with the natural remove of a child. Candles, leather books, obscure mutterings. And then, one night, he was shooed into the woods. *Go play. Go play back in there as you always do, but this time, don't come out. You understand? Your game must go on forever.* With only a look from his mother. A look of pain, of torture, of hope, of pride. Of all hope dashed and all hope still intact. The full expectation of defeat and the full expectation of triumph. Her eyes so wide and awash in emotion, he stared for a moment into her soul. Stared into a naked soul, and expected never in his mortal life to see one so naked again. A last look from his mother that he still carries with him, a psychological amulet.

This life on the run from the age of seven, because he was Jewish. Because he was something that he didn't even comprehend. He knew the fact but had no understanding to accompany it.

So Judaism was for him, more than anyone, an act of faith. When people called it a faith—well, yes, exactly, he was taking it entirely on faith.

He has had the sense it actually makes his faith stronger. Because he has never failed it, and it has never failed him. His heritage is for him *purely* an act of faith. Purely a belief in something greater. Something worth surviving for, yet something that he does not understand. It has no edges, no definition. So it's unconfined by definition. Bigger than that.

He knows next to nothing about Judaism. Which, on one level, is simply one of those wartime absurdities. Part of the suspension of rationality and reason and civility that is always a corollary of war.

For him his Judaism is nothing. Holds no meaning. And therefore is everything. Holds all meaning.

In a lifetime filled with the ironies of opposites, this one made all others pale.

At a social gathering once, after a lot of wine, when he mentioned to a young American rabbi this irony of no knowledge, no custom, and yet persecution, the rabbi—instead of nodding with the acceptance and understanding and blind respect that Peke was usually met with—told him the ancient legend of Rabbi Akiba. Herded out with captured slaves and criminals and enemies of the Caesars onto the blood-soaked wooden floor of the Colosseum, the frail, elderly rabbi had recited only the Shema, a Jewish prayer, over and over, and it could be heard above the bloodthirsty din of the mob, even as his skin was raked from his bones, even as the lions came roaring and charging. He told Peke that Judaism could be distilled to that single six-word assertion. *Shema yisrael Adonai eloheinu, Adonai echad.* Hear, O Israel, the Lord our God, the Lord is one. "That's all you need to know," the American rabbi said matter-of-factly. "That's faith in a nutshell. A simple declaration of the authority of the spirit. An acceptance of meaning—above idols, above objects, above kings and emperors, above facts, above actuality, above all." And with a friendly smile, the rabbi turned to engage in the party again, a particularly undevout rabbi, it seemed to Peke, flirting openly with the most provocative women, with their thigh-slit black dresses and sumptuous busts—quite taken with the party's secular pleasures. As if perhaps the few minutes with Peke had been an interruption to his fun.

The rabbi's nearly incidental Judaism. His natty houndstooth sport coat. But something about the moment, something about the rabbi's genial informality, had stuck with Peke. And as a result, Peke knew the Shema.

>>>>

The muscled middle one's inadvertent, absent "Nick said" points out to Peke that except for this apparent slip, he has not been touched or spoken to directly since being taped to the chair. It is obvious to him that, at least for now, there are instructions to that effect from the thief. The fact that he is temporarily off-limits, out of bounds, brings him no relief, though, because if that is the case, then it is likely a part of a broader arrangement, an implicit agreement struck, wherein at a certain point, the skinheads will get to finally exercise their side of the bargain. He has the sense that he is, for the moment, collateral. An object like any other that can be transported in the back of a truck.

So it's purposeless for him to be taped to the chair. There's nothing to learn from him, no interrogation. It is only a small torture. It is just a waiting. Quite possibly, a waiting to die.

While he can speak, while they must bear him, while he has the chance, this is the time to make inroads, he senses. Needle, wheedle, cajole, command, annoy. Become a thousand voices—a platoon, an army, a comedy, a tragedy. From the chair, unleash, use the only weapon he has. Mind and words. Both barrels. Fire at will.

So the Dutch Christian recites the Lord's prayer aloud. *Our Father, who art in heaven, hallowed be thy name. Thy kingdom come, thy will be done, on Earth as it is in heaven.* "Do you know what that is? You don't, do you? You're not Christians, are you? You're not decent, God-fearing, churchgoing Americans who accept Jesus. Jesus, our Savior."

They are trying not to listen, he can see. They want to respond, but they can't, and they have heard, no doubt, have grown up on the inanity that the Jews crucified Jesus, that the Jews despise Jesus, and a preemptive strike, allying himself with their beliefs, will confound them, he's sure. They have mothers, grandfathers, crazy aunts, who espouse their Christian fundamentalist tenets. Who may have driven these three along some winding thorny path to this. "You don't believe in Jesus? So you're heathen, then?"

The big, beefy one blinks, looks over to Nick's office as if hoping for help. It confirms for Peke some sort of arrangement that the beefy one is barely managing to live by. It is the first that Peke has seen him at all rattled.

Needle, wheedle, cajole, command, annoy.

Out the narrow slat of living-room window, which is all Peke can see of the outdoors from his nailed-down chair—his privileged throne—he watches the light giving out across the scarred land.

There is only a slow fading—no greater demarcation, no signal sunset, no great, colorful, dying end of the day. There is only the slow, indistinguishable turning of light to dark, day to night. Nothing to separate one from the other, to declare one day and one night, to label one light and one dark, except human judgment, an individual human decision. Light, dark, human judgment. The metaphors vibrate in Stanley Peke.

>>>

"I was a Nazi," Peke says. He looks around at the squalid room, darker now, layers of night's texture, a multiplicity of shadow cast by two floor lamps with dim bare bulbs. "I was a friend of Hitler, you know."

"Shut up," says the beefy one, with an irritation finally erupted, written on him.

"We knew each other well," Peke continues, thinking, in a whisper at the back of his mind, how that is partly true.

"I grew up under the Nazi system," he tells them, light, conversational, another tack, another tone. "I'm a child of Nazism. Which makes me more of a Nazi than any of you will ever be." True in effect. It was his world. He says it with exaggerated pride, chest puffed out against the duct tape. Watches while the tenuous logic seeps into them as if chemically.

They are afraid of listening. They are afraid not to. They are quiet. He is quiet along with them, for a moment, studying them.

"I have killed smarter Nazis than you. Real Nazis," he informs them flatly.

They can't help themselves. There is a flicker of interest from them.

He's never said it to anyone. Not Rose, not anyone. And he's going to tell this vermin? Is that one of God's cosmic jokes? That this scum in this godforsaken place will be his confessor? But he must engage them, to stand any kind of chance, he knows. Coddle. Confide. Infuriate. Humiliate. But engage—above all, engage.

The office door finally opens, and Nick enters, looks at them, looks at him, smiles urchinly. "Turning your crazy Nazi heads around, is he?" As if he has read their stricken expressions. Though probably he has simply overheard, while in his office in the next room. He is the one to deal with, Peke knows. But cautiously. Because Nick has the intelligence that, unfortunately, could translate into more effective and ingenious torture than these brutes are capable of conceiving.

Nick pulls a small table up next to Peke. Sets on top of it a small battery-powered clock, one with an analog face and a sweep second hand. They all look at it, not sure of its purpose, while Nick pulls from his back pocket a black wireless phone. Larger than a cell phone. Peke gathers—from his new familiarity with GPS and from his previous discovery that there are no cell towers or cell reception out here—that's it's a satellite phone. Nick looks at the clock as he dials. Obviously his purpose is to time the call. To not stay on long enough to trace.

Once he dials, he holds the phone to Peke's ear. "A quick, loving hello," he instructs Peke curtly. "Then it's my turn."

"Hello?" Rose's voice. In that one word, Peke hears so much. Confusion. Caution. Hope. Pleading. Paralysis. Femininity. Fragility. Beauty. The voice in his ear in the middle of the night for a lifetime. In overheated Village apartments. In high-rise hotels. In their Westchester bedroom for forty years. A voice woven into the fabric of his brain.

"Do nothing he tells you . . . Deny him everything . . . We've had a good life . . ." Peke tells her, an urgent rush of instruction, pointed and summary.

The satellite phone is pulled away. The thief is not angry, only annoyed, as he puts the phone to his own ear.

"That's just like him, isn't it, Rose?" he says with a familiarity, a presumptive intimacy, that Peke has not expected, that has Peke pulling fiercely, uselessly, at the duct tape on his wrists. "The hero. The lone wolf. Well, you certainly know we've got him. You know it's no impostor." He smiles at his own wit. "Childish, isn't he? Now, let's let the adults talk, you and me." Symbolically, he turns away from Peke, walks across the room—maybe also to keep Peke from hearing his wife's answers, to let him imagine them, to not know. Because Peke can no longer hear.

"You don't know who this is," Nick says, "but you know why I'm calling."

"I know who this is," she corrects him. "The moving man."

"You haven't called the police, have you? That would be a problem."

"The police weren't interested. An old man lost in his Mercedes," she says curtly, angrily. "But now they'd be interested, of course." He likes that—her anger making her honest. Honest even in revealing her intent to inform the police.

"Don't bring them in. It's not necessary," Nick says.

It will be a waste of their time, your time, everyone's time and energy, thinks Nick. *There'll be no chance for heroism. Because your husband will be dead by then.* He debates actually saying this to her, but it seems crude. "It will be easier without them," he says, cooingly, wooingly, and he turns back to look at Peke briefly—to frustrate him at being out of earshot.

"I don't want money," says Nick, looking at the clock, needing to stay on subject.

"What then?" asks Rose.

"I want my stuff back." Nick feels the amusement of it on his lips, at the back of his throat. "My abstract impressionists. My Louis the Fourteenth chairs. My nice things." He looks at the clock, picks up the pace. "Your job is to keep the police and kindly neighbors out of it. It should be easy—just tell them if there's any involvement from any of them, your husband will die."

He clicks off the satellite phone. There is a moment of stillness. Then, with an instantly summoned fury, called up like a skill on a resume, he smashes the phone against the little table. There is a splintering of the plastic. A plastic piece of the phone flies up off the table, pirouettes in the air. The little battery-powered clock jumps off the table as well. He continues smashing the phone against the little table until the table collapses, then smashes it against a doorjamb, until the phone's pieces are sufficiently numerous. A sudden fury, Peke knows, partly orchestrated for Peke's own benefit—showing Nick's brutal instincts, cutting off future communication, all that—but the destruction fulfilling a necessary function that he calmly explains in a moment.

"They emit a signal, you know," says Nick. "Satellite phones."

Peke thinks for a black, sinking moment that the thief must know about the other signal. That this is a fully intended ironic introduction to the thief's knowledge. But Nick says nothing more. And Peke gathers the secret might still be intact.

They all stare at the phone's pieces on the floor. Nick looks at Peke while he addresses his three witless Nazi rats. "We get my stuff back, then you can kill him if you want," he says emotionlessly. Making clear that his reasonableness on the phone was only for Rose's benefit. Rose's trust. "Or maybe we kill him, then get the stuff back. I haven't decided yet. Let me think about that." Is it a mockery of the inane binary logic of the skinheads in the car? *Kill first = no fun. Fun first, then kill.* Or is it a tacit endorsement of it? Nick heads back into his office.

Annihilation. Thoroughness. Peke was right about that. He read the personality correctly from two thousand miles away. The way the thief would come back for the contents of the safe-deposit box.

Taking everything. Annihilation—it was even in the very nature of the scam.

This is the beginning of the torture, Peke knows. A psychological torture tailored to him. Weighing whether the thief means it or not. To decide, to decipher, if it's only a game, or a plan. The thief knows it is torture of the most effective kind. For Rose to make a deal, to behave in good faith, and then to be denied. While Peke must witness the truth, must see the other side from his nailed-down chair, must hear the whispers behind the curtain, and then be hung with it.

For what is worse than death? Only one thing: death with foreknowledge.

>>>

She paces, distraught. She doesn't know what to do. Her husband, who in one sense has asked so little of her all these years, and in another has asked everything of her, has asked it all: her loyalty, her obedience, and now her willingness and preparation to continue without him.

Do nothing he says. Deny him everything. We've had a good life.

And should she obey her husband? Was it bluster and bluff for the kidnappers' benefit, or did he truly want her to say no, to refuse to cooperate? Did he simply want to control the situation, to win, out of some immaturity, some irremediable male impulse? Or did his wish reflect a higher moral stance? One that was somehow beyond her ken? Was he putting his own wishes ahead of his responsibilities to her, to his family? Or did he see one's greatest responsibility as being true to oneself?

Damn his history. Damn his past. It skews and burdens every judgment, makes it impossibly layered, textured. Should she call the police, try to save him? Or leave them out of it, as the thief warned?

Who is to be taken at his word here? The thief, or her husband, or neither? Hard to believe that she is treating them together, that they are two points of a strange, tight triangle, equal suitors to her "affections," to her reason.

She paces. She realizes there are no answers. You make a judgment and go on. Your own judgment is all you have.

She realizes that, from this thousand-mile distance, she has never been closer to her husband. To the ontological dilemmas of his barely spoken past. When there is no map, no guide. She is inhabiting a similar dilemma now. She is in a vast, featureless land of no answers. He entered it, inhabited it, from the very first years of his war-tossed life. She is finally forced to inhabit it only toward the end of her easy, civilized, coddled own.

She paces. She looks at the objects around her. The gilded, the polished, the cherished, the symbolic, the retrieved. All about to disappear again. The objects around her, mutely mocking her.

To all of them she says: *Good riddance. Take them all. Just give him back.*

30

Morning. Clean, sunny, deceptive morning. Merely a few jagged hours later. Rose sits in their other Mercedes, the sedan they bought to replace the one they sold in Boise. She is parked across the street from the police station. The quaint, old brick entrance, shaded by evergreens and deciduous trees, looks more like a stylish shop or a tony private school than a police station. She watches the doors. Secretaries, support staff, going in. A few cops—tanned, relaxed, ambling, friendly.

"Can I help you?"

Rose turns, and there is a cop—hang-jowled, sweetly hound-like, friendly—looking in at her through the passenger side. Smiling. A little flirty, even.

"I see you watching the station," he says, sufficient explanation for his inquiry. "Help you with anything?"

She looks, shakes her head. "No. It's nothing."

"You sure?"

She smiles in resignation. *My husband's been kidnapped. They've taken him to Montana. They stole all our possessions. He stole them all back. If I speak to you, they'll kill him.*

"I'm sure," she says.

His smile disappears. Goes flat, businesslike, competent, a little annoyed. He knows she is not saying something. "You change your mind, you try us."

>>>

LaFarge passes by Peke.

Peke looks at him. The friendly black one. Peke remembers. He knows LaFarge does, too.

LaFarge glances at him and glances away.

LaFarge, Chiv, Al—Nick has told them to stay away from Peke and the skinheads. He has told them this doesn't concern them. As if it is assumed that they don't have the stomach for this, whatever this will turn out to be.

LaFarge, who said that maybe it wasn't right to take the old man's pictures. Who bantered with the old man. Now the old man himself is here, tied up.

LaFarge wonders what Nick is doing. Couldn't whoever came for the old man's things the first time come back to get him? This is so risky, so unlike Nick. It could bring down the whole enterprise. Something has gotten under Nick's skin, LaFarge can tell. Then again, Nick probably has it covered: the old man is the collateral. Nick will make it clear: *you come for him, he dies.* But Jesus, it's all changed so fast. It ain't what it was.

LaFarge thinks for a moment about cutting the old man free. But he'd be caught. He'd be figured out. So does he cut the tape and leave? Walk out? Would Nick and the crew come after him?

"You're not so friendly now, I see," comments Peke.

LaFarge says nothing. Wants to say something, anything, but doesn't know what—and anyway knows he'd better not. He learned his lesson from Nick. Nick taught him his lesson. Nick knows what's right, what works.

"Nice chatting with you," says Peke, as LaFarge walks silently out the door into the yard.

Nick, passing by, suddenly sits down on the shredded-up couch nearest Peke. He assumes an air of familiarity. "You weren't following us. I would have seen you. How did you do it?" He asks it almost cheerily, a chipper interviewer, as if he never asked in the car. As if the question has never occurred to him before.

Peke stares, says nothing.

"You're going to tell me," says Nick, cheerily, undeterred. "I can't have that happening again." *I will be continuing in my mode of existence, even if you won't.*

Peke says nothing.

"You will tell me," the thief says confidently, with no sense of rush or urgency about it.

"You'll get nothing," Peke says defiantly. "My wife will respect the wishes of a dead man."

But will Rose listen to him? *"Do nothing he tells you. Deny him everything . . ."* Will Rose obey? She knows only generally where he is. Up at the fishing cottage, he never revealed exactly where he was going—the knowledge could have been dangerous for her. But now, her sum of not knowing, of desperation, might cause her to give in to their demands. To grab at their dangled promises. *Don't, Rose. Stand mute. Stand firm. That's what I want.*

You'll get nothing, says the old man, but he doesn't know Nick. He doesn't know how smart—how uncommon—a common criminal can be. Nick is already getting something from Peke. Peke is already giving him more than he thinks.

Nick is thinking about the old man's accent. An accent so slight you have to listen closely to be sure you really hear it. A slight accent—banished, buffed away to a residue. Left over from years ago. And that's the point.

What kind of rich old man risks so much—discovery, injury, his elderly neighbors' ridicule—to come after his things? What kind of rich old man doesn't call the authorities, doesn't leave it to the police? What kind of rich old man proceeds so intently? Goes to reclaim his possessions in the most primitive way, by simply taking them back just as they were taken? Not a conventional rich old man. A rich old man who's prepared to risk everything. Who fears nothing. But equally fears having nothing. The old man has revealed more than he might want.

Nick snickers to himself, shakes his head. A real Jew, Nick promised the skinheads. A Jew in a Mercedes, he told them, having in truth no idea at all about it, nothing but the money and the vague accent to go on. But now he thinks about that accent. And the old man's age. And the old man's distrust of the police. And the old man's absurd sense of self-reliance, his primitive notion of justice and setting things right and self-righteously coming after his belongings. The old man's arrogant belief in himself, his pride, his self-containment, even as he sits bound to the chair. Nick knows now that his little joke, his cynical, calculating lure to the skinheads, has ended up as truth. Nick the street punk doesn't doubt for a moment the world's death and chaos and stink. Nick the career criminal knows how deeply, how universally, such stink runs. He knows there are these people who escaped. This is a real Jew, he knows—the kind that came escaping Europe. Escaping death.

"When did you arrive here? Before the war, or during?" Expecting to surprise him with his civility, with his worldliness and wisdom.

Peke doesn't answer.

179

"Without a dime, I'll bet."

Peke stares steadfastly away.

Nick says it as it occurs to him. "Maybe without a mother or father."

Peke suddenly looks up at him, regards Nick as if he has seen him for the first time. "Yes. Without a mother or father." There is, however, no defiance in it. The hardness of the old man seems to instantly melt. The old man's eyes seem to float for a moment, warm and soft. It is as if by Nick's striking so close to the truth, the old man has suddenly—in this single instance—decided to concede it. To reward Nick for his intuition.

But it could be a ploy, thinks Nick. It could be a ploy on the old man's part, a ploy for connection, a ploy for mercy. Jews are extremely clever. That is well known. Clever enough to have found Nick here, by some method Nick still doesn't know. The man has cleverness enough to have fooled Nick once. Nick has to be clever enough not to be fooled again.

Yet at this moment, at this mention of mothers and fathers, Nick experiences some kind of shift, too. Nick finds—sitting opposite him like this—that he feels a connection to the old man. The connection he felt the edges of on the ride in the Mercedes. A sudden magnetic draw. Peke's arrival without mother or father; Nick's string of foster homes and foster neglect. But Nick thinks that their connection may go deeper than that. Because while no one ever beat Nick or abused him, people did not understand him and so stayed cleared of him, left him alone. So he existed without them. He raised himself. Alone. Running wild in the streets. And by the arrogant sense of self-sufficiency that he sees, he senses that the old man lived some version of that, too—if not in ancient European ghettos, then running loose in the cobbled streets of New York or Boston or Philadelphia or Baltimore. No parents: that is a sizable thing to have in common. Monstrously sizable.

Nick can sense that at the old man's fancy dinner parties, at social events, gatherings, even to his children, even to his wife, the old man doesn't say much, if anything, about that former life. As Nick doesn't say much, if anything, about his own.

But where the old man's silence arises from horrible truths, Nick's own silence is, he knows, centered on falsity. He doesn't like being cast back like this, because he is cast back into the falsity of his own life.

Bisexuality—a label whose inadequacy has always enraged him, ever since he came across it as a teen. A definition whose dryness is parched, useless. So at the moment of acceptance, he simultaneously rejected it.

The neat and orderly term for it came his way long after the disorderly urges. And whatever it is that the term dryly seeks to describe, it is as natural to him as breathing, and he hides it only because of how the world feels, not how he does. As natural to him as breathing, and as comprehensible to him, too. A sexuality that arises out of his own wanton need. Every need, every wish in him unfulfilled, unfulfillable. He is craving. He is need. That is the theme of his life, and though he senses by now that no amount of *stuff*, no breathtaking quantity and quality of objects, no magical ultimate item, will fulfill it, he is not free to abandon the pursuit. Understanding of is not liberation from. He is a junkie.

Bisexuality. Because he wants everything. Because he doesn't know what he wants. Nick is stricken by the clarity and symmetry of the thought.

And this old man who is willing to risk his life to have back the things he wants. To have his objects. Does this somehow ennoble, legitimize Nick's pursuit, that this man seems to crave the same? By that fact alone, Nick does not know of—cannot imagine—anyone in this world so much like him as this adversary. His prisoner, it turns out, is his psychological double. Is the old man taped to the chair now providing Nick a chance to further understand himself?

Nick wants everything, because he doesn't know what he wants. And is that, in essence, how it is for this old man? This old survivor?

An unaccustomed calm comes over Nick, brought on by the clarity of his thoughts, the simplicity of this human connection. Nick will cut Peke loose. Let him go. Cut through the layers of duct tape, help him unsteadily to his feet, watch the old man stand there—disoriented, stunned, confused to be free—before stepping tentatively forward. The old man's gait picking up speed while the reality sinks in—Nick likes picturing that. Is it somehow watching himself, the joy of watching himself freed from himself? He feels it. It feels good. By cutting the duct tape, severing the whole matter. To start clean, with a new theft, maybe, find someone less willful, more docile, more appropriate to and deserving of Nick's deviousness. Let the old man be like that special piece of prey that was impressive enough—remarkable enough—to be released back into the wild.

But that would negate everything Nick stands for. Everything that has brought him this life. His organization. His care. And God knows it wouldn't sit well with his crazy, shaven-headed partners. No, it is too late for changing the plan, releasing the prey. And this making Nick think about his own life, and consider alterations to the old man's advantage—maybe it's all just the Jew's cleverness, too.

And this man emerges from even a worse mess than Nick does, climbs out of the destruction and decay, and look what he has made of his life. Look at his home, the sunny family pictures on his Westchester walls. How did that happen to him and this happen to Nick? It makes Nick resent him all the more. He despises looking into this strange mirror. Distorting. Unflattering.

No, there will be no mercy today.

Today or ever.

With no final words, only a faint smile in the way of conclusion, Nick rises silently and heads back to his office.

The street punk, soaked in reality, knows: it is too late for anything else.

>>>

Rose lies on top of the bed, staring numbly at the ceiling in the dark. The nights, the weeks she spent without him when he traveled on business are many years behind them now. Since his retirement a decade ago, they have spent almost every night together. So while the daylight hours have been expectedly painful—a steady, drawn-out, moment-by-moment suffering—the darkness has brought on, almost unimaginably, an extra layer of anguish.

What is he going through? What is he subjected to? Kidnapping—like Bogota. Like Lima. Where they have to travel with guards. Yet this is America. And should she listen to the thief? Simply wait for the call? Organize the house? Prepare for the truck? Or find some way to rescue him? But how? Where?

Should she confide in the kids? They would be there in hours, from their scattered places across the continent, offering consolation, plans of action, contacts. But they would definitely, unquestionably, insist on bringing in the police—this sense of security, this wonderful enviable confidence in the system, in the omnipotence of the authorities, confidence and security that are a credit to the atmosphere her husband and she have raised them in, provided for them. But she knows it's not what her husband would want—*does no good, makes things worse, don't bring in the children or police, we have resources, we're still in charge here*. He got their things back himself. Certainly the record of his preference—the record of his life—is to do without help. And such a clear purpose of his life has been not to burden his children with his past. For them to have lives contrastingly untroubled, unencumbered, free. Such a clear goal has been for their experiences, their rites of passage, to have no connection to his own. She could never perceive much in him, but she can clearly perceive that.

So should she try to find the Mercers? She knows only that they've left for a vacation in Europe. But even if she could somehow track them down, they, like her children, would undoubtedly advise police intervention, and in their reassuring way, in their dulcet tones, they might even succeed in convincing her of it.

Events, of course, have shoved aside and submerged for now all her nervous ruminations about their marriage—her doubts and reflections about their silences and disconnections and an irremediable separateness from each other. Yet at the same time, those subjects circle back, come to the fore relentlessly again, because this after all is separation and silence and disconnection, magnified and writ large. Now life is physically playing out, it turns out, the psychological truth of their marriage—and this highlighting of that truth serves only to make the hours in the dark even more painful.

She can't escape the logic: if he were not a survivor, if he did not have his past, he would not have gone to retrieve his possessions, and this would not be happening. If he did not have his past, he would not have felt the same need to have everything back, nor felt the capacity or fierceness to get it all, and this would not have occurred, and he would be here with her. He brought this on. He tackled this. He made her explicit and implicit assurances: that if there was trouble, he would back off. And he didn't. And now look.

But here, she doesn't even have the right to her fury. She has to bury it in the moment, too, subsume it to the greater, more pressing needs of the catastrophe. Even in calamity, her life is about his. Even in crisis, when she is his only hope, he is still their life's subject. She is ashamed of the resentment she feels, ashamed to detect it in herself, and yet crisis makes it clear.

It's not resentment of him, though. It's resentment of how the world took him and held him and still takes him and holds him. Keeping him from her.

She has resented his slipping away, but now that he truly could be slipping away, she desperately wants him back. As if it is a test. A proof. As if he has arranged it.

For this calamitous moment, at least, she is a prisoner to his past as much as he. It is that powerful, that relentless, a past. And now she will play an unasked-for role in some twisted repeating of it. The world is proving as fragile as deep down she has always known it to be. A fragility that they have assiduously built a life to avoid, but that his past seems to have rendered unavoidable.

Damn his past. Damn his baggage. Damn his history.

The bedside alarm chirps suddenly into the dark. It startles her into alertness and fresh fear. She fumbles for it, shuts it off. Her heart pounds in its aftermath. She must have set it accidentally, fussing with the clock incessantly, checking the time while waiting, praying for a call. Her fussing, her turning the little clock in her hands. A modern, graceless item, plastic, functional. The alarm, chirping into the dark insistently like that, before she could locate and slide the button. A *chirp, chirp, chirp* of doom.

She blinks into the dark.

My God.

How could she have not remembered? How could she not have thought?

She throws herself across to her husband's side of the big canopy bed. Reaches almost desperately into the first drawer of the night table. Rummages through with just her hands, not stopping even to turn on the light, so focused, so hopeful is she.

But nothing. Kleenex, those little yellow notes, receipts, magazines, books . . .

She is standing up now, more effective, spry and awake, organized, the mild bedside light is on, as she tries the second drawer . . .

Clothing. She feels around it. Nothing.

Her heart sinks. *This is torture*, she thinks vaguely. Her own tenuous connection to the evil clevernesses of torture—to raise hopes and dash them. If that is its technique, then this, too, is torture—unintended, self-inflicted.

She tries the third drawer. Looks in, feels around frantically.

Finds it almost immediately.

The little device. The odd little radio-ish box.

She grabs it. Places it sacredly in the middle of the bed. Stares at it.

Touches the button.

But there is no little chirp.

She presses the button again. Nothing.

She taps at it furiously now, harder and harder, soon punches it desperately. She shakes it. But it remains silent. That stupid insistent chirping that she heard and hated for so long, that accompanied them for almost two thousand miles. Where is it now? Where is it now that she wants to hear it? *Please. Please chirp.*

Nothing. No response. The power light indicates that the problem is not with the unit she's holding. It's at the other end. The other end is not working. The other end is . . . dead.

She had thought for a gloriously giddy moment that he would prove to be here beside her the whole time. Here at her bedside. Waiting in the little box.

But he is lost. Lost like a little boy in the woods of Cracow. Lost to the earth's surface again.

And here is what she must wrestle with now:

Does it not work because its transmitting battery has died at the other end?

Or because it has been discovered?

She crumples to the mattress. In pure dread. In pure weight. In utter collapse.

In a minute, she lifts her head. A small act—functional, automatic, thoughtlessly willful. An action somehow separate from her.

His worn and battered address book is there in the bedside drawer, next to where the device had been. She begins to leaf through it aimlessly. Names of the departed, of the hospitalized, of the far-flung, names of a lifetime ago, a lifetime gone. His ancient address book is a mocking exercise—like the nonfunctioning device, another form of torture. Their friends are old, infirm. She turns the pages, coming across names that she expects and names that hold instant and surprising memories for her.

She slams the book closed.

It is midnight here. Three in the morning in the East. No matter. She is desperate. She will do anything. Disobey his deepest most basic wishes, risk contradicting what might be his instincts for survival (his proven instincts for survival), because that is what's required. Because she must act.

She dials.

A man's voice answers stumblingly. Three in the morning, distraught, confused, but alert somehow.

"I'm so sorry about the hour. He'd kill me if he knew I was calling, but I don't know where else to turn."

"Mom?"

"He needs you, Daniel." She pauses. She knows he understands. A tectonic shift occurs in an instant. "He finally needs you."

31

Peke opens his eyes and sees an older man standing over him. About Peke's age. A similar short haircut. Even, Peke notices, the same squinting, attentive regard as his own. A doppelgänger. And now Peke recognizes him. The old dishwasher from Freedom Café. Standing unstooped, transformed, in this Montana farmhouse. And Peke knows why. Knows only too well. It's because of the uniform the man is wearing. Lovingly faithful to the original, he can see. Worn proudly. And now, apparently, at last, with some kind of purpose. A Nazi uniform.

The three skinheads are behind the man. They are proud—expectant—showing off Peke, their prize catch.

He can tell instantly—by a certain opacity in the man's eyes—that this is a lunatic. This is not someone who has loosely adopted some ideas for their outrageousness. Not someone who lashes out with shoddy, half-conceived, lazy bigotry, angry and outraged, given too much alcohol at a bar. This is a zealot. Who has pondered and studied, deeply and perversely. Who has carefully arranged and organized his thoughts and actions around a system of beliefs. Peke realizes immediately that—despite the gulf of time and place and circumstance in this man's core being, or lack of one—this is a Nazi.

And taped up like this to this chair, he knows his only chance will be to strike out at those beliefs. Challenge, chip away—it's the only chance he has to do any useful damage. The only time he has is this short window in which he is being kept alive as collateral, a valuable item himself. Because he is sure—can tell even on awakening, by the tone of the farmhouse around him—that Nick and his crew are gone.

"Surprise," says the uniformed man, in a proud, commanding voice. "Are you awake? Or is it a bad dream continuing?" Smiling seedily at his own wit and putting a hand on Peke's undefended shoulder—the subtle implication of his close, physical domination. What would otherwise be a friendly gesture between men inverted, turned to mockery. Closeness turned to heavy-breathing threat.

Peke examines his uniform. A colonel's uniform. Colonel bars. *Needle. Wheedle. Cajole. Annoy. Jump in.* "Your collar insignias are wrong." Peke smiles, shakes his head as if with weariness at a world of incompetence. He looks close to suppressing a mild laugh.

The uniformed man withdraws his hand. Retreats into expressionlessness for a moment. Into the bunker, out of the line of fire.

The big skinhead stands up, ready to be directed to swing at Peke. To bring order.

"That's the wrong number of sleeve stripes for your command level. It's wrong for the rest of the uniform." Peke strikes again, using evidence, adding the weight of credibility. A survivor of the Nazis, establishing his authority.

The man glowers, unsure what to do. He has not met with quite the docile shock he seems to have expected. Peke would bet that the man's physical encounters so far have been limited, if not nonexistent, and though he can tell a man like this would acquire a taste for physical violence, he may, like most men, be repelled by the intense smell and feel and actuality of it initially, and this window of repulsion and discomfort could work to Peke's advantage.

The beefy skinhead steps forward, threatening, eager. Peke pointedly ignores him.

The Colonel shifts, considering a small act of discipline, Peke can tell—a small, symbolic act of retaliation.

So Peke strikes quickly once more. "I can fix those stripes for you. We can get you the right insignia. You'll have the only perfect uniform. It's up to you."

The man looks down at him mutely confused, assessing. Peke knows he is not really considering the offer. But he is, Peke feels sure, nevertheless picturing himself with the correct uniform. The man probably worked carefully from pictures. The artifacts are genuine. They were presumably extremely costly—Nazi memorabilia is. Maybe it took a lot to find them through the Internet. To negotiate for them. All of this Peke imagines the man is quickly, angrily mulling. All of this Peke imagines the man wants to tell him, to defend his appearance. And the man may also be stewing that he's been had. That it was for naught. He's probably also thinking how to cut off this line of inquiry.

The Colonel suddenly slaps Peke. A glove across the cheek. The skinheads grin gleefully, joy unpenned, the gate to the fields of play opening at last. But Peke knows this is his opportunity to go beyond the uniform—to move to something more fundamental.

"You're doing it all wrong," says Peke. "You should be ignoring me. We're lower than pond scum, remember—we're not people. You honor and respect me too much by engaging me, by speaking to me, by considering me," he says. "You're not a real Nazi. You're thinking about it all too much." And now another pinprick, another needle, further up, closer in. "This is not just some game, you know," Peke says sternly, hoping to steal the man's thoughts, the man's words, what the man was about to say reversing on him. "You can't play this like some game. This is serious. Life and death. You have to be real," Peke says.

Peke considers—*I know where to get you the right uniform. I know where to get the right artifacts.* But it's too early for these. These would be too obvious a bid for release.

The big skinhead steps forward and delivers a swiping blow across Peke's head. Much harder than the Colonel's slap. Demonstrating to the Colonel quickly and wordlessly and efficiently what works. How to do it.

Peke goes dizzy. For a long moment he feels close to passing out, but doesn't. The room rights itself. He is primally, exceedingly aware of the pain. The pain that remains, still sharp, still coursing. But the pain is at the same time somehow inconsequential, he notices. Secondary. Maybe that's an effect of being an old man. A survivor.

The thief and his crew are gone, and in their absence, the Colonel and the skinheads are adjusting the rules a little. Peke is not worried about the pain, per se. He's very worried, though, that they may overdo it. Misapply, overapply, the violence. Kill him inadvertently. They have no experience with this. He is very worried, not to say terrified, of that.

What are his children doing at this moment, he wonders? His daughter, perhaps feeding and watering a specimen plant in her beautiful garden. Smoothing the loamy dirt around its base, the dirt running through her fingers. His son, playing catch with his grandson, the steady, rhythmic thud of the ball in their gloves, the easy rhythm of wind-up and throw, father and son locking into it like figurines on a Swiss clock. His youngest daughter, out on a new lightweight racing bike with her biking-enthusiast friends on their morning ride, the cool air against their faces and limbs, the green woods rushing by.

While their father is strapped to a chair in Montana.

32

The white truck heads toward Southern California. Nick, Chiv, LaFarge, Al, the regular crew. The skinheads and that old nut are holding Peke, having their fun with him, despite his instructions, Nick is sure. He needed the skinheads to babysit Peke while he and his crew collect the Pekes' belongings once again. It's working, he thinks; the arrangement is working. And it's serving a couple of purposes, even beyond their watching Peke while Nick can't. First, it ingratiates him a little to their eccentric, fucked-up local community. Backwoods diplomacy. And it advances their cause—or at least they think so. The elimination of the unclean, the unchosen, even if it is one Jew at a time. But best, it puts them in his debt. They'll feel they owe him one. For including them. For throwing them one. Even for understanding them. Interesting that so much indecency could buy him so much goodwill.

He's not really worried they'll kill the old man. Although they might—it's obvious they don't know what they're doing. But that wouldn't derail his plan—the missus will assume her husband is alive, particularly since Nick will be there with her. She'll assume that Nick is keeping the implicit agreement in good faith—*you don't tell anyone, and I'll return him to you*—and there's no way an inadvertent death could get communicated to the missus before the moving truck has pulled away. Anyway, he'll be honoring his part of the bargain. *He didn't want Peke to die, he didn't do it;* hey, it was his idiot babysitters, his incompetent partners. His larger concern is that if the death does occur, they won't know how to handle it. What to do. How to proceed. And some representative of the State of Montana might come snooping around as a result of some foolish misstep they make. He figures he'll be back in time to take care of any incompetence, but it's still on his mind. Gross incompetence happens in a flash; its damage can last a lifetime. A lifetime behind bars.

He's upped the stakes, he knows. Skipped up a criminal category in the eyes of the law. You'd have to call this kidnapping, or abduction, unfortunately, even though to him it's just a case of temporary human collateral. Kidnapping, abduction—they have new rules, and you have to be especially careful not to count on the old ones. Nick figures he's pretty safe, though. This old guy Peke has already shown he's someone who doesn't call the police. Maybe has some ingrained distrust of police authority. Or else he's just a guy who lives by self-reliance. Solving his own problems. Like finding Nick, however the hell he did it. And hiring a truck to get his things back. That's a guy who's arrogant enough to think he can handle anything by himself. In finding and following Nick, the old man demonstrated his unshakable belief in his own abilities. Ironically, thinks Nick, it leaves Nick feeling pretty confident the police won't be summoned. Peke's arrogance is Nick's safety.

The Nazi nuts are on their own. He knows they'll feel freer, probably be crazier, more dangerous, off the leash, with him gone. *Jesus, don't burn the place down.*

Peke looks up, and the hazy forms come back into view.

He's aware of the throbbing welt on the side of his face. It has a pulse of its own. He can almost see it when he looks sidelong. He can't reach for it, of course, but he can still sense its contours, its outline, its raised reds and purples.

His vision is blurry now, but his head, his thoughts, are clear. They want to kill him, but that is so final, they don't want to just yet. And they don't know what they want to do with him in the interim. The Jewish problem, Peke thinks vaguely, with no amusement. Here in the Montana woods, they have their own unique Jewish problem.

Nick must know they might kill him. Nick is a professional. Nick must have observed their amateurism and known they might kill him, so it obviously doesn't matter much to Nick. This much is clear now to Peke, too.

Conscious again, he will not relent.

"You shave your heads," says Peke through the dizziness, the slight nausea. "Just like the Jewish prisoners. Why do you try to look like Jewish prisoners? I don't understand." *Keep up the connection. Keep needling.* It might seem like the wrong thing, to annoy them, opposite what one should do. *But engage, engage.* It makes him human and alive. The squeaky wheel. And if his strategy is wrong, if they are going to kill him anyway, at least he'll make his points, be himself, try to the very end.

There is a palpable degeneration as the hours click by. A human regression that both prisoner and guards sense equally. A steady descent into a rawness that Peke is aware of in all his senses. In the close scent of the farmhouse living room. In the raw rubbing of the tape against his wrists. In the increasingly guttural communications between the skinheads. An animal descent, a primitive vision, that he detects in them. That he detects in himself.

Because despite the pain they have haphazardly inflicted, despite the aura of threat and lawlessness and implicit finality that hangs over the living room, he finds he's able to handle it. To remain calm. Perhaps because he is not surprised by any of it. Expected it. Predicted it. It is the dark subcellar of human behavior; a dark, damp, unspecified corner of hell that Dante missed, but he finds he can function within it.

To be taped up like this, unable to move, it is like a paralysis, and the risk is that your mind will follow suit. At first you pull, you bristle, you bridle, with equal physical and mental vigor, but then paralysis and numbness set in and you begin to feel it is the order of things, that it has a certain inevitability; even, you begin to feel, a certain justice. But that is what you must guard against: lying back in the warm sun, floating powerless down the river on a current of suffering. *No. Resist. No.*

In that insinuating numbness, he is aware of his own brain beginning its little minuet with reality—its soft, creeping retreat from the horror of the here and now. He is aware of his own mind's recesses and caverns starting to gently taunt him . . .

Soon the sight of the two shadowed figures in the small, dim-lit kitchen in front of him, from the enforced viewing angle of this nailed-down chair, these taped-down arms and legs, his current fate of mere powerless observation, slants into a vision of two other figures, hulking and indistinct, in another small, dim kitchen, where he is similarly contained in—what is it? a hard-backed, homemade pine high chair?—and he hears the mutter of those voices, too, incomprehensible except as a river of familiarity, a tide of belonging. Olfactory memory assaults him from some preconscious place. He is suddenly bathed in the scents from that high chair—barnyard scents carried through the open curtained window; piquant root smells from deep within the dark kitchen; the thick, cloying smell of that ancient, reddish pine planking beneath him. And now those immense, dark-draped figures are moving lugubriously in front of him, their muted tones of dress and speech, their obsessive turning to regard and consider him, turning those huge brown eyes on him. *Mammen . . . Foter . . .*

He blinks. He shudders. An ancient fury resurfaces sharply to prick the vision, to pull him out . . .

The ending, the finality he faces here, feels suddenly more inevitable and conclusive to him by bringing him back to the beginning, to his earliest sense memories. The vision—still hovering, still reverberating—juxtaposes his current hatred with that long-ago love. Contraposes his will to escape with a tenor of belonging, a primal tug of home. Matches this present with that past—tauntingly, teasingly, meanly, absurdly . . .

Resist . . . Resist . . .

"I have to shit," he says. "Do you want me to shit myself and stink up your room? You couldn't stand the stench of this old Jew—believe me, you've never smelled anything like it. You couldn't stand here, torturing me with that stench. You'd miss all your fun." *Cajole, insinuate, prod. Worm inside their heads, peck at their brains.* The thoughts and words come easily, he finds. The filth, the absurdities, are readily available, as if dormant inside him, waiting for just such a release.

He has to shit. They puzzle over this. Absorbing the unpredicted situation. How to proceed. They've been instructed, he imagines, to never let the Jew out of their sight. Not for a moment. The wily, sneaky Jew.

He presses. He pushes. "I've got to go," he tells them. "I've got no choice. I'm going to have to shit my pants. And you won't want to guard me after that, believe me." An old man who can't control his bowels. An indignity of age. He adds some moans, some pained writhing, sounds of desperation that are easy to summon by their close relationship to the truth.

"Let's kill him before he has to shit," proposes the middle one. It has an appealing neatness to it, a Nazi problem-solving efficiency. But that is too sudden, too soon for the rest of them. It seems too radical a solution to the matter of shitting.

"We could give him a pot or bowl to hold under himself," suggests the skinny one.

"And which of you is going to carry my shit out?" Peke asks with rhetorical flourish. "Which of you is going to handle that task for me? Perform that service? Carry the shit of a Jew?" He punctuates the urgency once more with a long moan.

Absurdly, he has command. Improbably, he controls the scene. Tied in his chair, he holds center stage. And he highlights this absurdity, rubs it in, with a wildly stentorian, commanding vocal delivery. He gives his accent free rein, elevates it into caricature. To reinforce the absurdity of the situation. To reinforce the impression of his command. To challenge the Colonel with a direct mocking imitation of the Colonel's command.

"He goes to the bathroom." The old Colonel, wresting back control. "Where we all watch him." *In case you intend to try something, Jew. Something in the walk to the bathroom. Something with the bathroom window.* "We see how the Jew does it," says the Colonel. *We turn the occasion into an opportunity to demean you.*

With their hunting knives—knives Peke knows are as common as keys here in the Montana woods, part of dressing in the morning—the beefy one and the muscled one sever the tape across Peke's waist and thighs and knees with a purposeful air of carelessness, cutting him out of the chair. They leave his hands taped behind his back.

They lumber together—Peke, the Colonel, the skinheads—a humpbacked beast of hatred and antagonism, a perverse processional—down the narrow hall to the bathroom.

The bathroom—a narrow L, the toilet tucked into the elbow at the far end—can hardly hold five people, no matter how they arrange themselves in it, no matter what the circumstances, and the immediate uncomfortable looks exchanged between the skinheads and the Colonel seem a recognition of this.

Peke doesn't miss the opportunity. "And who is going to undo my pants for me?" Peke looks at them, challenging.

They have not thought of this, of course. As they have not thought of anything. But here they are in the bathroom, they've already cut the tape that was around his waist, across his thighs and calves, they've come this far, they will somehow see it through. Again, there is procrastination, inertia, a hope that the need for decision will disappear.

"Hurry. I feel it coming . . . ," moans Peke insistently.

Still he has the control. He is about to defecate in front of them, and still he has the control.

The big, beefy one seems to sense that, and can't stand it, and storms out of the bathroom in disgust, knocking aside the thin bathroom door so it trembles in his angry exit.

The Colonel makes no move but looks to the other skinheads. With what they must take to be a regard of authority, of hierarchy.

Because the middle-size one unhitches Peke's belt and pants top, then—pressing a black boot to Peke's stomach—kicks him down onto the seat of the open toilet. That's how he does it. How he wrestles back dignity from the situation.

Peke, forced suddenly into a sitting position, hands taped behind him, now attempts to wriggle his pants and underwear down his thighs as far as necessary. Shifting, twisting, he manages to pull pants and underwear sufficiently down his white thighs.

He leans back gingerly against the tank of the toilet to adjust himself on the oval seat. Then he hunches forward somewhat. Grunts, as if approvingly, at his arrival in position.

He looks up at them. They stare at him. Peke squatting on the can. His old man's genitals, gray-haired, hoary, pendulous.

"You like to watch?" Peke inquires. Turning on the accent even more now; it is overflowing, florid. He looks at the skinny, smallest one, positioned behind the others. "It's fun for you, yes?" He gestures to the Colonel. "But more fun for him, I assure you." The bluffest, broadest bathroom humor, from the rich Jew. It confuses them, he hopes, usurps them in their vileness, since they are supposed to be the vile ones.

"It's circumcised," he informs them, pretending to have seen them staring. "You know who's circumcised? Only two groups in the world. Real Jews and real Americans. The only ones. That's why the Jews chose America, you know. So we could hide among the circumcised cocks." He doesn't know where this comes from. He listens, amazed by this idea. At least as amazed as his audience. "Let's see yours," he says with seriousness, with camaraderie. "C'mon, let's see yours. Let's see if you're real Jews or real Americans. Or are you neither one? Is that why you're ashamed to show them? Because you're neither one?"

"I'm gonna tape his fuckin' mouth," says the middle one, shifting itchily in the little bathroom, threateningly, explosive. Realizing they have not done this right at all but are now stuck. Fuck—they are *his* prisoners. The skinhead kicks the wall in frustrated punctuation. "When we tape him up again, I'm tapin' that mouth."

There is silence as Peke shits. A holy pause, a moment of suspension and fascination. He mutters. He strains, for their benefit. They watch. "You see," he says, breathing, "just like you. No different. The same." Alternating continually, confusingly, purposefully, between the declarations they can't believe, and the assertions they don't doubt. *Needle, cajole, annoy. Engage, engage . . .*

A group of strangers watching you shit. Is that the opposite of aloneness? The opposite of lost? Or another variant of lost, of alone . . .

In a moment, waving his taped hands modestly behind him like a wagging duck tail—something mocking in its very motion—

he asks in a manner so cheerful, so succinctly crafted, that it is obvious he has been gleefully waiting for this moment to ask:

"So, who will wipe me? Who volunteers?"

They haven't anticipated this either. Once again, they don't know what to do. It is as if each succeeding moment has been calibrated to add another layer of incompetence and embarrassment. Should they cut his hands loose? But Nick must have said not to untie him no matter what, and they are already partly in violation of that, not knowing how else to accommodate the predicament. And anyway, which of them would even get near Peke's hands right now to cut the tape?

"Or should I come back to you unwiped, and we'll enjoy the scent together?"

Crasser than they. Less civil than even they can imagine.

It is too much for them.

"Wipe with your hands tied," the Colonel commands curtly, reddening, trying to maintain control and authority—a ridiculous aim, given the circumstance.

"Ah, so you've imagined me wiping and you think it can be done? You've had fun imagining me doing it . . ."

"Wipe!" the Colonel shrieks, nearly frantic, explosive. "Wipe!"

Peke looks at him and shrugs.

Hands behind his back, he bends down awkwardly, shuffles sideways, to reach the toilet paper roll perched on the freestanding plastic shelf next to the toilet.

He succeeds in unrolling a portion of it, pulling it off the roll.

He also feels for the nail scissors that he knows are next to the toilet roll. He finds them with his fingers, tucks them quickly beneath the palm of one hand, keeps them tucked in that hand as he manages to wipe.

The scissors that he saw among the toiletries on the plastic shelf when he used this toilet a week ago.

When he saw how narrow and uncomfortable the bathroom is. Thinking—while tied to the chair—how its narrowness and L-shape would necessarily limit the number of observers and the effectiveness of their observations.

The purpose of his trip to the bathroom was not primarily to shit, of course, but he waited until he could, to make that seem the purpose.

The little plastic shelf next to the toilet: on it the roll of toilet paper. Deodorant. Shampoo. Nail scissors. A spray disinfectant. More of the thief's organizational zealotry, he had thought, seeing it that first time, wondering for a brief moment about the thief's sexual preference, given this neat, prim arrangement of items next to the toilet, and the tasteful bedroom where he saw the jeweled watch. Such surprising touches amid the farmhouse's general male chaos.

There is, he realizes with gratitude now, nothing wrong with his memory whatsoever.

His body provides a natural shield from their seeing what he is doing. Amid his sputter of scatological jokes and speculations and barbs, they are not inclined to look too closely either.

If he smudges some of his own feces on the nail scissors, so be it. If he accidentally cuts himself in the unfamiliar simultaneous actions of holding the scissors and wiping his anus, so be it. They won't see any blood. It would only run into his pants. And he can work somewhat slowly. They will assume it is simply his wiping. They will assume it takes an old man some time to wipe. Especially an old man with his hands taped together behind him.

He stands up, leans partly forward, squats awkwardly, to accomplish the wiping.

Perhaps they think this is how any old man wipes.

Perhaps they think this is how you have to wipe with your hands taped behind your back.

Perhaps they think this is how a Jew wipes. Standing like this. Different from them.

As he finishes, he is able to drop the used panels of toilet paper directly into the toilet, grapple for and press the flush lever, even to pull his pants partway up, to his knees, before looking up at them, exasperated, that he can't pull his pants up all the way.

As the muscled one steps forward, Peke presses the scissors deeper into his own hand. The muscled one hitches Peke's belt loosely, and then—given the events and frustrations of the last few minutes, and the sense of belittlement where there should have been domination, and such proximity and opportunity—he kicks Stanley Peke in the gray, dangling, too-tempting balls.

Peke gasps. Falls back awkwardly onto the open toilet. The pain goes hot, searing, instantaneous through his body like an electric jolt.

In a moment, he realizes he has opened his hands. He's no longer gripping the nail scissors.

A new pain sears him inside his forehead, deep inside his chest. The interior pain of a crucial mistake—equally unbearable in its own way.

They must have dropped—to the floor, or into the bowl. He must not have heard them—it must be that nobody had—in the commotion and crash of his body against the toilet.

But when he desperately clenches his hand again, the scissors are still there.

A sticky edge of the duct tape around his wrists and hands must have held them stuck for that brief instant.

He grips them again. Holds them tight.

In another minute, Peke is back in the living-room chair, the nail scissors hidden beneath his taped palms.

O n a sunny California morning, at a beautiful oceanside home in Santa Barbara, the front doorbell rings.

The lady of the house rises to answer it.

She opens the door.

It's four men in crisp green uniforms, an immense white truck gleaming in the California sunshine behind them.

Rose and Nick stare silently at each other for a moment.

"We're the movers," he says. With only the trace of a smirking smile.

Their possessions in exchange for her husband's life. Reduced to those stark terms—things versus a life—it's ridiculous to even contemplate any other decision, no matter what her husband has instructed.

Of course this is what the thief is relying on, Rose knows. He knows there is no choice, really. Though he values the worldly things— values them so highly he has come for them again—he knows they will have no value to civilized people in comparison with a life. To anyone's life. It's easy for the thief. It's an equation he knows the answer to before the test is administered. A nondecision. For all her pacing, her sleeplessness, her replaying of that brief moment of insistent instruction from her husband, there really was never a decision.

The only question is, will the thief honor his side of the agreement? But why wouldn't he? What is in it not to? She could not see his face at that moment he proposed it—*your things for your husband's life*—but presumes that his coarse posturing over the phone was primarily for threat. His implying that it would be nothing—easy, unthinking, only momentary—for him to kill her husband. That is bound to be posturing. Necessary for him to do. What would it profit him to actually do it?

Now he is no longer a voice on the phone but standing in the California sun in front of her. Yet the question remains. Who is this man, really? This broad, squat, quick-grinned cipher?

She hopes his coming here, doing this, is pure vindictiveness on the thief's part. Because if it is vindictiveness, then the thief will want Peke alive to prove the point to him. He will want Peke alive to wander his own empty house. To live with the knowledge of who has won. She hopes, prays, for that vindictiveness, that meanness, that precise purpose in the thief.

"My men will be very careful with your things," says the broad, squat man now, holding his clipboard. "We wouldn't want to compromise their value in any way."

He smiles that narrow smile again.

The same men, she sees. The same uniforms. The same white truck. An eerie duplication of the original moving day, as if to mock them. A perfect reenactment. Making her watch in the bright reality of the California morning what she has already watched repeatedly in shadowy memory.

There was complete shock and surprise, of course, at the unpredictable conclusion of that moving day.

While this time—with every piece they pack and carry—she already knows that it is gone.

The loading begins.

>>>

Who is this man, really? The question becomes immediately more pointed, because this man with his clipboard, she realizes soon enough, is going to stand beside her the whole time. It begins as hardly noticeable, but he is soon a pressing presence.

In case she tries to say anything, she's sure. In case there's been an arrangement with the police. So that he can monitor her. So that should anything happen, he can grab her, possess a fragile, useful hostage. He is not foolish, this man. He is a tactician. So would a true tactician really see murder as a tactic? What tactical purpose could it serve?

Estelle Simon, neighbor and casual friend, wanders up the bluestone walk, her exaggeratedly puzzled look clearly the excuse she is wearing to approach. Rose breathes deep to calm herself, to prepare for this first test that she knew would come from somewhere.

"My God, Rose. You can't be moving!"

Rose smiles. "No, no, just putting a few things in storage."

Estelle stands and watches for a moment. "Such a big truck. It confused me."

Rose shrugs, smiles. "I don't know why they sent such a big truck. Maybe they make a few stops."

Estelle watches the loading, looks in the rear gate of the truck. "That's a lot for storage."

"Well, we're really redoing it. The whole place. You'll see. You'll love it."

"And where's Stanley during all this?" Slightly disapproving—as if she knows the answer can't justify his absence.

"Golf with friends. He'll be back."

"You let him?"

Rose shrugs again.

The thief is sitting in the kitchen nearby, looking at his sheaf of papers, pretending not to listen, listening intently.

"Well, I was just checking. We didn't want to lose you and Stanley so soon," says Estelle. And smiles at Rose. And smiles, too, at the broad, squat, nice moving foreman sitting there studiously over his paperwork, who smiles pleasantly back at her.

P eke is back in the chair. Worn down from the stealth of the
event, the tensions of the effort, the lack of food, the lack of
rest. But if he falls asleep, his hands will relax and the scissors will
drop. He can't count again on a lucky edge of tape.

They have not said it specifically, but he knows. That the truck
is on its way to his home in Santa Barbara—or is by now even making its return. That Rose is doing everything they ask, in the hope
of getting him back. That she is not listening to him. That she is
denying his explicit wishes, for perhaps the first time in their lives.
For perhaps the last time in their lives.

He still assumes that the skinheads and the Colonel have been
instructed to keep him alive, so the fact can be proved to Rose if
need be, with a phone call where she hears his voice. *You see, Mrs.
Peke? Everything is as promised, everything is as planned, a simple
exchange of goods—no reason to involve the police.*

At least until the truck is loaded and closed, its big diesel engine
started up, and it pulls away from the Santa Barbara curb. Then he
is instantly expendable. Then he can be left utterly to the narrow
imaginations and devices of the skinheads and their Gothic commandant.

His captors might in fact be waiting for that phone call. Letting them know they can do whatever they want with him. And what would that be, exactly?

》》》

The offhand slaps and punches, occasional, unpredictable, are becoming more adept—and more enthusiastic. To him it is clearer than ever that they signify waiting. An aggressive, brutal ticking of the clock. A violent, impatient marking of time. He finds he can bear the individual blows. Each like a wave of pain, thick and liquid, rising up, washing over him but washing past. It's their cumulative effect that is wearing him down, exhausting him. Can he pretend to sleep? Can he pretend to without actually falling asleep?

His captors have not slept either. They are amped up, stimulated by events. Their normally sluggish, inalert patterns are temporarily suspended. But they will have to revert at some point. Sometime soon, they will want—need—to sleep. Come down. He has to make it until then.

Or else take a chance when there's no one else in the room. When they're eating something in the kitchen, for instance. Ignoring him for a few minutes. It's happened before. He can reasonably expect it to happen again. That will be much riskier, but it may be the only chance he has.

He tries to calculate when the truck will be back. How long it has been away. It's difficult. A couple of the blows have actually knocked him out, and he doesn't know whether for a moment or for longer. They've taken his watch. He has only night and day to rely on—morning and afternoon shadows in the yard outside the dust-caked living-room windows—and the patterns of his captors, who are largely patternless. By his estimate of when the truck left (he heard it pulling loudly out of the yard) and how long it would take to drive to Santa Barbara, pack, load, and drive back, they will return here by morning. By his rough and unreliable calculation, he is coming into his last few hours of opportunity. Maybe his last few hours of life.

The skinheads clearly have not heard yet from the thief. It seems they will wait for any greater action, any higher violence, until they do, and if the thief doesn't call, that could mean waiting until he is back. Peke feels sure the thief will want to see him, show Peke that the mission has been accomplished, wave an item or two under his nose, before he nods to the crazy Colonel and the skinheads to do what they wish, as the thief turns away from Peke for the last time. Peke feels sure that the thief will want Peke to suffer such a moment.

Peke pitches his head forward.

His breathing evens out.

Sleep. Not sleep.

So that he is merely half-aware of the Colonel's, the skinheads', eventual wandering away.

He must wait.

He mustn't wait.

The impossible discipline of half-awareness returns him to the drift of visions, turns his mind loose to play. He finds himself, in this susceptible state, left dangerously exposed to the old ambivalences, to the ceaseless, restless confusions—to all the old questions that an active lifetime could somewhat hide, could tamp down if not fully extinguish. But a chair in the dark, an atmosphere of finality, calls it up for assessment, wraps him in it like layers of tape across the chest.

Those indistinct figures in the long-ago kitchen, remembered only in a detail here or there, are by now merely stand-ins for something else, mythic, visionary, unreal. *They abandoned me to save me. Saved me by abandoning me.* The ancient, banished thought turns in him like a child's rhyme. *Saved by being abandoned. Abandoned to be saved.* Once again, he tries to imagine the commotion of the village, to imagine the approaching terror, preceded by the credulity and affirmation of horrifying tales—and what portion of those tales was mere rumor, paranoia, inaccurate hysteria? Would he have been better to stay with them? To be with them forever, whatever form forever ultimately took?

Yet what choice was there? None. None but survival. And that survival's necessary and subsequent rending of his previous universe: a wolf child, creating his own authority, his own morality, his own existence . . .

»»»

Night falls flat over the 150 acres of scrub.

Peke finds himself alert again. Time must have passed. Peke in his suspended state, thoughtless, imageless, a trick of his childhood existence, a reexperience of time that he learned when lying in cold fields, staring at faraway stars.

The old Colonel is lying on the sofa, asleep. One of the skinheads, the small, skinny one, is somewhere out of sight, crashed on a bed, he presumes.

The other two, though, the muscled middle one and the big, beefy one with the swastika on his forehead—the two most aggressive ones—are eating something in the kitchen.

They haven't offered Peke anything. He's starting to go weaker from his hunger, he can sense. They've given him water grudgingly when he's asked for it—small half cups—not wanting him to urinate, not wanting to again deal with his bodily needs, not wanting to see his cock again.

The novelty of the prisoner is wearing off. It is obvious they are waiting now only for permission. Only for the go-ahead.

The two are in the kitchen, laughing, guffawing meanly. The kitchen is close, but there is a wall. He can hear jars opening and closing, the refrigerator opening and closing, the clatter of plates and cutlery. It sounds more elaborate than a snack. That's good. That's a little more time. Rock and roll blares on the radio in the kitchen—a hostile, high-speed noise. Noise—that's good, too.

He unwraps his clenched fingers from around the scissors slowly, aware that his fingers will initially be cramped and useless.

He almost drops the scissors anyway, his fingers are so unused to moving after being clenched for so long.

He exercises his fingers a little individually, limbers them, tries the scissors motion, prepares. Because once he starts, there is no going back. Anyone will see that the duct tape has been cut. The secret will be revealed.

Nail scissors. A little tool of civilization. We trim our nails in respect for one another, to greet one another civilly, to touch one another gently. A tool to keep us from growing the claws of animals. Nail scissors—a representation of civilization, and maybe his one chance to return to that civilization.

Can he even cut the tape at all, with these little nail scissors?

He works the sharp tips into the tape between his wrists carefully. This gives him a starting point. He begins to slice outward from there, working against the tape's interior edges with the inside edge of the chrome blade. Holding the scissors in his right hand, he closes the blades, helping the little scissors by tilting them slightly as he goes, letting the scissors tear at the tape as well as cut it.

He feels the tear in the top layers of tape. He feels the top layers begin to give way, layer by layer.

It's too slow.

His heart pumps. He tries to remain calm, but he must work fast.

The radio plays. Sends out a pulsing, tinny cacophony. The mean laughter, the brusque eruptions from the kitchen, continue. He is acutely aware of them, but at the same time not aware of them at all, as he works the tape with the scissors, small snip by small snip, layer by layer.

Suddenly, his hands are free. It's a surprise to him. It feels odd, like a mistake.

The suddenness of it so alarms him, he drops the scissors.

But they fall directly beneath him, under the chair, and, hands now free, he quickly scoops them up and, not pausing, begins to use one blade to rip at the bands of duct tape around his waist.

It is no longer snipping. He is slashing fiercely with the little scissors, slashing at the many layers of wrapping across his waist and thighs, across the knees and shins. For some of it, where there are not as many layers, he needs only one neat, sharp cut, like a mad surgeon making a single seam, opening the patient up. But most of it takes more than that—slashing, jabbing, poking, ripping, tearing. If he were to pull the tape quickly, the loud, hollow rips and zips might be heard, even over the pulsing radio. And peeling off the many layers slowly, quietly, would take too long. He must work between these two extremes. He is still limited to the blades of the little scissors and his maniacal silent surgery.

His waist is done.

His thighs are done. He has reached his knees.

"I mean, fuck, I ain't takin' that shit; I don't care who it is . . ." The voice rising above the manic jungle thump of the radio, perhaps even driven by it, then settling down again . . . The voices in the kitchen go more muffled once more.

It's taking too long.

He's running out of time.

Faster, faster. He is not thinking anything.

And then, incredibly, his knees, his feet, are free.

He sits in the chair a moment, briefly uncomprehending, momentarily startled that this has worked . . .

The sudden physical freedom causes a sensation of floating, after hours, days, pinned to the chair . . .

And then, as he has imagined a hundred times before, as he has calculated and repeated incessantly to himself so that he would not forget when the time came, he takes the three long, quick steps to the back door, grabs what is left of the roll of duct tape that wrapped him, grabs what he knows from his previous visit is the key ring with the barn key, hanging there on the hook, steps out onto the rickety wooden back landing, closes the door quietly but firmly, and stumbles directly into the night.

"Hey, Lee, that you, you shithead?" Called out in a moment from the kitchen.

The big, beefy, tattooed skinhead comes around the corner when there's no response.

The big skinhead looks at the broken tape, at the empty chair.

And grins.

The old Jew has escaped.

Now he can go ahead and kill him. Now it'll be OK.

35

The packing is not as careful this time. As Rose expected. The possessions that have less value are rushed into the truck, loose. But it is still as thorough, she notices. It is still everything. As if to make a point. Not so the thief has it, but so the Pekes don't. She hopes it's a point the thief wants to make to her husband, not just to her, or only to himself.

Her heart still pounds tensely, slightly painful. It has pounded like this—she's been aware of it—all day. It didn't increase when Estelle Simon approached or relent when she finally wandered away. She watches through the kitchen window. The crew has loaded the last of the possessions and closed the gate of the truck, but they have not yet locked it.

From the kitchen window, she can just see the rear gate of the truck in the gathering twilight. She roughly calculates—they'll drive all night. Arrive by morning.

She'll have the embarrassment of reporting it again. Dealing once more with the police. Telling them that she had no choice, that her husband was held hostage. The insurance companies will not be so understanding this time. They could deny the claim completely, insisting that she should have called the police. But what does any of that matter? It is all mere aftermath, when her husband is back beside her.

If her husband is back beside her.

The thief still stands next to her in the kitchen. His three men are now all in the doorway. Childishly, she counts them. Just to be sure. Ridiculous. She knows it's the four of them together. She's watched them all day, and here they are, all four.

"Counting us up?" asks the thief. "Worried there are more of us?"

She's startled. He's seen her counting—unconsciously nodding at each one. "You think there's gonna be someone staying and hiding in the closet?" He smiles archly at her.

She pretends to ignore it. "You have what you came for," she says. "Now it's yours. When do you return what belongs to me?" Pointedly, defiantly, from a position of weakness, but as if from a position of strength.

Nick says quietly, "We'll see." As if to a demanding child.

A stab of pain goes through her. The fact that there is no completion. That she doesn't yet know.

The truck pulls out. She has held up. Held it all in. Now she falls apart. Cracks completely. Crumples to the floor, her sobs pyramiding into wails, chaotic, patternless, echoing in the newly empty room.

She crawls to the telephone in the center of the empty room, the only object still in it, curls up next to it, to do all she can do.

Wait.

Wait for a call.

Just as the Colonel and the skinheads were waiting for a call.

But, of course, they are no longer waiting.

36

L et's take the dogs! They'll smell him!" Excited voices on the back-porch landing, the harsh porch light sending sharp, slanted shadows stabbing into the night.

"Get him! Get him!" they command, their excitement uncontainable, and it is enough. The dogs understand. They hear the extremity of tone in the commanding voices, the fever pitch, and they understand from merely that. The dogs take off barking, paws splaying comically, cartoonish, as they seek traction in the dust. Twin black bullets of aggression. An animal translation of the bloodlust the skinheads feel.

Night. Running. Dogs. The beams of flashlight lanterns dancing in the leaves.

He has come full circle.

But he is not an agile, feral seven-year-old. He is more than sixty years older, much slower. In good shape, yes, in good health for a man in his seventies, only a little bit arthritic, after all. But he is no agile child.

Fortunately, he has cased it. He has been here before. Sitting in the chair with the scissors tucked into his palms, eyeing the prefab barn's keys on the nail on the wall, he has been picturing it all. Remembering it from his aimless wandering of the grounds as his own men loaded their truck. The barn—its bays empty of his belongings for the moment. He has been picturing, remembering it all.

He is no agile, feral child. But he has a plan.

>>>

The pond is glassy black in the cloudy, moonless night. A black, eerie liquid surface one comes upon suddenly. When he reaches it, he stares for a moment at its pellucid, frightening beauty. Then removes his shoes, as if in a rushed ceremony. He wades slowly, silently, into it. No splashing. No sound. He feels the cold, clammy water climb his body, envelop him in its chill, devour him in its darkness and mud. He thinks of the crystalline pool off the back deck in Santa Barbara where he does his morning laps, the water so clear you see through it beneath you to the immaculate bottom. It's hard to believe they're both called water. There should be different subsets of such a variable substance. It's like the descriptive inefficiency of calling a twenty-two-year-old Montana skinhead and a seventy-two-year-old Jewish war survivor the same species. He feels oddly, momentarily calm, in the water.

They are not trained dogs. They may smell him initially, but his scent will disappear at the edge of the pond, and they will not know where he has emerged. They won't know his exit point. Untrained dogs, they may not be able to pick up his trail again at all, crossed as it will be with deer, muskrat, rabbit, the wildlife that certainly comes to drink at the far side of this pond. And that will buy him some time. Anything to buy some time.

It's not that the knowledge is coming back to him. It's that it never left. It is still somehow in him, in the quick of his being, from the time he was seven, and something in him so long practically qualifies as instinct.

The pond, it turns out, is shallow enough to walk across. It never reaches higher than his chest. He is able to hold the shoes up, wade across through the muck, pebbles, rocks, weeds, frogs, and snakes to the other side. Better not to have to swim. Better to conserve his strength.

He works his way through the night around to the barn. Comes at it from the far side, to minimize the chance they will see any movement in the charcoal dark.

He can't outrun the dogs. It is open land right here, low scrub, so he has to keep moving. While he might make it to the woods, might even make it through the woods to a road, might get a ride, the odds are good that they will eventually find him, by alerting the rest of their crazy militia to keep an eye out for him, by using his escape as a chance to awaken the bloodthirst of a hundred waiting soldiers. Whereas if he stays within the compound, he has to deal only with them. Within the compound, he is their problem to solve. An enemy now known to him. And there is a lot of acreage.

He remembers lying in open fields, sleeping in them, but there is no option of that here. They are too close to him already. They know he is here, and they are looking.

Lying in open fields, in cold, in fear. Feelings, memories, he has pushed away. Now he will not merely remember it all. Now he will relive it.

There were barns then, too. That winter—huddling into the stenchy warmth of the sheep. With Abel, only two years older than Peke, sneaking into a barn when the lights of the farmhouse went out, leaving it at the first crowing of the roosters, their strutting alarm clock hustling Abel and him back out into the cold fields before the farmer arrived. Once, exhausted, he and Abel overslept. The farmer came in before dawn, before the rooster's crowing. Peke opened his eyes to see the farmer staring at them. And then the farmer turned away wordlessly and went about his work as if he had never seen them.

He and Abel came in the next night, and in the morning, the same thing happened. The farmer stared, then turned away and went about his work. This time even leaving the barn before Peke and Abel did.

This went on, might have gone on indefinitely, until one morning Abel asked, with an overweening politeness and deference—a nine-year-old's best effort at formality—if there was something, anything, for them to eat or drink.

The farmer began screaming, cursing, throwing hay at them. As if his fury had been building, and yet he did not lash out in any physical way, and once he had finished his round of furious cursing, he turned to his chores once again, just as before. And as for the hay he'd thrown—they had to suppress their laughter.

They discussed whether they should continue to sleep in the barn. The farmer, for all his cursing, had not hurt them, after all. But Abel with his caution prevailed, arguing that despite the bitter cold, despite sacrificing the warmth of the barn and the docile sheep's thick winter coats, they should sleep at the edge of the field. The seven-year-old Peke had protested violently. Even hardened to it as they were, the cold was almost unbearable at that time of year. But Abel remained firm.

In the morning they awoke to a military truck pulling up to the barn, and voices. They could just see, over the tops of the protective weeds, three uniformed soldiers and the farmer, talking, gesticulating.

Their small, skimming lives were lived dodging, skirting, alert for those big, uniformed, hulking, gleaming presences. Their shiny belts and boots, their ruddy faces, their big, gruff voices, their sheer size, their pure power. A seven-year-old boy and his barely older protector, always watching them. Gauging their every mood, their every movement, reading their gesticulations, their tone. A necessary preoccupation, for the purpose of survival.

They're the champs, the winners, thought the seven-year-old boy. He wanted to join them, be part of them somehow, but Abel said he couldn't.

The soldiers made some final gestures of annoyance to the farmer and got back into their truck.

Peke and Abel would have been finished. But Abel saved them.

And when the time came, Peke could not do the same for Abel.

Peke knew barns. A barn could be sanctuary, salvation. A barn could be a trap, a cemetery.

>>>

In the dark, he slips the key into the padlock. He unclips the padlock, quickly works off the metal strap beneath, pulls the heavy door open, slips behind it and into the darkness. He pulls the door closed and feels around on the door's inside to see if there is a hook to clip the padlock to and lock the door from inside. Yes. Good. They'll have to work it off, bend the lock, maybe destroy the door's hardware. It will give him another minute or two. Maybe more.

He remembers there is a path, an unobstructed aisle, down the center of the barn. He feels his way along that, knocks his foot on an object or two, but it doesn't stop him. Nothing will.

It is unfortunate his own possessions are gone. He knows where particular things might be. Tools. Wire. But there must be much else to choose from here. Barn implements. The possessions of other victims. If he could just see. Because it is pitch black. The cloudiness, the moonlessness, is an advantage in being unseen, a disadvantage in seeing.

Before, while he waited here in the barn for the truck to arrive, to load his things, he saw the generator at the back. Rusty orange. Substantial. Survivalists, off the grid, he remembers thinking on seeing it. A generator—of course. The lights undoubtedly connect directly to it. If he turns on the generator, though, they'll come running when they see the lights. But it would give him a chance to find things. A minute or so. Maybe less. To cobble together some kind of defense. Locate some kind of weapon. He has no idea what he'll find. But this is a barn, after all. He will be prepared to think fast—to improvise, to think ahead—in that minute or so of light.

He stumbles along the aisle to where he remembers the primitive generator. Feeling the objects, trying to see anything, as he makes his way along.

He reaches where he remembers the generator being. Tucked at the bottom of a ladder leading to a small loft. He reaches out blindly to where he saw the generator, and his hands soon find its cold metal surfaces.

He takes a breath in preparation. It will be a moment of light. A moment of illumination that—ironically—will summon the Nazis. That will bring the dogs. That will bring an unknown outcome charging toward him.

He feels around the generator's bulky shape to find its start cord. He grips it, pulls hard. Nothing. He feels a wave of panic rise in him like liquid. He struggles to quell it, to push it down. The night isn't cold. It should start. He pulls hard again. The generator rumbles on. The overhead lights flicker, then glare. The light visible, he knows, through the high slats at the crease of the barn's roof.

He hears the barking immediately. A bloodthirsty chorus. Next to the generator, leaned against the ladder, there is a rusty old spade. A pile of old tire chains. A sledgehammer.

Some coils of rope a few yards away. He hustles over to them, throws them over his shoulder, hustles back to the generator.

The dogs are coming closer. It sounds like only a couple hundred yards now. The fragile, rusty inside lock will not keep them out for long. But maybe long enough.

In the light, he can see the generator's little choke. He pulls it, and the generator momentarily runs on high, spewing smoke and fumes into the barn. He lets go of the little choke lever in order to trace the path of the wire that runs from the generator to the wall—obviously the wire for the lights—and at the point where the wire reaches the wall and begins its climb up the side of the barn, he slams the spade's blade several times into it, until the wire severs. He is plunged into the safety of darkness. He leaves the generator running. In the dark now, he feels for the little choke again, pulls it to spew more smoke, more fumes, more noise into the barn. This time, he wedges a little piece of wood from the barn floor against the choke lever, to keep the choke on high. To keep the smoke, the fumes, the noise, spewing maximally into the closed barn.

Pork finds the barn's side door wedged shut. He struggles with it uselessly. "Fuck." The old Colonel, the three skinheads—all awake now, all together, all invigorated by the chase—walk once with their flashlights around the barn, a building they don't know, have never been to, and determine that the side door is the best possible entrance.

So they return to it. "Fuck." Big, beefy Dustin rams himself into the door repeatedly, furiously, to no avail. "I could drive my truck into it," he says angrily. But the Colonel holds up his hand, turns, and silently jogs—with a concise, purposeful, military confidence—the hundred yards or so to his own pickup truck. He returns with some heavy screwdrivers. They begin the process of prying the door off its hinges, the dogs barking furiously, annoyingly, around them.

When the door comes off, the skinheads hoot with victory like Indian warriors. The smoke tumbles out. But that hardly deters them.

The dogs rush straight toward the noisy, belching generator—the source of commotion, the logical place to charge to—then stop there for a moment, confused. They smell nothing but smoke. They can hear nothing but the loud, belching machine. Their two acute exploratory senses—smell and hearing—are momentarily useless. Their sullen looks betray that, and their next sense, sight, is as inept in the dark as it is for the men who come up right behind them.

The three skinheads stumbling in on the heels of the dogs are not much different from the animals preceding them. Packed together, plunging forward unthinking, newly motivated by increased proximity to the prize, the increased excitement of the game. They have quickly blocked the door, to not let the Jew escape, and in moments they stand at the generator, alongside the dogs, their flashlight beams eerie—and not much use—in the smoke. The old Colonel, only a little bit slower, is right behind them.

The barn lights are out, but the generator is humming. The light switch must be near the generator, because the Jew must have started the generator to briefly switch on the lights, before switching them off again. They will turn on the lights and find him, hiding somewhere in here. That must be why he turned the lights back off.

Lights off, lights on. Darkness, illumination. People of the darkness, people of the light. The chosen, the unchosen. The children of God, the seed of Satan.

From amid the smoke, a heavy, rusty black object swings and lands against the big, beefy skinhead's skull. It catches him fully, resoundingly, on the side of the skull, and he crumples silently, doll-like—that outsize form, that blustery, ceaseless aggression, so powerfully present until the previous moment, and then so utterly absent in the next.

Before any of them can understand what's happened—as the dogs bark in blind, confused reaction, as the other skinheads and the Colonel turn instinctively amid the generator smoke and noise and thick dark to process what has just occurred—the object lands against the skull of the second skinhead. The force of the spade—the Colonel can make it out this time, a rusty black spade—makes contact with the second skinhead's skull, and his flashlight goes flying into the smoke and across the barn.

The flashlights are like convenient beacons, the Colonel will soon realize, guides in the fog, helping the spade accurately land its blows.

The second skinhead, Pork, the muscled one, staggers a moment, standing stunned—the side of his face in a single stroke a paste of bone and blood and torn flesh—then kneels, then curls to the unforgiving barn floor in anguished moans.

Amid the smoke and darkness and generator noise, they realize there is a small loft above them—its hollow black entrance just above the generator. They hadn't thought to look up—why would they? In the smoke and dark, it just seemed like a low ceiling. And there was no ladder. How did he get up there? He must have pulled the ladder up with him. The clever Jew, hiding in the loft.

The dogs are barking and snapping insanely—frothy, leaping, now pawing at the loft above them.

The Colonel and the third skinhead squint up into the smoke, trying to see into the loft's dark opening.

The third skinhead, Lee, is slower, more deliberate. He pauses a moment longer to comprehend. To take in the suddenness of events. In a moment, he bends down to the generator, finds the emergency shut-off switch, finally turns it off. In the relief from the generator's loud wail and rumble—despite the barking of the dogs, despite the dark—he can at least begin to think. He and the Colonel can at least communicate. The smoke starts to clear but continues to hang in the corner of the barn.

The Jew put himself up there so the dogs couldn't reach him, the skinhead realizes. So none of them could.

And for whatever reason, the Jew was able to function in the smoke. The opening into the loft is narrow and low, the skinhead sees. He realizes it might have kept the smoke out. Maybe there's an opening up there in the siding of the barn that lets in enough fresh air.

So they can't smoke him out. How will they get him out of there?

They could toss a torch up there, drive him out with fire, but the whole wooden barn could ignite, along with all Nick's valuables that are stored in here. Nick might actually kill them—although it was maybe worth Nick's fury to burn the Jew out. Or fire a shotgun up into the floorboards. Although if the loft is full of storage, the Jew could probably get up off the loft floor to protect himself. And if one of them drove off now to find a gun, could the other one hold the Jew up there alone? Because Dustin and Pork are down . . .

These strategies, these fragments of vengefulness crackling through the smallest skinhead's brain, never occur to Pork, the muscled one, who—face bloodied, adrenaline surging—is up off the floor moments later, screaming furious and raw, and who now leaps blindly, impressively, up at the loft's opening. He dangles there for a moment, hanging by his fingers.

Jesus fuck! He's fucking insane! The black spade will land any second on his fingers and break them, Lee knows.

But, inexplicably, the spade doesn't materialize to crush his fingers. Miraculously, the muscled skinhead, fueled by the rush of pure rage, has the chance to pull himself up to a crouched position in the dark loft entrance and takes a step into the ominously quiet loft. Has the Jew already moved defensively to the back of the loft? Is he already cowering rat-like, Jew-like, in the corner?

It happens in the next moment. Even from down here, he and the Colonel can see that the attack doesn't come from the deep blackness in front of the muscled skinhead, where he is looking, where anyone would look. The spade swings at the muscled skin-head unexpectedly from the side.

He staggers back a defenseless step, then falls out of the loft backward. He lands on the barn's dirt floor eight feet below. His shoulders and neck hit first. His body bounces once. Then doesn't move.

The Colonel and the third skinhead stare wordless, paralyzed.

The Jew resisted the temptation of those grasping fingers, Lee realizes. He waited patiently for the skinhead's moment of maximum stupidity. To inflict maximum damage. He waited until the idiot was standing defenseless in the loft door.

>>>>

Rage seeps up in the third skinhead, fills him, replacing the caution inside him with its quickness, its darting, manic, random bounce. Though the barn has gone suddenly quieter—minus the generator, the dogs sniffing now amid the clearing smoke, pausing to concentrate, trying to figuring it out—the chaos is generated from within him now. This old Jew who has done this. This old Jew who has done this out of the smoke and dark and from the safety and invisibility of the loft. Sneaky, unfair, cowering in the shadows like a rat. Just like them. Just like he's always heard about them. So the stories are true. The fury gathers in him, a rage not unfamiliar to him, rage at the injustice and unfairness of the world always in him in a low simmer, but now uncapped. Rage waiting just for this.

He's up there. He can't escape. But they can't get him. God, does he want to pepper the floor of the loft with a shotgun, fire along its length and width.

The dogs continue barking, leaping, frothing.

The beam of the third skinhead's flashlight finally finds the light switch, then shines on the severed electrical line below it. He shines the flashlight along the underside of the loft, following it to the darkest corner of the barn, looking for another entrance, a weak point, to find any way to get at the Jew. Nothing.

He needs to get up high enough to at least see in, to see what he is dealing with up there. Here on the floor of the barn, he can see with his flashlight, there is a piece of furniture, a chest of drawers, positioned several feet back from the generator. Safely out of range of the swinging spade.

Climbing up onto the chest gives him enough angle to shine his flashlight in.

He sees the old Jew's eyes glowing like a rat's caught in the light.

He's out of range of the rusty spade.

But he's well within range of the loft's heavy ladder.

It slides out at him furiously, along the loft floor, at the perfect height to catch him in the neck.

The smallest skinhead is knocked cleanly off the wooden chest, and his head hits the edge of the old generator as he falls.

The ladder is pulled back into the loft several feet. Then it slides down from the loft to the floor. Its top leans against the loft entrance, as it must have originally.

"Christ," says the Colonel, backing away.

He finally materializes from the loft's shadows. He steps halfway down the ladder, facing out, the spade still in one hand. The dogs are barking fiercely, snarling, dancing below him as if beckoned.

Which is exactly what the man in the loft has wanted, apparently. Because he swings the spade hard at the first dog and catches it in the flank. The black dog goes flying. The insult stirs it to even higher paroxysms of rage. The same dog lurches back, yelps, paws up at Peke once, and he catches it with the spade again.

The second dog trots, as if leisurely—and with inarguable intelligence—out of the barn and into the night.

The first one limps out after it.

Partly reluctantly, partly ceremonially, somehow inevitably, the Colonel draws the polished, elegant Nazi dagger from its leather sheath. A Third Reich artifact, more ceremonial than useful, he knows, its handle inlaid with semiprecious stones, an oath to the Führer engraved in its glistening blade. But it will be little use in reaching the Jew holding the rusty spade. The garden tool with an impressive record. Like the reaper's sickle, swung out of the dark. Meting out justice, counting out revenge, in single thudding strokes.

The Colonel holds the dagger up, waveringly, unsure . . .

The Jew takes the last few steps down the ladder, strides toward the Colonel, confident, emboldened, making clear that the Colonel's dagger is of no consequence. The Jew briskly pulls a fabric kerchief down from his mouth. It must have helped protect him from the smoke. In three quick steps, the spade poised defensively, he is opposite the Colonel.

He holds the spade; the Colonel holds the knife. The Colonel tries to figure out how to lunge for him, but the spade seems to give the Jew the irrevocable advantage, keeping the Colonel at a distance.

"You have tangled with a superior species," says the Jew, and the Colonel can hear in the ironic tone of voice that the Jew finds both absurdity and truth in the statement, and means for the Colonel to hear that, too. It sends an extra shudder of fury and fear through the Colonel—he can't separate the two. "Your inferiority will cost you now," says the Jew.

The Colonel lunges and slashes futilely with the dagger.

Slap. The dagger is gone from the Colonel's right hand, and he yelps and grabs at the searing pain in his hand in the wake of its departure. Pain like he's never known.

"How stupid you are," says the voice—its detached, calm tone infuriating, humiliating. "Proving your stupidity so quickly. . ."

And with the pain of his hand still throbbing, still primary, the Colonel becomes aware of the spade at his throat.

"Take off your clothes," says the Jew.

The old Colonel looks at him. He thinks he may not have understood. He is afraid, though, that he has.

"Off. Everything off."

The spade is pressed harder against the Colonel's throat. He feels its rusty edge—smells its life of dirt and dung.

"Spades. Shovels. Ropes. These were my weapons. These were my existence. We caught and ate wild dogs. We trapped and roasted cats. We roped a boar once. I remember all the knots. I remember everything. Undress. Faster." Even being so close, a few feet from the Colonel, it is still a voice in the dark, in the inky barn.

The spade prods the commandant's ribs forcefully, painfully.

"You have unleashed an animal," the voice warns. "And you will not get it back in its cage."

>>>

Nick dials the house from his cell phone. Lets it ring.

"Christ," he says.

"What?" asks LaFarge.

"No answer." He shakes his head. "Looks like those crazy fuckers couldn't wait." He puts the cell phone back on the dash. Looks slightly pained. "I told them to wait." But he seems only slightly annoyed that they disobeyed his order. It seems he half expected it. "Well," he shrugs, "makes things easier."

LaFarge wants to know what he means, but he no longer dares to ask Nick any uninvited questions. He doesn't want to ponder the details of what Nick might say. And thinks maybe Nick doesn't want to either.

>>>

The Colonel is roped and taped to a chair near the center of the barn. Naked.

The skinheads are all tied where they fell. Which ones breathing, which ones not, the Colonel can't tell.

The barn lights are back on. They shine brightly on the Colonel's naked, white body, soaked with nervous perspiration yet shivering in the cold.

A fully uniformed Nazi colonel stands over him.

>>>

He smooths the flanks of the uniform, admires it, feels the ruthless, raw, animal power coursing down his spine, tingling wildly in his ancient balls. He has waited to wear this uniform. Eyed it, desired it, since he was seven.

He banished such thoughts and feelings, forced them down, and then, unable to anymore, at the safe remove of a new land and a new life, began tentatively to read about these urges, to explore them privately, like pornography.

The psychiatrist he finally went to see—just once, in a serene, minimalist office high above Manhattan—merely, but sympathetically, confirmed Peke's speculations. They discussed, like colleagues, Stockholm syndrome—by now a well-documented phenomenon, he was assured. Adapting the beliefs, the mores of the oppressor, the captor, the torturer. Making a complete identification with the aggressor. But Peke resented the dispassionate, academic tone of the articles he had found and the cool, scholarly pronouncements in that sparsely furnished Manhattan office. Even learning that each case is to some degree unique, that each person concocts and suffers his own version, the explanation still fell short for him. It was nothing so simple, he knew. It was nothing with such an easy label. It was, Peke could see, hopelessly more entangled and complex. Tied up with larger subjects. Authority. Belonging. A hunger for order. For deliverance from inexorable chaos.

What is that he feels as he smooths these flanks? As he inhales with pride, in relief that the uniform is finally on him, as he regards and inhabits its utter familiarity and utter strangeness, what does he feel?

He is quite outside himself, yet he still occupies himself. But which self? A new one, or a previous one always lying in wait for this? He is using the uniform for the crafty purposes of survival, for shock, for a lesson, but aren't those all excuses to let this moment fulfill its subtler purpose? A greater, personal, primitive, ineffable purpose?

The psychiatrist steered the discussion to the two absent figures. He could sense the man's eagerness to explore there, a belief in finding hard-won answers there. *They abandoned me to save me. Saved me by abandoning me.* The syllogism that might solve the puzzle at the core of his being. *Saved by being abandoned. Abandoned to be saved.*

He feels the uniform. He loves the uniform. He despises the uniform. Attracted, repulsed, aware of the pornography, unable to resist.

How could he ever share it with Rose? How could he share it with anyone? It is the past that will not be consigned to the past. That refuses to become history. So he has carried his past silently, alone, because it has remained too present.

He has survived. He has survived again, escaped again. How can that be? How is that possible, when so many have not escaped, have not survived? It is unfathomable that he has done it again, that he does so apparently every time. He cannot accept it. He cannot accept the unfairness of it again. The overwhelming unfairness to so many others. To so many millions gone.

This time, he will not escape. He is determined not to escape. He is determined to stay within the fatal loop of his past, the loop his past has evidently confined him to, the dark, closed circle of seventy-two years. The uniform will certainly help assure that he will remain in the past—long enough to get it right? Long enough to triumph? To provide some sort of completion?

He feels only barely in control. Untethered. Unmoored. Cut loose from all logic, reason, civility. It is the animal existence he once knew—unleashed, returned, surging up. The strange physical repetition—the woods, the farmhouse, the barn—is only the surface of it. The sense of precariousness that he knew as a lupine child in the woods and fields—that precariousness, that anarchy—has been reawakened and is as wholly familiar to him as a long-lost friend, and he greets its familiar energy, its addictive drug rush, and fears it as much as anything so far.

"And now," he says, listening to the icy, preternatural calm of his own voice, not knowing exactly whose words, whose thoughts these are, "I can show you the real thing. I can teach you some real Nazi games. Perhaps you've heard of some. I'll bet you haven't, though. Now you get to play them. Just as you've always wanted."

Just as little Stanislaw Shmuel Pecoskowitz has always wanted . . .

The Colonel is taped to the chair identically, in a perfect mirroring, he notices, of the way the Jew was taped not a half hour ago. He watched the Jew wrap each of the skinheads with rope and tape, binding their arms and legs tightly.

Taped to the chair, the Colonel watched it all. He is sure that his watching was the intent.

The Colonel begins to whimper.

"Whimpering is how we begin," the voice says.

>>>

From brutal woods to brutal woods. From persecution to persecution. Has he moved nowhere in more than sixty years? Has he not advanced?

His life has come full circle. And a little bit more, hasn't it?

He remembers the games, he finds. Games that involve fingernails. Toenails. Fifth fingers. Earlobes. The tongue. The tips of ears. Artful scarifications with a knife on white skin. Hearing about them first, boys' holy voices in the dark. And then seeing them played— with, against others—watching from the distance and safety of the darkness, mesmerized, transfixed.

He remembers the games. Buried deep, stored, waiting— whether they only seized and irreparably deformed a childhood imagination, or whether they were observed and suppressed, or whether in some now-indecipherable mixture of the two, here they are, pure, unchanged, recalled, returned to him, summoned up complete like nursery rhymes. His own peculiar nursery rhymes, his own strange childhood games, like songs not sung in a lifetime, and one is amazed to hear oneself sing them first note to last without missing a word or a beat.

He is outside himself. He is someone else. He has stepped whole, weirdly, unnaturally, into the slanted shadows, the opaque blackness of his past, and then beyond it somehow. There is a narrow, pale, small remnant of who he actually is, standing by inert, observing but barely there. Someone else will carry out these duties. Someone, it seems, who has stood by patiently, waiting to carry them out. Someone he doesn't recognize but who has apparently been there all along.

In a part of his brain—a human, reflective part—he knows it is some kind of dissociation, because he senses himself looking on from a distance. Maybe through the distance of time. Maybe through the distance of history. Someone else is taking over from Stanley Peke. And Stanley Peke hardly dares to interrupt.

He can see already, before he even begins: droplets of blood binding in globules, like mercury patterns, on the cold floor of the barn.

Fingernails. Earlobes.

The authentic Nazi experience, with all the trimmings.

He can provide it undiminished, unabbreviated, to the naked, shaking, sobbing man taped to the chair.

The big white truck rolls up to the barn at dawn. Nick makes a quick three-point turn in the dirt—truck ballet—and backs the white beast toward the overhead doors.

LaFarge jumps out, goes behind the truck to unlock and pull open the barn bays.

LaFarge is slightly nervous. He remembers the last time. When the last load suddenly wasn't there. But this time, he notices, the dogs are barking, scampering in the yard as usual when they arrive. Roaming and guarding as they're supposed to be. A sign of normal. He herds them into their pen, the way Nick likes, getting them out from underfoot before they begin unloading.

In a perfectly coordinated effort, as LaFarge is hiking up the first of the barn's overhead doors, Chiv pulls open the rear gates of the white truck.

Four men in black ski masks leap out.

One of them lands on top of Chiv, and Chiv crumples. He is on the ground, in the dusty dirt, almost instantly, and as he struggles to get up, a swift kick to the stomach and then the groin puts him back on the ground.

The dogs howl ferociously, attack the fencing of their pen uselessly.

LaFarge looks around from the overhead door to the truck in time to see a black-ski-masked man coming at him full speed, and there's hardly time to put up his arms to defend or swing before the man's body plows into his. Though LaFarge manages somehow to remain upright for a moment, blows start landing in his solar plexus, swift and hard, and he is down, too, moaning into the dirt, his hands taped behind him in an instant. He doesn't know yet it's with packing tape.

Hearing the dogs' ferocious howling, looking in the driver's side mirror, Nick sees LaFarge go down, a black-hooded figure over him. For a moment, it doesn't seem actual—it's something occurring only in the mirror. He doesn't know what's happening, or how, or why, but he nevertheless responds intuitively, slamming his palm at the truck's big gearshift, gunning the truck forward.

Too late. Another black-hooded figure is already up next to him, as if suspended outside the driver's side window. Still partly mesmerized by the implausibility of events, a half-beat behind in shock, Nick watches the figure pull the cab door open, and—holding the steering wheel, unable to defend himself—Nick watches a boot get pressed against his rib cage, forcing him out of the driver's position and across the truck's bench seat. As Nick reaches to the glove compartment for his gun, the black hood, now fully inside the cab, elbows him hard in the diaphragm. *Uhhh . . . Smart . . . ,* Nick thinks, as he fights for breath, and the man applies the brakes and brings the truck to a stop. Then he kicks Nick—still struggling for oxygen—hard against the passenger door, and somewhat awkwardly pulls handcuffs from his belt behind him, and cuffs Nick to the passenger door's interior handle, before sliding the truck's key out of the ignition. It is he, not Nick, who pops the glove compartment to take the gun he correctly assumed Nick was reaching for.

Al must have been put down, too, Nick thinks vaguely, somewhere along the passenger flank of the truck.

The dogs snap and snarl, howl with frustrated fury.

It is all instantaneous. Over in moments. The advantage of surprise.

And despite its admirable efficiency, Nick senses something loose about it all. It's not a sleek, professional violence. It's more passionate. Like a bottle uncorked. Barroom brawl–ish. Enthusiastic.

And Nick—a tactician even amid this confusion, this disaster—has a single refrain looping in his head, pressing hard against his skull:

How in fuck's name is this happening to me?

38

Days earlier, at his folder-strewn wooden desk in the plant's still-modest back offices, Daniel hung up the phone, stunned.

They've taken him, his mother said. They called to prove they had him. In her voice was a peak of franticness that she was fighting to quell. Attempting to suppress insuppressible thoughts and images. They want their things back, his mother said. That's how they put it. They want their things back.

But even as she was speaking, even as she was whimpering over the phone line, struggling not to break down, to remain at least coherent, even as Daniel was processing the fact that she had finally picked him to call, as had his father, each unbeknownst to the other—even as Daniel was trying to allay her fears and feeling his own fears forming, even as he was on the verge of tears himself, thinking of it—*my father, after all he has suffered and survived*—even with all of it, the plan was already forming in his head.

They want their things back. So they'll come in their truck, reasoned Daniel.

He gets up from his desk, heads down to the loading dock.

Grady. Where's Grady?

He passes, as he walks along the loading dock, dozens of the immigrants working there, a haphazard UN, their workforce a rough-hewn experiment in discord and harmony, a spicy human stew, rough and tumble, as such men generally are. A hiring practice begun by his father—in sympathy, in connection—and a tradition continued by Daniel. He has transformed the business, but hasn't altered the philosophy.

Daniel finds Grady, pulls him aside. They kidnapped the old man, Daniel tells him. They called my mother. And if they smell police, he's dead. Crazy fuckers, they're coming to get everything again.

Quietly: I need you to go again. To take a truck again. But this time, it won't be our truck.

Grady looks at Daniel, waiting for more.

And this time, there's going to be a fight.

Grady doesn't flinch. Seems, if anything, a notch more interested.

You don't have to do it, says Daniel. Knowing that it's the only way he can think of. The only way there is.

You'll hide in the back of their truck, Daniel explains. Jump in the back when they've finished loading, when they're in my parents' house, making a last sweep. My mother will help you. She'll know. It's the only way we can find out where they're keeping my father. It's probably the same place you were, but might not be. This guy is careful, a planner, pretty sharp. He may have other places, other hideouts. And we can't risk being wrong.

Grady shrugs. It's cold enough out, he says. We won't melt like Mexicans crossing the border. We'll stretch out on the furniture. Bring battery lanterns. Radios. Relax. Grady's blue eyes twinkle. He gives a quick bravado smile.

Who do you want? asks Daniel.

My same crew, says Grady.

You want more? Take more.

Grady thinks a moment. Maybe Avi, he says.

Daniel looks at Grady for a moment. The hothead Israeli? The most erratic personality on the loading floor? Compounding risk with risk?

Then again, no one's more ready for a fight.

Sure, Daniel says. Take Avi.

The crew decided, Daniel is already on to other things. Logistics. Timing. Not thinking about Avi or the others anymore, but about the plan.

>>>

At the same time that LaFarge and Chiv have been put to the dirt and Nick has been cuffed to the truck's passenger door, another figure in a black ski mask hikes open the overhead barn door that LaFarge had just finished unlocking. Traveling in moments from the darkness of the truck bed to the sudden daylight of the Montana morning, and now into the barn's deep interior dark, the black-ski-masked, charging figure at first has difficulty seeing.

But as his eyes adjust, there is little doubt about what he sees.

The sight penetrates his experience, awakens his history, nauseates him.

There is an old man bent in a chair, naked, and a Nazi in full uniform standing over him.

Avi stares, thunderstruck.

The loading-dock joke is that Europe couldn't handle him, so he went to Israel. Then Israel couldn't handle him, so he came to them.

Daniel, son of a survivor, student of survivorship, sees it differently:

There are three kinds of survivors. There's the Stanley Peke kind. Who arrive with nothing and remake themselves from nothing, succeed on determination and intelligence and sheer will, make you believe anew in the power of the human spirit, in the triumph of man. Walking miracles.

The second kind—no less remarkable, in a way—arrive with their old-world crafts and old-world beliefs and set up shop and set up house and continue their lives as if nothing has happened, as if there's been no upheaval, no rupture at all. There was a jeweler in the town he grew up in—Itzhak something, his father knew him—who was that kind of survivor.

But the third kind of survivor. The third kind never again find who they are. Never regain their footing. Spend their days and nights lost, adrift. Furious at what has been taken, angry at the universe that has robbed them, trying to get even. Lurching desperately from difficulty to difficulty, place to place. Trying to find an existence. The congenitally lost. The severed. Avi is one of those. So Daniel takes him in. As he has seen his father do. He will try to help whomever, though this third kind of survivor is a far different proposition than the other two. Orphaned Avi, who lost all four grandparents and numberless aunts and uncles and cousins in the camps, and then lost his destitute settlement parents—scraping a refugee existence from the desert land—to a Syrian raid in the months before the '67 war. Daniel thinks about Avi's parents—cast off from a continent penniless to meet extermination on another continent a generation later. Avi, who has stayed lost. Drifting in and out of a succession of menial jobs—grocery clerk, bike delivery boy, landscaping crew—lasting only weeks at a time, until some fistfight or other infraction ends it. Daniel can't begin to know what that is like. He can at least try to help. Who would he be if he didn't try?

It is like a rip in the fabric of time. Like a living exhibit in a perverse museum. Or an incriminating snapshot stumbled onto in a raid. Or a painting, its dramatic, self-conscious interplay of light and dark, its admirable fidelity to the past, evident in its detail—the authenticity of the dagger, the naked torso's glistening sheen. A moment of capture, a captured moment—the uniformed Nazi and the prisoner both looking up, united in their surprise, actors in the same drama, their performance intruded upon, their script interrupted.

Time is stopped, suspended, but emotion is propelled headlong. Revulsion. Shock. All the immediate feeling the painter surely intended. The scene is magically static. But the emotion it produces tumbles and screams, bounces and sears.

Avi feels his fury surge. He knows his own fury well, and though it has been his continual adversary, it has also been his constant companion.

He has the knife. It is for self-defense, they've said, but he has it, and from the moment he has held it, it has felt comfortable, has felt right. And he is in his black ski mask, unrecognizable, worn to give them all the element of surprise and the aura of terror, worn to free them up for any action necessary, but the point is, no one knows who he is.

And here is a Nazi. A Nazi torturing an old man.

He sees the dagger sheathed in the Nazi's uniform. Technically, it is knife for knife, but the dagger is nothing, he knows. Avi is faster, stronger, than the old Nazi.

History has cursed him. Now it offers him sly redemption.

History has abused and humiliated him. Now he can get even with it.

You've been a fuckup all your life. Here's your chance at last.

All of it in a mere beat, a single pulse. Almost instant.

We're commandos, they'd said quietly into the blackness, sprawled on the moving blankets they'd pulled off the furniture, arranged in the back of the truck. Repeating it into the dark, a half joke, but only half, a mantra to summon their own bravery. Taking leaks in the dark into the empty bottles of soda they'd already drunk.

At a certain point, Grady's cell phone had gone out. They'd lost touch with Daniel. We're out of cell range, Grady had told them. It means we're getting close.

Yes, a commando. With a black mask and knife.

Crouched, sharklike, unthinking, a honed weapon in human trim . . .

And now he draws his knife and presses forward to a swift, silent justice . . .

To reach its blade across a generation. Across history. A small, quiet retribution across time.

"Do it now!" the naked man screams—all his suffering of the past hours, the past night, rolled, apparently, into a single note of retaliation.

As Avi draws back his knife, the Nazi officer starts to recite it softly.

Maybe he means it to be too soft to hear.

Avi will wonder about that, in rooming houses, on loading docks to come. He will reflect on it, sitting alone in bars, stretched out on benches in closed city parks at night, staring up at the stars.

Because it will seem so unlikely to him, ruminating on it years from now, that he—who never listens, never hears, who his whole life has been accused of paying no attention—should hear it. Oh, it will eventually make at least some sense to him: to experience at that intense moment a hyperalertness, a heightened receptivity of the five senses, that a mammal—a man, in this case—discovers access to, on decisive, life-and-death occasions. He will learn eventually that it is an effect well documented by those in certain lines of work—mercenaries, rescue workers, emergency personnel, Special Forces soldiers in close combat. Human beings in extreme situations.

But the question will remain. Did the old man in the uniform intend him to hear it? Or intend him not to? He will never know.

But Avi does hear it.

"Shema yisrael, Adonai eloheinu, Adonai echad." Little more than a whisper.

And Avi looks into the uniformed Nazi's eyes—black, liquid, floating, warm, he will reflect. As he will remember the uniformed Nazi looking back into his own eyes, isolated and exposed in his black ski mask.

He has never practiced his own religion. In truth knows little about it. He knows his own rage at what it has cost him, knows its ultimate cost to two generations of his family and therefore to his life. But the actual religion itself has played no role in his upbringing. His own life has been entirely secular, nonobservant. Taken up with arguments with neighbors and bosses, fights with landlords and lovers, with recklessness and insolence, with the difficulties of living.

But though he knows nothing of his own religion, he does know that.

It is the prayer of Jews at the moment of death. A declaration of faith at the moment of expiring.

Tears well up. Tears he didn't think he possessed after all that has happened to him, after the tangle and tumble and harshness of his life. Tears that run from those black exposed eyes down his cheeks, beneath the black ski mask.

Thank God he knows that stupid fucking prayer.

He feels his right hand shudder for a moment, involuntarily. The hand holding the knife. An uncontrollable physical shudder, from somewhere beyond him, a shudder sent from the past. A shudder of consolation and retribution, of righteousness and evil, rolled into one.

He straightens. Breathes deep once. Pivots. Steps toward the naked man taped to the chair.

The rest of his crew are still occupied outside. He is fully aware of the figures on the floor, as he is somehow aware that they are of no consequence.

No one will see except the two of them: the Survivor wearing the Nazi uniform, and the naked Nazi whose uniform it is.

You are the people of darkness. We are the people of the light. The ugly children of Satan, the chosen children of Adam . . .

He holds the knife to the naked man's throat.

He looks at the Survivor.

Who looks back at him, and turns away . . .

To some other place, some other world.

With a single, clean, fluid stroke, Avi slashes the naked man's throat.

>>>

When the overhead door had opened and the light had flooded in and Stanislaw Shmuel Pecoskowitz had turned to see the charging, black-hooded figure, he had known it was the devil's messenger. An angry God's emissary. His escort to hell, here at last. He'd been expecting this, in some form or another, all his life, and he stood fascinated, momentarily transfixed.

He had discovered he could not do it. Could not, would not, go through with the Nazi games. He had every intention. He had started. Taken off an earlobe, held its softness in his fingers. He'd begun with that, knowing that it hardly hurt to lose an earlobe, caused relatively little pain, but it would have the requisite shock value, the desired effect, to hold it in front of the victim, as a starting point. *I guess you hear me now. I guess I have your ear now.* The shock of flesh: a little test for the victim, and the perpetrator, too.

And there, something had stopped him.

He doesn't know what, exactly. He will never know. The Colonel's terrified screams as he approached, which were after all only screams of anticipation? Maybe a sudden sense of futility, of uselessness, in holding that small piece of flesh? Or simply some sudden realness of events—some wave, some assault of actuality, of the here and now? The vivid realness of the past days and hours, after being so long without it.

Or simply his life, he will think later. Its comforts, its pleasures, its vistas, its minutenesses, its dailyness, its ironies, its tenor, its confusions, seeping into him steadily, inevitably, over the past sixty years. Its continual washing up against previous events like cool, clean water flowing over a hard rock. Smoothing the edges into a new shape, barely recognizable.

Or Rose. Maybe it was simply his Rose.

Whatever the reasons, he can't do it. The fingernails, the toe-nails, the scarifications, any of it. Each time he approaches the naked Colonel, knife drawn, intent, he finds he cannot. Can't, or won't. (He knows he will never be able to sort out the difference, the relationship between the two.) Although the Colonel, perma-nently shivering with cold and fright, seems sure Peke will pull away each time holding another piece of him, Peke discovers that he can't—but notices that he nevertheless retains his threat.

Anticipation. He knows its power. Thinking in some sense all his life that they would come for him at any moment. Living a lifetime with hot breath at the back of his neck.

Anticipation. The fear of what's coming, which can be as ter-rifying, as effective, as what does eventually come.

Which is when it occurs to him. Something much simpler and more apt. Something that lets him move away from the Colonel, move back, makes any of his actions seem purposeful, pointed. Something that gives him the time, the reason to continue to wear the uniform. To experience, to understand the urge. And maybe to feel the lessening of its effects, of its aura, by familiarity with it, by the steady loss of its allure.

Something more satisfying. Perhaps by being more insidious.

"Dawn," he says to the Colonel simply—a single word, leaning forward, serving it up on a pleasant little smile. "Dawn."

No light penetrates the barn. And as dawn approaches, he can even throw a tarpaulin over the Colonel's head. A sensory deprivation, so the Colonel will not know when dawn arrives. Can only . . . anticipate.

Precisely what the Colonel and the skinheads inflicted on Peke only hours before, as they had been marking time until Nick's return, waiting for the appointed moment, the permission to unleash. The marking of time, the excruciating ticking of the clock, now turned neatly back on the Colonel.

"Dawn," he repeats to the Colonel as he walks by him.

The implication clear. An appointment with mortality. A long military tradition of such appointments, thinks Peke in his uniform. And no one knows military tradition like the Colonel.

Dawn. Meaning night for you, Colonel. Eternal night.

Dawn. A beginning that means the end. An irony of the spheres. The misty meeting point of day and night. *You are the people of the darkness, and we are the people of the light.* Oh yes? Then we'll meet in the middle, rendezvous at dawn, when it is something else—not day, not night, not darkness, not light, but both and neither, inextricably . . .

He secures the ties on the neo-Nazis. Climbs up and lies down in the catwalk loft. And mutters the word as if under his breath, as if with pleasurable anticipation, within earshot of the Colonel:

"Dawn."

When we fulfill tradition.

Having no clear sense, of course, what dawn will actually bring.

And wishing—vaguely, uselessly—that dawn will bring some kind of dawn for him.

>>>>

And through that strange, fractured night in the barn, up through roiling floodwaters of memory released by the night's events and by the barn itself, it surfaced. It loomed up, rendered visible at last in the contrast provided by this reliving, the contrast between this time and that time, this barn and those barns, between now and then. A tiny darkness that had plagued him, inexorable but unnameable. The little black secret that had torn at him for more than sixty years, gnawed at him across a lifetime:

It was fun.

For a seven-year-old boy, pure exhilaration. No rules, no laws, no conventions, no boundaries, the rule only of stark feeling and brute impulse. A rawness, an impulsiveness of existence. Every morsel a feast. Every sip a coursing pleasure. Every moment pure excitement, an adrenaline thrill, a boy's wild dream. Existence itself as a never-ending game. *Fun.* God, what fun! Induplicable. But how could you tell the stylish guests in a chandeliered room it was fun? How could you tell guests in a chandeliered room—or your sweet, smiling child in your lap, or your wife curled snug against you in bed—that it had been fun? That the violence, the passion, the surprise, the energy, had galloped through you every moment. How could you describe the rush of feeling—the exhilarating confusion, the wild pound of blood—when that old guard strolled beneath the underpass and you and Abel dropped the stone? Watching the old guard crumple instantly, silently, into a puddle of coat and backpack and boots and gun. A perfect hit. A stunned exhilaration coursing through your seven-year-old body. A shock of elation that a seven-year-old body isn't built for. The suddenness of power, the momentary reversal of all your weakness and fear. Delivering a mortal blow from above. Godlike.

How could he explain that? Killing when there was no threat, killing for no reason. How that had been some of the best fun of all?

Abel had been shot the next day. Unceremoniously. No warning. An impulsive round fired by a frustrated sergeant, fed up with these ragamuffins, these trash-bin scavengers. A single bullet, while Abel's wild young companion looked on.

There the fun had ended.

And the two events—the stone dropped from the bridge, his friend's execution—had linked into perfect justice in the mind of a seven-year-old. Perfect justice, retribution swift and precise. The truest evidence of Nazi power: to render justice in even the darkest forgotten corner, even to little boys. Oh, they were powerful. Oh, they were righteous. Oh, he longed for that power.

The simple psychology of the seven-year-old: *I want that. I want what they have.* But attached to what a seven-year-old should never have to attach it to. Should never have to know in a lifetime, much less live by hour to hour. Life. Death. Oh, to control life and death like that, in warm uniforms and shiny boots.

And then to drop the stone off the bridge—challenging, undermining, the very power you crave. In that victorious instant, to experience triumph yet suffer shame, and then a swift, godly seeming retribution—all packed together in a single drop of the stone. A stone dropped off a bridge. A universe falling into a void.

As he lies there in the dark barn, pondering those stark boyhood joys and their stark ending, the games come floating back to him. Not the Nazi games. Boys' games. A world of games that ended only with the game of the stone. Games of aggression and dominion and camaraderie and trust and testing that boys play. With one twist. Playing them for real. *Go out in the woods and play. Go play, keep playing, don't come back.* His mother's final instruction. Her last words, with meaningful looks, to her dutiful son. *Go out in the woods and play and don't come back.*

But he disobeyed. Disobeyed his mother's explicit instructions and went back. In a few days wound his way back, with a boy's growing competence in the woods.

Entered stealthily from the backyard bramble. Moved cautiously around to the front of the stone farmhouse. Stepped up the familiar rough-hewn stone front steps to the stone-and-timber landing. Stepped over the shards of glass from the broken windows. Stepped in through the wide-open front door, its wooden panels smashed. Looked numbly at the casually burned interiors. Regarded the patterns of black char.

There was nothing there. The young boy understood. Everything of value had been taken. The paintings. The silver. The objects and possessions of his parents' pride. He knew what those were. And saw they were gone. He experienced not disbelief at what had happened, so much as a wholesale evaporation of the idea of believing. He had entered a realm of dream, and he had the sense—even then, as a seven-year-old boy—that to some degree, he would never leave it.

He walks, of course, down the dark hallway to his bedroom. He steps over the shattered lamp—the lamp in whose flickering light his mother once removed a deep splinter, freeing him suddenly from pain. He glides past a broken hallway table—the little round chestnut table where the family left each other notes and jokes and riddles. He runs his finger along the hallway wall as he always has, but this action from before does not restore anything from before, nor does it help to tether him to the ground. He is floating. He is disconnected from himself. Taking exactly the same steps that a little boy who once lived in this house took, but he is someone else, someone ancient, coming to look, temporarily retracing a little boy's footsteps.

The bed is upended. The toys are scraped from the toy shelf in what is clearly a single, summary motion. The clothes have been taken in a single armful from the narrow closet and tossed onto the floor. He is surprised that they have found his little sanctuary at the end of the hall. He had always thought it was safely hidden, tucked away, forgotten even by his parents. It will occur to him later that they were only there looking for valuables—salable treasures that the clever, deceitful Jews might have hidden in a child's room. He will understand later that such searching is why the bed's mattress is so brutally punctured. But that is not what the seven-year-old boy thinks then, seeing all the mattress's wounds. He thinks it is him they are looking for. Hoping to puncture him. Stabbing at his ghost.

His home is gone, his parents are gone, his toys are broken, his bed is upended. But those facts aren't separate from one another. Home, mother, father, room, bed: it is all the same thing to a seven-year-old. All tendrils of security, of being, of one's place in the world. Home, mother, father, toys, things: all hopelessly inextricable and intertwined, all lost together. Everything, gone. Everything in his life—except his life.

It happened early to them, he would later learn. His family was among the first. It was perhaps a local, specific vendetta—he would never know, of course. Yet his mother had anticipated it, had powers of intuition. Perhaps that was her legacy, his only inheritance: an intuition for survival.

He stood alone in the ruined, looted house. (His feral friends, a couple of years older, had hung back, afraid of ghosts or some kind of spooky contagion.) He felt life shift inside him as profoundly, as suddenly, as his life had externally changed. He can't articulate—even to this day—precisely what that change was. But he felt it. Felt its rearrangement even physically.

Had he misunderstood? Had he played too long? Had he missed her call to come home? *Go out in the woods and play and don't come back.* He had heard her say it, but he now doubted that was what she had said. It seemed impossible now, too unlikely, and yet the words rang in his head. And he had gone out in the woods and played the games so long that the games had become real.

Uniformed men. The empty house. It had happened to him before.

But he never saw the uniformed men. He never saw the truck they loaded. He never saw his parents again.

Gone, swept violently off the shelf of existence, packed up and carted off as if with their belongings, as if along with the valuables, with the items he was always instructed not to touch.

What is all this, really, here in the woods of Montana? Seeking a second justice for Abel? Seeking a second justice for himself? Or merely, futilely, seeking a resolution that can never come?

>>>

In a moment, he knows what it is that has come charging into the barn.

No supernatural emissary. No divine escort.

It is simply the world. The world beyond the barn. The world as always. Here to save him. Here to imprison him again.

The Shema. The prayer by which they died. The prayer by which he lived.

Bursting into the barn moments later, the blue-eyed, black-ski-masked leader drops his backpack of bottled water, flash-lights, half-eaten sandwiches, Dramamine. He rips off the ski mask. Reaches deep into the backpack, pulls out a satellite phone, and dials.

"Got him," says Grady. His familiar Irish lilt, in just those two words.

Never more sparkling or twinkling, thinks Daniel on the other end.

"And he's OK?" Daniel pleads, heart beating, breathing labored, back muscles like broad arcs of pain, they are so tense. "He's OK?" Asking again, to be sure he's been heard as the signal bounces across the sky, to be sure he can believe the response.

Grady looks around. Takes in the scene. Considers a moment. Sees now that they have some work to do. A few things to take care of. They will need a vehicle to get out. He sees immediately that the blood is fresh, and knows that Avi did it, and can tell by Avi's silence and shrugging stance that Avi plans to say nothing, to imply—or say outright, if forced to say—that the man was dead already. Avi has upped the stakes, hasn't he? It doesn't surprise Grady. It doesn't unnerve him. Grady is up to it. He welcomes it. All the better. But he doesn't mention any of this to Daniel. Nor does he mention the German uniform. Why confuse the moment?

"Yes," says Grady, in his twinkling Irish lilt. "Yes, your old man's OK."

The local police, having received an anonymous and suspiciously well-informed tip, will two hours later find a black man and two white men arrayed in the dirt around the truck, their wrists and ankles bound with packing tape. They will find a barn filled with stolen goods. They will find blood on the barn floor but no figures to attach it to. They will reasonably suspect bodies somewhere on the compound, but how would they ever find them? One hundred fifty acres of Montana scrub. How could they even begin to search it?

For the next two years, they will field calls from insurance companies and small police departments across the country. Rich little enclaves that they never knew existed. They will be busy, so busy they will grow somewhat resentful, but that will be tempered by their reception as heroes, which they will find absurd and ironic, since they were simply responding to a phone call from someone with some kind of English accent whom they will never meet and never see. Their investigation into whoever made that call—which they can't trace and therefore assume was a satellite phone—will go nowhere.

They will know immediately of the disappearance of three local skinheads, troublemakers they'd been watching anyway. One of the skinheads' beat-up pickup trucks is gone. Maybe they drove it into the gorge. Maybe they've skipped town. Maybe there was some conflict between the skinheads and one of the local militias. Some white-supremacy dispute settled among themselves. That wouldn't much surprise the local police. That wouldn't surprise anyone. No one will be too upset if they rid the world of each other. In any case, there is never much motivation to find them.

The empty handcuffs in the moving truck will always intrigue them. Not because of how whoever was in them got out of them. That was obvious. The crowbar must have been kept under the bench seat, and that must have done the job, though not without considerable pain. But what happened to whoever was in them. His name was Nick Pelletiere, according to the black man and the two white men. But what happened to him, they couldn't say. Their own faces had been put into the dirt. They couldn't see. They didn't know. Probably wouldn't ever know. Because if Nick escaped, the black one pointed out from his holding cell, he wasn't about to contact any of his old crew anytime soon.

Wrists searing with pain, the left one broken, he thinks, stomach still knotted and burning from the blow, Nick trots, bent over, toward the woods. The pain rips through him, encases both hands, climbs up his forearms, shoots rampantly around his body.

His timing, though, is perfect. Through the truck's rearview mirror, he watched the black-ski-masked leader heading into the barn, then saw the other black ski masks enter the barn a few moments later, probably called by the leader, at which point Nick—simmering in pain, pain so great he is fighting to stay conscious, but now with a chance, a chance—slipped down from the cab of the truck.

Now, he ducks into the woods. The foliage hides him momentarily. He has made it to the woods, knows the temporary safety of the tree line, where he stops for a moment to breathe and to assess.

He looks back. He sees it all. Everything. Everything he has, everything that's his, in the middle distance behind him. The truck. The barn. The crummy house. The thousand objects inside them.

Everything is gone now. Everything has been suddenly taken from him. He hasn't even got a wallet or a dollar of cash. Nothing. He has nothing. He is starting over. But he can do it. He will limp, tramp through the woods to the roadway. He will commandeer or sweet-talk his way into a ride. He will reach Freedom Café. He will make it. He will live.

Peke is standing outside the barn when he hears the barking suddenly intensify and sees the dogs' noses jerk in their pen. Exhausted from the long night, he has been waiting out here, as instructed by Grady, who is in the barn with the others, attending to whatever it is that he doesn't want Peke to see. So Peke has been watching the dogs, listening to them bark at him in frustration, in misery, still out of their reach. He has been vaguely pondering the dogs' possible fates, for no matter how fearsome, they are innocent creatures, after all. And then the barking intensifies and their noses shift. Something—some movement, some smell detected by these highly tuned black machines—has triggered it. He remembers hearing the soldiers' dogs in their pens. Learning to tell if they had heard you or not. If it was you they heard, or something else.

Peke trots around the corner of the barn in time to see the movement of the trees and tall grasses across the muddy expanse. In time to see a brown jacket moving against the green. In time to see the thief, hunched over, scurrying awkwardly into the woods.

At the moment, his rescuers are all occupied inside the barn. If he goes into the barn to tell them, to get their help, it will give the thief too much of a lead. Peke will lose sight of him. The thief will get away.

Peke can see the spot where the thief ducked into the woods. Peke heads after him.

»»»

Nick stumbles on, bent over, awkward, but less dizzy, he notices, his various pains settling into a steady pulse now. He stops for a moment, listens, hears nothing.

Through the pain, he feels a moment of relief. A vague satisfaction, stronger at the moment than any regret. He is going to make it. He is going to make it out of here.

His wrists still sear, they are still on fire, but he finds he is somehow adjusting to it. He feels again the cold, rough iron of the crowbar against his wrists. He is like a dog, he thinks, chewing its leg off to escape a trap.

His abdomen still cripples him with deep swaths of pain. He is still doubled over. But he turns and stumbles on.

The old man must be dead in the barn. That must be what the black ski masks discovered. He has little doubt that the skinheads—impatient, frenzied, insane—finished off the old man. The black ski masks must be dealing with the skinheads now, probably more brutally than they dealt with Nick and his crew. Because now—if they've discovered the old man dead—their response is propelled by revenge.

Nick keeps moving, heading deeper into the woods. He starts to think about water, and food, and the cold temperature. *Good. Beginning to think like a survivor.* Thinking about these woods, in order to make it out of them.

The woods are marshy, swampy underfoot. There is a smell that hovers between fetid and sweet. He stumbles on.

»»»

Peke feels himself fly over the wet earth and packed leaves, fly past the black and gray tree trunks. He has not been in or moved through woods like this for over sixty years. Of course, he has occasionally hiked a manicured trail with his wife. Played a game of hide-and-seek with his children in a tame local wooded park, walked in a hundred yards to see their elaborate stick forts, to see the handiwork of their imaginations. But those were not woods like this—wild and vast, directionless and dense. He has not run through woods like this since he was seven. Woods where now, once again, life and death are in the air.

He moves lithely. He surprises himself. He slips through unknown woods that nevertheless feel familiar. The woods where he began. The woods where he survived.

He is a child again. He feels Abel beside him. More than that. He can practically see Abel's spirit next to him. But of course—Abel's spirit has never left the woods. It has stayed here for more than sixty years, waiting for scrawny, clever little Pecoskowitz to rejoin him. He runs with Abel. He feels Abel next to him. In him.

And what will he do when he finds the thief? Is this some ultimate test of his humanity? Some final test of his being? A chance to rectify, to correct, in some broad way? But what is the rectification? What is the correction? He knows now there are limits to what he'll do. And the seven-year-old wolf child in him knows—instinctually—that such limits pose an intense disadvantage.

And something else the wolf child knows, something else beneath expression: he's been permitted to experience survival. To experience it again. But you are not permitted it indefinitely.

All of it charges dimly through his mind as he runs.

In a few minutes, he stops. Listens. Hears nothing. His pounding heart, his invigorated chest and torso, nevertheless feel pressed in by dejection and defeat.

He suppresses his own heavy breathing for a moment, to listen again. He hears it now. Off to the right. Maybe fifty yards away. The awkward scrape of brush. He can tell it's the scraping, the awkward movement, that results from injury. He can hear it is the scrape, the movement, of desperation. He can hear it. He can feel it. Like being attuned to the weakness of prey. Fifty yards through the woods. He moves lightly, silently.

»»»

Nick struggles through the woods, and in a terrain where thick layers of leaves cover tree roots and stumps and fallen branches, he trips on a stump and falls. In his extreme state of pain, the tripping and falling—which would otherwise be nothing—is a major event. He cries out involuntarily. He hears his own crying out echoing around him, and echoing in his head. The fresh pain threatens his consciousness, flirts and plays with it. He finds himself on his knees, clenching his stomach. He is sickly, woozily aware of the soaking, marshy ground less than a foot in front of his eyes. His hands sink into it. It fills his senses.

He waits a moment there, gathering his senses and his strength. He pushes himself, like a rising hero, up off the ground, manages to straighten, and looks ahead.

There is a soldier in a uniform—a formal, old war uniform—standing ten feet in front of him.

Nick sucks in his breath in startlement.

Amid his pain, he blinks to focus.

It is the old man.

»»»

Last seen taped to the chair. After that, Nick only imagined him. Only vaguely. Not vividly enough. Not as vividly as now. The uniform is only the most obvious difference about him, Nick senses a moment later. Something in the old Jew has changed. He is livelier.

Energized. Is it the uniform, or the woods, or both that have brought this new aliveness into the old Jew? The old man's eyes stare at Nick from somewhere else.

Nick watches those eyes travel coldly, appraisingly around Nick's face and body. Taking an inventory of Nick's injuries, Nick can see. Nick remains hunched over in abdominal pain. His face is creased with his anguish. There is no hiding his injuries from the old man.

The old Jew holds a long stick at his side. A staff that seems as natural, at home, in the old man's fist as the old man somehow seems in these woods. In that strange, old military uniform—like a ghost or creature that has inhabited these woods forever.

Both are aware of the shift. Peke, the hunted, is now the hunter. Nick, the hunter, is now the hunted. Both can see awareness of the shift, of the reversal, in the other's eyes. This reversal creates a kind of balance to events, presaging some sort of conclusion. Both know the end of the story is near.

Something primal will take place here. Something above words, or beneath them. So nothing is said. Whatever happens now, though neither knows what that will be, both know that words are superfluous.

>>>

He feels as if he has ceased to exist. As if he has died, and returned as a mythological creature. A dybbuk from Jewish myth, roaming the woods. But he is a unique creature of modern mythology. Half-Nazi, half-Jew.

He stands in front of Nick. Physically and symbolically blocking Nick's motion in any direction.

He begins to move around him as if around prey. Aware of that sense of it. He imagines that Nick senses it that way, too.

Nick is panting. Still gasping deeply from the fall, from the wounds, from the pain; from the searing wrists, the left one probably broken, judging by the angle of it; from the blows to the abdomen.

Peke, in contrast with the heavy panting and gasping, is preternaturally silent.

They both listen to Nick's gasping, his labored breathing.

A thief, he thinks, looking at Nick. A particularly cunning and adept one, but nothing more than a thief. Through some obsession, some compulsion, this thief took Peke's things, and Peke was clever and determined enough to get them back.

A thief is low in the order of things. A thief is hungry. It is a hunger of some sort. Peke has known hungers, too.

But then the thief took Peke. Tied him to a chair, rendered him chattel, a slave, to negotiate his precise value with Peke's wife, to terrify her with the tactic. Was it still mere thievery to the thief? Or was it then about vengeance? Was it then about teaching the Jew a lesson? Understanding it or not, the thief put himself into a deeper alliance with evil.

Peke feels all his civility, all his rationality, still pushing at him from some neat, organized place within him, despite this charged moment, despite the forces now unleashed, like ghosts and spirits suddenly alight in the woods.

He feels all his rationality, his understanding about the thief seeking vengeance, the clear logic of the argument. But all that rationality and understanding seems irrelevant amid the ghosts.

He begins to sense it is not the thief who is caught out here in the woods. It is him.

>>>>

It's lying there in the leaves, Nick knows, just a few feet away. It's long enough, thick enough. It's closer to him than the old man is.

Nick knows it's there—right there—because he is meant to survive. The sticks, the downed branches that cover the floor of the woods— one tripped him; this one will free him.

He senses, from the old man's moving around him from several yards away, a hesitancy, the old man's lack of a plan, and Nick's street-kid instincts tell him to capitalize on that indecision.

Nick lunges for the stick and straightens against his abdominal pain, and now stands armed. Nick—racked with pain, but much younger and much stronger than the old man. Cornered, but with clearer purpose.

It is now some mechanism deeper than consciousness. Nick feels no hesitancy, no confusion. For Nick, it is survival. That's the difference between them here. That's what the old man hasn't calculated, hasn't understood. Maybe the old man has confused this with some other time, some other event—certainly the uniform indicates that. But this is now. It's this event. And here, now, it's a matter of Nick's survival—not the old man's.

Brandishing the stick, swinging it warningly, Nick begins to move around the old man, edging steadily toward the deeper woods that the old man had blocked. The old man backs up a couple of steps. Nick sees, feels, an invisible corridor opening to him. A path to freedom. But the street kid in him senses that the path still leads over the old man.

It has all caught up with him as suddenly as he's caught up with the thief. The weariness, the exhaustion, seem as sudden as an ambush. Running through the woods, everything felt the same, but everything felt different, too. The night in the barn has worn him down. The effort of survival. The peeling, raw layers of memory. And what exactly is he doing here? What course of action does he have? Trying to block the thief's escape indefinitely? Trying to lead the thief back? He won't, can't, do more than that. The quotient of violence is already so high.

Running through the woods, Peke has felt himself shuttling oddly, uncontrollably, between his seventy-two-year-old and his seven-year-old selves. He knows it's some sort of collapse, some sort of melding that has waited for so long, the pressures of his stoicism, the pressures of his memory, folding in on themselves, but recognizing such a collapse doesn't mean he can control it. It is some kind of integration—or disintegration. Some kind of final tumbling-out . . .

He is weary. He is done. He wants rest. He is no longer seven. That sensation of seven was momentary, fleeting. He is seventy-two. Maybe he's survived enough. Maybe it's someone else's turn to survive.

He holds the stick up, but purposelessly.

Weary, exhausted, foggy, unsure, he wants to lower it, drop it at his side. Let him go.

》》》

It's at that moment—when Nick might limp on and Peke might watch him go—that they both hear the dogs.

Those stupid fucking dogs, thinks Nick.

Someone opened the pen. Someone was smart enough to let them out of the pen, smart enough to put them onto the trail. The dogs will lead the black masks right to Nick. Nick can tell, by the frantic barking, that they have picked up the scent already, maybe Nick's, maybe the old man's, either way giving Nick away. They're closing—maybe a quarter mile off, he'd guess by the sound.

He can't outrun his own dogs. So he can't outrun the black masks following them. He's seen enough of the black masks' violence to predict what will happen when they arrive here. He knows what happens when bloodlust is unleashed like that.

He knows what he would do if he were the black masks.

Only then does he realize: his dogs will arrive ahead of the black masks. Far enough ahead for Nick to have an option: to turn the dogs on the old man. Only Nick knows the command drilled into the dogs by that crazy off-the-grid skinhead who trained them behind his broken-down trailer. When the old man broke into the farmhouse, Nick wasn't there to deliver the command. But he's here now. Nick, from amid his pain, feels himself smile.

Peke hears the dogs' barking grow closer.

The wolf child in him knows how the dogs rely on scent. How they recognize and respond to it. When the skinheads first let the dogs inside to circle and snap at his chair, maybe they remembered his scent, and the sweet special meat he'd brought them, and maybe were waiting for more. But since then, they've been unleashed to chase him through the night. Since then, he has swung at them with the spade, caught one in the flank, sent both whimpering and scurrying. They barked frantically, leaped furiously at him against their pen as he waited for Grady to finish in the barn. What will they do now? Which Peke will they remember? Though he realizes, darkly, that his own scent is now probably unrecognizable, erased, because he is wearing the uniform of the Colonel. He is clothed now in the Colonel's scent.

The barking grows louder. The two black bullets are closing in.

Is there a chance to bargain? Can Nick grab the old man, hold him, and with the threat of commanding the dogs to attack the old man, can Nick bargain for his own life when the black masks arrive?

No. Because if the black masks are armed (and certainly they will be), they can simply dispense with the dogs, leaving him no threat, no leverage.

So he has no choice, really: he'll have to turn the dogs on the old man when they arrive, ahead of the black masks. With no chance to bargain or negotiate, that will be Nick's final act. The black masks may ultimately take him, but he will take the old man with him. They will enter eternity together. An odd notion. A strange couple.

And again he knows what he would do if he were the black masks. He wouldn't pause to negotiate. He knows what happens when bloodlust is released.

And if that will be his final act, then he will initiate it now, before the black masks arrive, to assure its completion, to pave its way.

An inextinguishable fury has propelled Nick into the streets and through this life—a fury that he has made his partner and ally. His fury serves him now, as he seizes upon this moment of pause, of indecision, of the dogs' relentless approach—and he roars through his pain and lunges at the old Jew, swinging his stick furiously, an animal unleashed.

Whether by mere suddenness or fury or skill, it drives the old man back farther. And Nick, student of the streets, won't miss his chance. All animal fury and adrenaline—the pain channeled into rage—he keeps coming and leaps at Peke, preparing the prey for his dogs, taking control of his own mortality.

>>>

Peke falls backward into the hard mud and rolls, instinctively protective, to the side.

The thought is brief but crisp, dizzy but sharp:

The Nazi soldier has finally fallen. What the seven-year-old has always wished for, beneath it all—for the Nazi soldier to fall, the soldier whose bullet pierced Abel. But isn't it actually the seven-year-old who has fallen? The seven-year-old pretending to adult power, donning it, but found out at last. The seven-year-old, back on the familiar, cold mud floor of the woods. Looking up from the mud floor into the years of fear. Because you cannot defeat them.

And that is when the dogs finally appear. Charging at him, snapping snarling raging muscle and bone. They bark furiously at him, pawing and pedaling around his head. Black-pupiled empty-eyed soulless ferocious machines of teeth and jaw and snout and eagerly dripping saliva—savagery sharpened to a polished point. He suddenly knows: this is the end always meant for him. Like a final scene carried patiently in his own genes, and in theirs. A scene handed down genetically for eventual enactment, from his perse-cuted ancestors to him, from the dogs' ancestors to them.

Snapping. Snarling. They are fury itself. But they haven't touched him. Because they are waiting. Waiting as they have been trained to. Waiting as they have been waiting all along. Waiting for the command.

Nick stands over the old man. He looks at him for a moment. "I was an orphan, too," he says.

The old man looks up at him.

"That's how I guessed that you lost your parents. Because I recognized it in you," he says flatly, over the fierce racket of rage, standing above the pawing, rippling, eager black forms.

The old man stares up at Nick. As if uncomprehending. As if momentarily lost.

Another orphan. Alone in the woods.

It must be Abel. Abel, out here with him, in pain. Out here for years, and runty little Stanislaw doesn't recognize him.

He understands now. Understands at last. A German soldier is on the ground, and an orphan stands over him. It's what he's always wanted—unspoken, unrecognized. It's what the seven-year-old has unconsciously waited for, for sixty years. Completion and revenge, all in one. The Fates, the cosmos, have clearly weighed in, just as he suspected all along. He feels the elation rise in him. Relief. Resolution. *Yes, Abel. The German soldier is on the ground. Go ahead, Abel. Take your revenge.*

>>>

Nick senses the black masks closing in.

This is his only chance. It's all the diversion and distraction he has available to him. He must time it exactly right.

He says the word he's never said before but has always remembered, from the look in the crazy skinhead's eyes, proudly demonstrating the dogs' abilities.

Remembered it as someone else might remember a prayer.

"*Angriff!*" Nick shouts to the dogs.

German for *attack*, the crazy skinhead had said.

And it's only at the moment he says it that he finally, fully realizes that the old man is wearing a German uniform.

Which only confirms for him the old Jew's wiliness.

>>>

"*Angriff!*"

A phrase uttered at the moment of death.

A phrase lodged in thousands of Jewish souls.

Just like the Shema, thinks Stanley Peke.

An inverse Shema.

A last thought.

The opposite of a prayer.

Stanley Peke curls into his seventy-two-year-old body and enters the darkness.

He tucks into his body, tucks into his past, tucks into the darkness so deeply, so far, he is barely aware of the shots.

A few of them. He hasn't heard shots in over sixty years, but their sound hasn't changed. They're fired from close by, he knows from over sixty years ago. Close as Abel. Close as the shot that took Abel.

He can feel Abel next to him. Can feel his breath stop. Can feel the last beat of his breath. Can feel Abel collapse on top of him. Abel's warmth. Protecting him again.

Stanley Peke stays curled in the darkness. Until he feels a hand on him. A big hand, like those unknown hands that passed him in the wooden trunk to safety, pulling him up again.

Through a haze of being—an uncertainty that is at once physical, emotional, and mental—he is only partly aware of the dogs' bodies lying next to him.

The warm blood. The stink to come. Abel. Oh, Abel.

"Walk away, Stanley," Grady says, the gun in Grady's hand. Peke hears the words, the unplaceable lilt of them. He looks up to see the thief limping desperately away, hunched over, already fifty yards ahead.

Grady turns, narrows his eyes at the thief, turns back to Peke, and instructs him again, the brogue not lilting or sparkling but brusque, urgent, stern. "Walk away, Stanley. Time to walk away. Time to walk out of the woods."

And only half-aware, Stanley Peke does begin to walk away. Still curled partway into the black, but then—beginning gradually to see, smell, taste the woods around him—uncurling slowly from the blackness.

He sheds the uniform. Rips the polished buttons open, tears off the stiff epauletted jacket as if sloughing a diseased, relentlessly itching skin. Without looking, he lets it fall to the ground. He feels the shock of brisk Montana air on his arms and torso. The blackness still lifting, he senses a kind of levitation of both body and soul, a sudden, weightless moment of profound calm, of grace, that he will liken, in the days ahead, to what others refer to as religious experience.

Shedding the past—literally. Leaving it to the mud and rain.

In a minute, he hears one more shot. A last shot, ringing through the woods, as if merely ceremonial. It is, he senses, the last shot he'll ever have to hear.

Stanley Peke hikes back through the woods. In a few minutes, he emerges from them at last.

He sees a familiar figure across the muddy field.

He thinks he must be mistaken, or delirious. But in a moment, a few yards closer, he knows he's not.

It's Daniel. His son, Daniel.

Something in the vision of his only son solidifies the world around him, brings it back together before him.

Daniel. Here. With him.

The doorbell rings.

Stanley Peke moves to the big door slowly. He finds himself moving everywhere a step slower these days.

He opens the door. A man and woman are standing there. Small, dark. South American. They are tentative, nervous. They both stand with shoulders slightly hunched forward, in a kind of static bow—a modest, deferential immigrant stance.

"Mister Stanley Peke?" the man asks tentatively.

"Yes," he says cautiously. *What now? God, what now?*

The man smiles. "We look all over for you."

And now Peke focuses on the carton in the man's hands.

"We are driving across from New Jersey to Los Angeles, and we play football in a parking lot—getting gas and hamburgers, you know?—and our ball go into a Dumpster, and I jump in to get it. And this"—he holds the carton—"this, it's what I found," explaining in a rush. "Is your box. Is your pictures."

The thief. The thief, for some reason, must have cast it off along the way.

Peke is stunned. Confused. "How . . . how did you ever find me?"

The man smiles proudly. "We look through. And, sir, see here . . ."

He takes out a photograph from his shirt pocket. It is Daniel's high school graduation. Mortarboards, gowns, a family snapshot, and the name of the high school and the town and state lettered proudly on the banner draped in back.

Place. Belonging. Identity. Home. Some powerful amalgam of them all kneads within him, fills him instantly.

The man smiles. "We call to your town. We tell them what we find, where we find it. They believe it, I guess—is so crazy, you know? They know where you are moving to. So when we are coming out here, to seeing our cousins, we are coming to see you."

Resourceful. Resourceful immigrants in a new land.

"Where are you from?" asks Peke.

"Peru," they tell him.

"I came from Poland," he tells them. And realizes: he's never told another immigrant that before.

He looks at the carton. At them.

"And you . . . you brought these to me." He states the obvious, summarizes foolishly, because he can think of nothing else to say.

"What good they gonna do to us? Is your pictures! Your things! You gotta have them." As if the alternative is unthinkable.

He understands who is standing there. He understands completely. It is him. In a different skin, from a different hemisphere, a half century later, but the same. He feels some unspoken comprehension pass between the short, dark-skinned man and him. Something travels the vast and inconsequential distance between the man's brown eyes and his own. He knows it.

"Would you . . . would you like to come in?" he asks them.

"Oh, no." They smile, big, deferential grins, stepping backward. "No, thank you. We just happy to bring you pictures back."

He is hurt for a moment. There is so much hospitality he could show them. A tall, cool drink. A comfortable place to rest from their long trip. But he sees that is not how they have imagined this. They have imagined it their own way—without imposition, without asking a thing.

He takes the carton. "Thank you."

They are still smiling broadly. The compact man and woman. Unable not to. "Yes. Yes. Thank you." Holding to that slight bowing. Their awkwardness, their charm.

>>>>

In the decade still ahead of him, lying awake in the dark at night, he will sometimes ponder the thin veneer of civilization. The nature of loss. The complexity of memory. The porousness of time and place.

Caught in the crosshairs of history, he will think. The phrase will echo in him, haunt him. *Caught in the crosshairs of history.*

But he will feel the sunlight every day, and the cool Pacific breeze every evening. And the skin of Rose, his wife—the still-beautiful, swooping planes of it, hot, cool, variable, infinite, soft, sweet, alive.

He will return to his dinners with close friends. His wines. His reading. His high-spirited visiting grandchildren. His life.

Treasure it. Love it.

Know security. Know serenity. Know peace.

A version of it, at least.

ACKNOWLEDGMENTS

Many friends and readers championed this book along the way. Special thanks, though, to Liz Paley, Jim Todd, and Jacques de Spoelberch, for their active support, unflagging enthusiasm, and unwavering belief.

Special thanks also to Clay Stafford and the whole gang at Killer Nashville, whose writing contest emboldened me to pull this unwanted, abandoned manuscript out of the drawer after *twelve years* (actually, to retrieve it from an old flash drive), send it off to Tennessee, and voila!

And to the memory of David Brown, legendary Hollywood lion, whose offhand suggestion led to this book's ending. A belated, distant, thank you, sir.

ABOUT THE AUTHOR

Sue Stone, 2013

Jonathan Stone writes his books on the commuter train between his home in Connecticut and his advertising job in midtown Manhattan. Honing his writing skills by creating smart and classic campaigns for high-level brands such as Mercedes-Benz, Microsoft, and Mitsubishi has paid off, as Stone's first mystery-thriller series, the Julian Palmer books, won critical acclaim and was hailed as "stunning" and "risk-taking" in *Publishers Weekly* starred reviews. He earned glowing praise for his novel *The Cold Truth* from *The New York Times*, which called it "bone-chilling" and added that "Stone plays cruel and cunning mind games." He's the recipient of a Claymore Award for Best Unpublished Crime Novel and a graduate of Yale, where he was a Scholar of the House in fiction writing.